INTRODUCTION

Mountain Wishes by Kimberley Woodhouse
Karon Granger has a life wish and wants to show her doctors and family that she's not a fragile piece of china. She's a cancer survivor. And she wants to climb Denali—the tallest mountain in North America—to prove it. Karon's brother joins her on the climb, but when he falls and breaks his leg, they must rely on mountaineering ranger Zack Taylor to rescue them from the weather-crazy Alaska wilderness.

Daring Heights by Ronie Kendig
Heiress and experienced climber Jolie Decoteau doesn't believe in coincidences, so getting acute mountain sickness shortly after her father is found dead convinces her that someone is trying to kill her. Denali Base Camp ranger David Whiteeagle is sent to rescue Jolie, but he's stunned to find that her condition is significantly worse than reported and, as they navigate their way through the storm back to safety, that someone else is on their trail. . . .

Taking Flight by Ronie Kendig
Deline Tsosie is the sweetheart and flightseeing tour guide of Talkeetna, Alaska, but she's going nowhere fast. Ranger Logan Knox is brilliant with wolves, mountains, and money but feels inept with people. He uses his financial investments to fund hiring Deline for tours to the glaciers. But the ice he'd like to melt is in her heart. Then when a series of incidents puts her in danger, his protective instincts fly to the surface to save the business and the girl.

Denali Guardians by Kimberley Woodhouse
Although Josh Ric[...] eering ranger for six months, he'[...]ob, the family of rangers. . .and m[...]a lives in fear of the stalker who t[...]ars ago. She's changed her name [...]remote job at the Talkeetna Ranger Station, but it's not long before her past catches up with her and she must rely on love to conquer all.

D1115803

DENALI DREAMS

DENALI DREAMS

FOUR-IN-ONE COLLECTION

Ronie Kendig
Kimberley Woodhouse

BARBOUR
PUBLISHING

Published by Barbour Publishing, Inc., P.O. Box 719, Uhrichsville, Ohio 44683, www.barbourbooks.com

Our mission is to publish and distribute inspirational products offering exceptional value and biblical encouragement to the masses.

 Member of the
Evangelical Christian
Publishers Association

Printed in the United States of America.

MOUNTAIN WISHES

by Kimberley Woodhouse

Dedication

This book is lovingly dedicated in memory of the real Karon Granger, who went home to be with the Lord after her long fight with cancer.

Karon, I can't wait to hug your neck and sing with you again. Precious friend, you are missed.

A Note from the Author

I'm so thankful you chose to journey to Alaska with us and spend time with the amazing rangers. Our family lived for many years in that great state known as the Last Frontier, and even with intense research on top of that, I need to give you a disclaimer: Any inaccuracies are all my own.

Karon, the heroine in this first story, is based on a real person with the same name. An amazing lady who passed away several years ago, but lives on in all the lives she touched with her vibrant personality. To the thousands of you who knew Karon personally, please remember that this is to honor Karon and her life, but it is also a work of fiction. Prayerfully, you will get glimpses of her throughout the story, and will smile in remembrance of our beautiful friend.

This book could not have been written without the help of my wonderful friends up at the Talkeetna Ranger Station. Those people are amazing. If you ever have the chance, go visit Alaska, visit the station, and say hi to Missy for me. And for fun—take a gander at the Clean Mountain Can (CMC).

Enjoy the journey,
Kimberley
http://kimberleywoodhouse.com

Chapter 1

Cool air fanned her face as Karon Granger leaned back in the rocking chair. The ceiling fan spun above her, helping stave off the always-humid, always-warm Louisiana air. She scanned her flower beds from the front porch and leaned forward again. With her small stature, her feet only touched the ground in the forward position, and like a child, she loved to rock with vigor. So she was just a little kid in a thirty-two-year-old body. That was her story and she was sticking to it. Even though everyone knew Karon's love of rocking chairs.

Her thoughts jolted back to the present. This particular rocking session meant more than comfort or relaxation or fun. This was a thinking rock. She'd made a big decision and wondered how on earth to share it with her friends and family.

Karon considered the changes that had occurred over the course of her illness. Everyone coddled her, protected her, treated her like a fragile porcelain doll.

Could she really blame them? They did it because they loved her—and because she'd almost lost the fight. So she didn't mind, at least she kept telling herself that. But how would they all react to her new adventure? Would they think she'd lost her mind?

Her brother, Clint, would react the worst to the news.

Even with all her training, all the research, all the gear—she knew it wouldn't be pretty. She needed to prepare herself for battle.

Battle. A familiar word now. But this time was different. This battle wasn't *for* her life, it proved that she wanted—no, needed—to *live* her life.

A long sigh escaped, splitting the silence. Leaning forward, elbows on her knees, she stopped the rocker. Strong willed might not be everyone's normal description of her, but she had a lot of gumption. Cancer had changed everything. This was a fight she wouldn't back down from—not even with Clint. The thought of ticking him off made her heart ache. Especially after all he'd done for her. But she'd have to cross that bridge when the time came. God had gotten her this far. He'd take her the rest of the way. *One step at a time* was the motto of her faith—she needed to keep heading toward the finish line.

Little Braiden from down the street rode his bike up to her front steps. He hopped off the seat and unsnapped his helmet, letting the bike wobble back and forth on its training wheels. "Did you see me, Miss Karon? Did ya? I rode all the way here *all* by myself!"

"Wow. That's a long way, B. I think that deserves a cookie." She gave him a wink and hopped out of her chair mimicking his actions.

"You mean, your special cookies?" His eyes grew large.

"Yes, sir—I just pulled another batch out of the oven about fifteen minutes ago."

"Wait till the rest of the kids hear I got a cookie!"

Karon giggled at his enthusiasm and tousled his hair. "Let's go inside and call your mom, okay?"

"You think she'll let me have *two*?" He grabbed her hand as they walked inside.

Her heart melted. She'd always wanted a family of her own. The small hand in hers generated that longing again. She smiled down at him. "If not now, then I'll send some home with you for later."

"Thanks, Miss Karon. You're the most awesomest lady on the block. When I grow up, I wanna marry you."

Oh, the innocence of youth. "That's quite a compliment, B, but why don't you focus on finishing first grade, and then you might want to graduate from high school and go to college."

He stared at the cooling racks filled with cookies. "But I already know. You make the best cookies in the whole universe. And you look real purty with your hair growin' back."

If only that made her marriage material in real life. She shook her head and tweaked his nose. "Thanks, B. But I thought you liked my hat collection?"

"Oh, I do! Your silly ones are the best, but I like your curly hair better." He climbed onto a stool and reached up to touch one of her short curls.

Leaning down, she touched her forehead to his. No one could duplicate the unconditional love of a child or the pure compassion. Her illness had never been a secret. Braiden had often come to give her a hug and rubbed her bald head when he told her that he and his mother prayed for Karon every night before bed.

Karon straightened and reached for the phone. She winked at B as she dialed her friend's number. "Hey, Lisa."

"I'm assuming you have an admirer at your house?" The soft voice laughed.

"Yep, and I'm wondering if he's allowed to have a cookie or two?"

"You're spoiling him, Karon, but you're the first person he wanted to ride to. Don watched him from the garage."

"So, that's a yes?"

Lisa laughed. "You bet, as long as he brings one home to his mom."

"Of course."

"Thanks, Karon. His dad is coming down there to walk around the block with him." Her voice quieted. "How are you feeling?"

The dreaded question. Everyone asked it. All the time. "Great. I feel great. The doctor has cleared me for everything."

"Oh, that's awesome! Just don't overdo it, okay? Let me know if you need anything."

"Sure thing. . .let me get back to B. I think he might start drooling soon." She tried to keep her tone light.

"Thanks for being so sweet to him. I'll talk to you later."

Karon hung up the phone. Would no one ever see her as whole again? Wasn't it enough she felt broken? Did they have to keep reminding her?

Braiden tugged on her jeans. "Miss Karon, did ya see my new knee pads and elbow pads?" He ripped the Velcro apart to show her his prize.

"Those are super cool, B." She handed him a soft cookie. "Your dad is coming to take you around the block, so I'm going to put a few in a bag for you to take home, okay?"

The treat disappeared in seconds. Chocolate ringed his lips and a large smudge graced one cheek. "Thanks, Miss Karon. I sure do love you."

She grabbed a paper towel and wet it down. "I love you, too. Let's get this chocolate off your face before your dad gets here."

As they walked toward the front door, Braiden turned and headed to a corner of the couch. "Hey, what's that?"

She glanced to where he pointed. A new pair of crampons and an ice axe lay next to the rope she'd just purchased. Oh boy.

A knock on the screen door saved her from explaining. But as Lisa's husband entered the living room, he spotted what caught B's attention. Don narrowed his eyes. "Please tell me that's not what I think it is."

She smiled. Maybe she should leave *now*. Not tell anyone where she was going.

"Karon?"

"Look at this, Dad!" Braiden held up the book she'd left on her coffee table. "It's all about climbing tall mountains."

Ratted out by a six-year-old.

Braiden's dad cocked an eyebrow at her and crossed his arms.

Great. If her friends and neighbors reacted this way, how would her brother react?

Chapter 2

"You want to do *what*?"

Even worse than she expected. Karon braced herself for the rest of the tirade.

"You're out of your mind. There is no way I will allow you to do this."

Karon's ears rang from the shouting. Her brother, her *only* brother—the one who stood by her side through thick and thin, the one who was there for every chemo treatment, the one who encouraged her to get on with her life after cancer—was treating her like a child. Well she wasn't one. At thirty-two, she could very well make her own decisions.

She'd been prepared for a mild scolding. The "Are you sure you're ready for this?" or even possibly "Maybe you should wait a while before you try it." But she had not expected Clint to pitch a fit in the middle of her living room. Granted, she'd just dropped a pretty large bomb at his feet, but he'd always been supportive. Why couldn't he just suck it up and go with it? Karon clenched her fists as she listened to him rant and rave. She allowed the rage inside to burn, let her temper flare.

So baby brother thought he could be her parent? News flash—their parents died sixteen years ago. The overgrown two-year-old would *not* tell her what to do with her life.

Deep breath. She could do this. With or without him. "I don't just *want* to do it. I *will* do it."

"Karon, this is crazy." Hands on his hips, Clint towered over her. "Do you have any idea what it takes to climb a mountain? Good grief! You're a kindergarten teacher. What will the parents of your students think? And you're so tiny.... You're still recovering." He stuck a finger in her face. "And don't you roll your big brown eyes at me. When I told you I had lots of paid vacation I needed to take, I was offering to take you to Hawaii or something. You know, to celebrate your one-year remission—but this?"

Karon stood and mustered up all the fight she had left. "Let's get one thing straight right now. This has nothing to do with your offer of a vacation. It's something *I'm* doing. With *my* vacation time. You are *not* part of this decision-making process. You are *not* in charge of my life. And you will *never* speak to me that way again."

Clint's eyes grew round, his eyebrows raised. "What are you saying?"

Hardheaded little punk. "You heard what I said, Clint. I'm not going to repeat it like you are one of my five-year-old students. Get over it, and move on."

He had the nerve to laugh. His eyes met hers again. Holding up his hands in submission, Clint wisely stopped laughing. "Wow. I guess you have the right—"

"You *guess?*"

"All right, fine. You *have* the right to make your own decisions." He turned toward the window. "You've been through a lot. Maybe this is just some weird desire you have right now, and you'll change your mind after you've had time to think about it and go through all the training. Until then, I will support you." He put a hand on her shoulder. "I've never seen you so riled up before. Maybe you should sit down."

Ooh, he made her so mad. She flung off his hand and straightened her shoulders. "Get out, Clint." Mr. Know-it-all thought he could boss her around. What did he know anyway? She'd already started the training.

He swung around. "Karon, you can't be serious."

"Oh, I'm serious. In fact, I'd like nothing more than to punch you in the nose right now. Get out." This felt entirely too good. Maybe she needed to vent more often. She felt so. . .alive.

He turned those puppy dog eyes on her. "I'm sorry—"

"Too little, too late." She shoved him toward the door.

"Wait, Karon, be reasonable." He back-stepped to keep his feet under him.

"I'm done being reasonable. Don't you get it?" She yanked open the door. "I almost lost my life. Yes, you were there for me. You've always been there. But you're smothering me." She pushed him through the opening. "I am not fragile. I don't want to live in a bubble. And I definitely don't want to sit here for the rest of my life wondering if or when the cancer's going to come back."

"Karon—"

"Don't *Karon* me. I want to live, Clint. I want to experience life in a whole new way. I want to take risks. I want to enjoy myself. I want to fall in love and get married and have a family. And I want to climb the tallest mountain in North America."

His mouth dropped open. He closed it.

Their eyes locked in a stand down.

Silence. Blessed silence. Maybe she'd finally gotten through to him.

Clint placed a hand on her shoulder again. "Okay."

"Okay? Okay what?" She crossed her arms and stared him down.

Mirth replaced the shock in his eyes. "Okay, you win."

Karon allowed a smile to reach her eyes. "Denali, here I come."

"Here *we* come. I'm coming with you."

Chapter 3

Y ou did *what?*" The voice crackled over the line.

"Mom, I need you to let this go." Zack Taylor rubbed a hand down his face. So much for an innocent Mother's Day call.

"Let it go?" She huffed. "You haven't called me in six months, and you have the gall to call me on Mother's Day and tell me this?"

Okay, so he stunk at being a son. "I'm sorry, Mom."

"Sorry?" Her voice sounded teary.

Great. Now he'd made her cry. Again.

"I worry about you all the time. You never let us know where you are. I check in with the rangers just to make sure you're still alive."

Oh, the guilt trip. "Mom, I'm alive. I'm calling."

"Zack, I know that. Don't get smart with me. But I just don't understand why you insist on doing all these crazy things."

"They're not crazy—"

"Don't start, Zack. They may not be crazy to you, but to us *normal* folks, let's face it. They're crazy."

Maybe she had a point.

"Every time you climb that insane mountain, I worry. Every time, you're gone for weeks at a time. . ." Another sigh.

Great. She was gearing up for the rampage. He braced himself against the kitchen counter. Stared out the window to his mountains. If only he could get out there today and do some serious climbing.

"...You always have an excuse for why you don't call. You always have an excuse for why you won't settle down. You always—"

"Mom, please—"

"Don't interrupt me, young man. Why can't you just do something normal like your father? Get a real job?"

Now she'd crossed the line. "Mom"—he grit his teeth—"I *have* a real job."

"Don't talk back to me."

His mother continued to rant in his ear. "Mom, I wanted to wish you a happy Mother's Day."

She stopped. Great. Now the silent treatment. Guilt trips or the silent treatment—his mother was the queen of both. While there was a pause, he continued. "I have a real job." Would she ever listen to him? "I love what I do. But I wanted more of a challenge."

Mom grunted.

"I'm trying to share with you how I feel, Mom." That should get her attention. How often did he get letters saying he never shared his feelings with her?

"All right, Zacky. Go on."

He let the nickname slide. He wasn't four anymore. Would she ever realize *that*? "I needed to do this. I've trained a long time for it." He played his trump card. "I was hoping you'd be proud of me."

"Oh, of course I'm proud of you!" The ooey-gooey mom voice took over for a moment. "But isn't that the most dangerous job?"

"It's not about danger, Mom. It's about saving people's lives." He'd never tell her the truth of the matter. Flying the rescue helicopter into one of the most dangerous places on the planet was his choice. His friends all told him he had a death wish—going from one extreme thing to the next to get his thrills—but he'd never tell his mom that. He needed her to think he was doing something noble. Saving lives was noble, right?

"Fine." He imagined her pressing her lips together and shaking her head. "As long as I don't see you one day on a crazy reality show where they follow you around with a camera and show how incredibly stupid you are doing the job you're doing." She paused for a loud breath. "I don't want all my friends to be asking why I let my son do something so wild and foolish."

Let him? Incredibly stupid? Good grief. "Mom, why don't you say how you *really* feel." She'd be sure to take him to task for his sarcasm. On Mother's Day, to boot. But he'd already crossed the line and, besides, she'd riled him up. So it was *her* fault. "I'm thirty-six years old. Seriously—"

"Don't take that tone with me, young man. I carried you for nine months and then had a forty-eight-hour labor trying to bring you into this world. I know exactly how old you are. It wouldn't hurt you to take your mother's advice every once in a while. It might keep you out of trouble."

He doubted it. For ten years, he'd been conquering Denali—the tallest mountain in North America—the High One. With weather extremes that far exceeded Everest, Denali was also taller from base to top. He'd climbed it fifteen times. Summitted twelve of those. He tried the West Buttress, the West Rib, Cassin Ridge, and Muldrow several times a piece. He'd even conquered Sultana—The Wife— one of the steepest and worst climbs in the world.

His appetite for extremes only grew; he couldn't seem to satisfy it. So he became a mountaineering ranger for Talkeetna Ranger Station, the headquarters for climbers in Denali National Park. When that failed to fill the hole in his gut, he trained to be a rescue helicopter pilot. Once the job was confirmed as his, he'd finally told his mom. Not that he'd expected enthusiasm, but Zack always hoped one day she'd understand him. Even though he didn't understand himself.

"Zack?" his mother's voice cut in. "Zack, are you even listening to me?"

"Sorry, Mom." He pinched the bridge of his nose between his thumb and middle finger. "Look, I know I ruined your day, but my intent really was to wish you a happy Mother's Day. I love you." He hung up before she could say anything else.

A twinge of guilt filled him. His mom would never understand him, and he'd just hung up on her. Good job.

The radio on the table crackled to life. "Ranger Taylor, you're needed at the station ASAP."

So much for being a good son. Well, at least he had his job. He grabbed his jacket and headed out the door to do what he did best.

Chapter 4

Karon shifted her weight to her left foot and breathed in the brisk Alaska air. She'd done it. Traveled all the way to Alaska by herself without anyone breathing down her neck about her health. No one on the flight knew her. No one knew that she was a cancer survivor. No one knew the battles she'd faced. And won.

A new person. With a new life in front of her. That's who she wanted to be.

Clint would be joining her for the trek up Denali, but she'd left early to do her own thing. He wasn't happy about it, but too bad. He had his job to worry about. That was the great thing about being a teacher, since it was summer she didn't have to take any time off for her adventure.

The time exploring Anchorage had been fun, but the drive out to Talkeetna took her breath away. This was where she belonged—she could feel it the moment she saw those mountains.

As she headed to the ranger station in Talkeetna, she took in the views around her and the quaint little businesses. Denali, still a good distance away, stood tall and immovable to the northwest. Snow covered the High One, and his shoulders were draped with clouds like a regal robe. She ventured farther into the tiny town and spotted Tsosie's Café. Her stomach rumbled. Might as well try it out.

The door creaked and a small bell rang above her head as she stepped in and inhaled. Wow. Whatever this place served smelled great. And it was packed. Always a good sign. A young native woman behind the counter waved her in.

"Hey there, what can I get for you on this gorgeous day?" The woman's long black hair shone.

"Well, I'm new in town. I'd love something new and different." Karon hopped up onto a stool at the counter and ran her fingers through her hair. The natural beauty of the woman in front of her caused her to feel frumpy and out of place.

"New to Talkeetna, or new to Alaska?" The woman's genuine smile calmed Karon's uneasiness.

"Both." Her excitement surged again. Karon felt like a kid in a candy shop.

The lady's eyes sparkled. She wiped a hand on her apron and held it out to Karon. "I'm Deline; my dad owns the café. Welcome to Alaska. It's the greatest place on earth."

A smile lifted Karon's cheeks. "Nice to meet you. I'm Karon. And I'm beginning to think the same thing."

"Good." Deline winked. " 'Cause it is." She placed a menu in front of Karon. "Coffee?"

"Yes, please."

Deline plopped a cup in front of her and filled it. "Have you ever had reindeer sausage?"

Karon stirred in sugar and cream. "You know, I saw it on the menu in Anchorage, but hadn't worked up the courage yet." The coffee slid down smooth and robust.

"You've got to try it. My dad makes the best. Although it's a little spicy—you okay with that?"

Karon laughed hard. "I'm Cajun—from south Louisiana—I don't think it will be a problem."

Deline patted her hand. "I knew I liked you." She pulled a pencil out from behind her ear. "You want eggs and sourdough pancakes with that?"

"Ooo, that sounds amazing. I've never had sourdough

pancakes before. By the way, this coffee's amazing." The half-empty cup testified for her.

"In my opinion, it's the only way to eat pancakes, and my dad's sourdough starter is forty years old."

In the middle of a swallow, Karon choked out, "What? I'm not sure I want to eat anything forty years old."

Deline just smiled. "Oh yes. You do. I promise. Now, do you want fireweed honey, fireweed jelly, salmonberry jelly, salmonberry syrup, blueberry syrup, or blueberry jelly with that?"

"Um. . .surprise me. Whatever you think goes best with the forty-year-old pancakes."

The waitress laughed hard at that one. She shook her head. "Eggs?"

"Not this time. But I'd love some sausage and a refill on this coffee."

"You got it." Deline turned and yelled through the window behind her, "Order of hots and links!" She turned back to the counter and sat a carafe in front of her. "Help yourself to as much as you want. So, what brings you all the way from the bayou to igloo country?"

Karon's insides flip-flopped. She hadn't said it out loud yet to anyone here. "I'm here to climb Denali with my brother."

Deline's face registered a bit of shock. "Wow. I'm impressed. Have you done much climbing?"

Karon giggled. "Only in the last twelve months to prepare for this trip."

"Whoa. That's intense. Are you ready?"

"I'm ready for anything."

The doubt on the waitress's face said it all. "I'm amazed you even want to try it. You're so tiny." A smile accompanied the comment.

But it still felt like a punch in the gut.

"Well, chemo and radiation will do that to a person." The words were out before she could stop them. She closed her eyes. How could she allow herself to admit that to a stranger?

Deline's face turned serious. She leaned over the counter and whispered, "Are you telling me you have cancer and want to climb the High One?"

Karon straightened her shoulders. "No. I'm sorry. I shouldn't have blurted that out. I'm a cancer survivor. Emphasis on *survivor*." She brought her coffee to her lips hoping to dispel the awkwardness of the moment.

A hand came around hers when she set the cup down. The dark eyes looked away, but not before Karon saw the cache of pain.

A moment passed. Then two. Deline focused back on Karon, poked a finger in her face. "You climb that mountain. And you'll summit. I just know it."

For the first time in a long time, it'd been her *choice* to tell someone about her cancer. No one blurted it out, or explained her situation in a whisper behind her back. No one told her she didn't look good, or asked if she wanted to sit down. Deline had looked upon her as an equal. As a healthy person. She didn't know whether to choke up and cry, or rejoice. And she wasn't sure she could handle the emotions either way just yet. "You know, I wanted to do some sightseeing first. In fact, since you're from here, maybe you can direct me to a good flightseeing service. I'd love to see the mountains from the air."

Imagining herself on top of Denali made her heartbeat race. She would do this. And prove that she wasn't fragile like a piece of china. No longer would she face life with timidity. She'd take the proverbial bull by the horns and tackle it. One day at a time.

"You're in luck. I just happen to be a pilot with a flightseeing operation. This season has been pretty crazy, but since this is normally my day off from flying and I like you, I'm pretty sure I can fit you in." Another wink. "You wanna go today?"

"Seriously?" Karon jumped off her stool. "That would be amazing! I can't believe you have time to do this." She swallowed her emotions. "Thank you."

"It *will* be amazing—that I can promise." Deline untied her apron. "Let me get your food, and then I'll prep the Otter—that's my plane—while you enjoy." She pulled a card out of her jeans pocket. "Here's my cell. Just call me when you're done."

"You mean, we can go now?"

"Shhh, don't want all the other tourists to hear. Yes, we'll go this morning, but you've got to eat first. Don't want you getting sick up there. I'll even let you sit in the copilot's seat."

Karon caught Deline's arm before she could race out the door. "Why are you doing this?"

Deline straightened and smiled before looking away. "Because you're living your life."

☙

Zack watched from his truck as the petite brunette left the café. Her aviator sunglasses hid her eyes, but the smile couldn't be mistaken.

Jeans, a T-shirt, and a fleece vest were her wardrobe. Just like him, she looked like she enjoyed being comfortable. Her tiny feet caught his attention. He'd never seen a pair of hiking boots so small. Maybe she shopped in the children's department.

As she strolled down the street with her arms swinging by her sides, he watched. Something about her struck him deep inside.

A knock on the passenger window jolted him. Kyle, a

fellow mountaineering ranger, stood with hands on his hips, grinning like the Cheshire cat. "You gonna unlock the door?" he shouted. "Or should I wait until she's out of sight?"

Zack allowed a laugh and hit the UNLOCK button. "I don't know what you're talking about."

"Yeah, uh-huh. I watched you." Kyle climbed into the Dodge 2500. "So. . .who is she?"

Zack shifted into DRIVE. "I have no idea."

"Gonna meet her?"

"Nope."

"Right." Kyle drew out the word.

"Come on, man. You know I don't introduce myself to women. Don't have time."

"Yeah, but you've got enough time to try and kill yourself every chance you get."

Zack shook his head and drove toward the station. Was that what everyone thought? "I am not out to kill myself."

"Fair enough, but you never seem satisfied. You're always after the next great adrenaline rush. Like you just want to be as careless as you can."

Ouch. Maybe it was true. But he didn't know everyone thought that. Couldn't he just be labeled an *adventurer*? The alternative sounded. . .pathetic. "Hey, it's who I am." He shrugged, trying to get Kyle's words to roll off his back.

"Zack, you know that's not true. As a ranger and a pilot— you're top-notch. But your *adventures*, as you call them, are not who you are. You're trying to fill a hole that can't be filled with all the adrenaline in the world."

Kyle was a good guy and he meant well, but Zack didn't think anything could fix him. Especially his friend's preaching. The beautiful brunette came back to mind. He wished *she* could heal his heart.

But no. He'd be trying to fill that void till he died.

Chapter 5

The ranger station stood in front of her. A relatively small building with its wood beams and front porch, the adventure it held beckoned to the deepest places in her heart. Stepping inside, Karon took in the rustic atmosphere. The huge close-up shots of the mountains she'd just flown over, the bear track samples, and the front desk.

Behind the desk was the climbing board. Posted were the stats: mountains, climbers for the season, how many were on each mountain at the time, and the one that mattered most—how many had summitted.

Karon wanted to add one more to that last number. She *would* summit. They'd planned a private, twenty-eight-day expedition to allow for weather conditions and acclimatization. This wish would come true. It just had to. Even though Clint insisted on paying for them both and their private guide, this was *her* dream.

An adorable woman with a name tag that read Missy came to the desk.

Karon smiled. She'd been waiting to meet the ranger friend for over a year. The familiar, high-pitched voice she knew from their many phone calls was a balm. "Welcome to the Talkeetna Ranger Station. How can I help you?"

"Missy! I'm Karon Granger from Louisiana." The woman's face lit up in a smile and Karon reached over to hug the woman. "I'm so excited to meet you finally."

"Same here. I didn't expect you for a few days."

"I decided to have some fun by myself before my brother came up for the climb." She rolled her eyes. "You know men. Anyway, I need to properly thank you. You have been a lifesaver."

Missy just laughed. "You don't have to thank me, Karon, you already—"

"Nope, don't even go there. You answered every one of my calls, helped me with all my questions—good grief—you totally made this a reality for me." Her emotions got the best of her and tears sprang to her eyes. Karon hugged her new friend again. "All these months, you've listened and been there."

Missy leaned close. "Well, you've worked hard for this. I'm happy to help out. And don't worry—only the personnel scheduled to be at Base Camp and High Camp during your climb will know any details."

"Thanks. It's nice to just be Karon and move forward from here."

Missy smiled. "I don't want to overstep my bounds, but I did talk with our head mountaineering ranger about your situation. Follow me. I want to show you something." She led Karon into the great room. "You see all these?"

Flags covered the walls. "Wow. Are these all expeditions?"

"Yep. They represent summits and safe climbs. And look over here." The ranger paused. "These are people with prostheses." She pointed to another set. "Cancer survivors. . . people like you." Missy turned and captured Karon's eyes. "They're all proud of what they've overcome. Proud of their accomplishments. Proud of the strength it took to do what you're about to do."

Shame filled her gut. And here she'd been hiding. Afraid to tell the truth. Afraid someone else would try to convince her not to go. Afraid of being seen as less of a person. Her eyes roamed the flags, reading each one. She bit her bottom lip and nodded. "So, you're saying you think I should be bold about it. Not scared of sharing it."

Missy squeezed her arm. "I'm not going to tell you what to do, Karon, but I think after all the conversations we've had, and meeting you in person, you should know that what you're doing is something to be proud of, not something to hide."

Karon's insides tumbled. Wow, she was nervous. She'd always thought climbing Denali would prove to people that she was okay. But what did she really have to prove? Hadn't the doctors cleared her? Hadn't she survived? Wasn't she living her life already?

One burning question remained. Why did she care so much about what other people thought? As the reality of her own inner struggle settled in her gut, Karon found a chair and sat.

Had she really turned into a people pleaser?

Missy smiled. "I'm going to give you a few moments alone. I've got a list a mile long. But I'll be back."

Voices argued inside Karon's head. All this time. Had she been fighting herself? Holding herself back? Was that why people coddled her? Because they knew she didn't believe in herself?

Blaming other people had been the easy way out. The way she'd coped. But the truth shone a bright light on all the fog-covered thoughts and ideas swarming in her mind.

The only one holding her back was *her*. Resolve shot through her veins. She would stop hiding behind her lame excuses. If she wanted to live life, she needed to live it. She *was* a cancer survivor. No shame in that.

Her faith had taken a huge blow with the cancer diagnosis three years ago, but thankfully, God never gave up on her. And through it all, she'd grown closer to Him. But her confidence had been shattered as she watched people she cared about retreat from her life. The roller coaster of emotions it created hadn't been a fun ride. Self-doubt battled with her confidence of who she was in Christ.

But no more.

Karon walked back to the front and found her ranger friend. "Thanks so much, Missy. You've made me think." She pasted on a smile. "I know you're busy, so I'll come back tomorrow. And I'll be seeing you in a few days for our briefing anyway."

Missy winked at her. "Anytime. I'll talk to you soon." She nodded to the customer she was helping.

Karon turned to the entrance and allowed her excitement to bubble up. This was her dream. God had given her this chance; she wasn't going to waste it with doubt or a pity party. She couldn't wait to get out to the mountain.

"Excuse me." Another ranger sidestepped her.

Karon looked into his eyes and stopped. The fierceness and intensity took her back. As his gaze swung to Missy, Karon studied his profile. Strong jaw, chapped lips and cheeks, wind-mussed blond hair. All business. After a quick word with Missy, he turned to another ranger. The man's serious demeanor and strength were a magnet for Karon. What made that guy tick?

He probably never had confidence issues. Wouldn't that be nice?

She shook her head. The expedition ahead needed her focus. Not the incredibly handsome, brown-eyed, blond-haired—

"Hi." The subject of her thoughts stood in front of her and reached out a hand.

Karon blinked. Stuck her hand out in return.

"Zack Taylor. I fly one of the rescue helicopters."

She shook his hand. Kept shaking. Up. Down. Her voice

had mysteriously disappeared. She swallowed. "Karon Granger."

"Nice to meet you, Karon." With a nod and a small smile, he turned on his heel and left.

What on earth was that all about? Karon glanced at Missy whose eyes had widened. Then she giggled.

"What?"

Missy cleared her throat. "Oh, nothing. You're just the first woman Zack has introduced himself to since I've been here. And I've been here a long time."

Karon shrugged the encounter off and tried to suppress the excitement in her stomach. "And?"

"Well, that's a first. That's all I'm saying."

Maybe the guy just wasn't a natural at friendliness. He did seem a little on the reserved side. "Okay. I'll have to take your word for it. That's definitely the shortest introduction I've ever heard." But he'd taken the initiative to introduce himself to *her*. She ran a finger through her hair. Glanced at Missy.

Her friend was all smiles.

A glance out the front window showed Zack talking on the porch with another ranger. He looked toward her and smiled.

A spark flickered in her heart. Dare she hope?

Chapter 6

Zack fought the urge to look back to the station again. He'd seen the woman earlier leaving the café and then exiting Deline Tsosie's Otter. Her laughter rang in the afternoon air and stayed with him until he'd seen her again. At the station, of all places. He'd done a double take. Three times in one day. Her short curly hair, tiny feet, and beautiful smile captured his attention. What was it about her?

He shook his head. There wasn't time for a relationship. And he didn't have the heart. His life was too much of a disaster. Besides, no one wanted to get involved with a guy whose insatiable desire to risk it all numbed him to any and all feelings.

But as he glanced through the window one more time and caught her gaze, something in him wanted to take a chance.

David Whiteeagle, another ranger, poked him in the shoulder. "I think I need to meet this lady. You've smiled twice in one day. That's got to be a record."

"Yeah, whatever."

His friend grinned then headed to the door.

"Don't do it."

"You gonna stop me?" Nobody messed with David. He was huge.

Zack growled. "Fine. Her name is Karon."

"And?"

"That's all I know! Other than the fact she has tiny feet and a beautiful smile."

David smacked him on the back this time. "I knew it! You like her. Let's get to the café for dinner and you can tell me all about it."

"How 'bout we just get dinner? We've got lots to review for the season."

"Two incredible bachelors like us?" David jangled his keys. "Nah, your love life is way more interesting. Considering there's never been one before." He laughed. "Besides, I don't want to talk shop. There are too many tourists right now, and a bunch of rich kids climbing my mountain that we'll probably have to rescue."

David's grousing about the climbers on "his mountain" was a standard at the ranger station. Hearing him grump about it made people think he was in the wrong vocation. But when it came to teaching and rescuing, he was one of the best. David hated for anyone to get hurt on his mountain. "What about *your* love life? Why can't we discuss that?" Zack said.

"Nice try, Taylor. I'll make you a deal. When someone catches my attention, you have full permission to grill me."

"Deal." Zack's stomach growled. "Let's get some grub. I'm starved."

❧

Check-in day. Karon's heart soared. And plunged. All at the same time.

Clint hopped out of the rented SUV and walked with her to the door of the ranger station. "You ready?" Ever since his arrival in Alaska, he'd been back to his usual supportive self. Maybe her little temper tantrum had done its job.

"As I'll ever be. We've checked in our equipment with AMS; we've trained; we've prayed." She giggled. "I'm ready to get to the mountain now."

He opened the door for her. "I hate to admit it, but I'm really looking forward to this."

"So you're admitting I had a good idea?"

He grinned. "Nope. I'm just gonna beat you to the top." Make that his usual-supportive-*competitive* self.

"Not a chance, you wimp." She poked him in the side and laughed. "I'll be the first one to—" Her face collided with a backpack before she could spit out the word *summit*.

Attached to the backpack was ranger Zack Taylor.

Heat flooded her cheeks.

He frowned at her and walked away.

Her heart sank. So much for the hope he found her attractive.

Missy waved from the desk. "You guys here to check in?"

Karon straightened her shoulders and attempted to banish Zack from her mind. "Yep! We're ready for our briefing."

"All right, follow me." Missy led them into a conference room.

Karon sucked in a small gasp when she saw Zack leaning over the table discussing something with another ranger.

He looked up.

Missy spoke, "This is Zack and John. Two of our best mountaineering rangers. Zack is also a helicopter rescue pilot. They'll be doing your briefing today." She turned to leave and smiled at Karon.

"Thanks," Karon croaked.

Zack straightened and crossed his arms. "So it's just the two of you with your guide?"

Words wouldn't come.

Clint cleared his throat and gave her an odd look. "Yes." He reached out a hand to Zack. "I'm Clint Granger."

John smiled. He shook Clint's hand as well. "Nice to meet you." He turned to Karon. "And you are?"

Cotton. Her mouth was filled with cotton. How did Zack hold the power to tongue-tie her every time they met? She blinked. Swallowed. "Karon." She stuck out her hand as well. "Karon Granger." Great. Clint's eyes drilled holes into her. He knew. Ugh.

John turned to look at Zack and then sat down. "Well, why don't we begin? We've got your paperwork. You're registered with AMS guide service. They'll take good care of you, but they're not babysitters. They know their stuff, so listen to your guide carefully."

Karon nodded. John continued to talk, but Zack drew her gaze like a magnet. Why wouldn't he look at her? Why was he frowning?

". . .I'm assuming you've practiced with your equipment and understand how to use the CMC?" John was looking at her.

"Um. . ."The CMC. Oh, right. The Clean Mountain Can.

John plopped one on the table. The green plastic container and black lid looked a little small.

Focus, Karon. All she needed was for the rangers to think she was a total nincompoop. Then she'd never realize her dream. "Yes. The CMC. We understand the 'Leave No Trace' policy." She wouldn't look at Zack again.

"Good, you'll each be issued one at Kahiltna Base Camp."

Fun, fun. They had to pack in and pack out everything they had. Including human waste. Karon didn't even want to think about the equipment she'd had to purchase to help make that possible. Practicing with it was even worse. But it'd be worth it once she reached Denali's summit. She just had to keep telling herself that.

Tuning back in, she realized they'd moved on from sanitation to other topics. Clint was talking about their equipment, the color of their tent, and type of stove.

She really needed to pay attention.

John asked about their food and fuel.

Zack continued to frown.

The senior ranger went on to talk about the route overview and various hazards they could face, camp etiquette, and the different weather conditions. "Basically, you need to be prepared for anything. This climb is unlike any other in the world." He turned to the brewing ranger at his side. "Zack? Why don't you take the rest."

Zack's frown deepened. Then he dove into the National Park Service's regulations and medical rescue policy.

"You need to be prepared to be self-reliant and to self-rescue." He looked straight at her. "Your husband may not be there to save you."

So that's what had turned him into a grouch. He thought she was married! Karon placed her palms on the table in front of her. "I'll have you know, that my *brother*"—she made sure to emphasize the last word—"and I have trained long and hard for this expedition. We know how to self-rescue, and we are very self-reliant." She shot Zack a long look.

His neck turned red. Then his face.

John chuckled.

Two and a half hours after they'd entered the conference room, Karon and Clint walked out with permits in hand.

They were cleared to climb Denali.

But even better than that? The triumphant feeling as she watched Zack's face when he realized Clint was her brother.

A warm rush of butterflies filled her stomach. The handsome ranger was attracted to her.

Chapter 7

*I*diot.

The word should be tattooed on his forehead.

That's what he deserved for even allowing himself to be attracted to a woman. To make matters worse, he'd have to spend two days with her at Base Camp. His ten-day shift started tomorrow, and she'd arrive the next day. With her *brother*.

John reached around him for the CMC. "So. . .you gonna fill me in on what that was all about?" The seasoned ranger stacked it on the shelf and reached for the paperwork on the table. John was the father figure of the rangers, and Zack knew he was in for a scolding.

"Nope." It'd be all over the station by the end of the hour anyway. It wasn't that they were gossips, the office just wasn't that big. And the whole station looked after one another like family.

John walked toward the door then turned back and sat on the corner of the table. "My advice to you is simple: next time you want to come to work acting like a grizzly and jam your foot in your mouth, stick your head in a pile of snow and rethink it. Don't offend our climbers." The warning given, John stood and exited.

Short and sweet. That was his way. But Zack still felt the sting. This was why he never let his emotions get involved. In anything. Because he simply couldn't handle it.

Kyle's figure filled the doorway. "I hear you've had quite a morning."

"Don't even start."

"John asked me to finish briefings with him today. You're on equipment duty for Base Camp." No trace of a smile remained on Kyle's face.

Zack swiped a hand down his neck. "Great."

"Look, I don't know what crawled up your shorts, but this is busy season. Everyone needs to be on the top of their game."

"I know that, Kyle."

"I know you *know* that. I'm trying to be your friend here."

Guilt flooded Zack. What was his problem? He knew better than to insult the climbers. "Sorry."

Hands on his hips, Kyle looked down. "Taylor, we need to talk. Lunch?"

As much as he hated to admit it, Zack needed someone to talk to. "Fine."

His friend left the room, and Zack stood. How could one woman turn his world upside down just like that? It wasn't as if he had everything under control, but at least he managed okay. So he liked to take risks on his own time. He'd never put anyone else in any danger. In fact, just the opposite. Didn't he save lives for a living?

A stark realization hit him square in the face. All the excuses in the world couldn't answer the question *why* he couldn't get enough. Why he risked his life again and again. Kyle was correct, the hole inside Zack couldn't be filled—it was bottomless.

Missy rounded the corner and entered. "Hey, Zack, since you've been rescheduled to be at Base Camp this week, I need to give you some information about one of our climbers."

Back to business. "Okay, shoot."

"We've got a cancer survivor, age thirty-two, in excellent health and in remission for two years." She handed him a paper.

"Any meds?"

"None."

"Good, that makes things easier. What's the name?" He perused the sheet.

"Granger. Karon Granger."

❧

A chair scraped across the café's wood floor. Zack didn't take much notice.

Karon was a cancer survivor? She seemed so vibrant and positive. So healthy.

So happy.

Cancer. The word alone stabbed his heart. His grandfather had died of cancer. But the cancerous attitude of his mom and dad through the battle had destroyed more than the disease had, in his opinion. Mom and Dad had divorced, Dad moved away and drank himself to an early grave, and Zack's own relationship with God suffered.

It hadn't just suffered. Zack turned away.

That was when he'd turned to extreme mountaineering. K-2, Everest, Aconcagua, Denali—they'd all been challenging. He'd used up fifteen years of his life looking for the answer— trying to fill the hole in his heart.

"Hey, man." Kyle patted him on the shoulder.

He nodded. Hadn't even realized Kyle had shown up.

"You look deep in thought." His friend sat down. "You ordered?"

Zack leaned back in his chair. "Nah, been waiting for you."

"Good. 'Cause what I've got to say needs your attention."

He looked up. "Go for it. I got nothin' to lose."

"You know what I'm going to say."

"Yeah, you're gonna preach at me and tell me the only way I'm going to turn things around is to turn back to God."

Kyle smiled. "Preach? Seriously?"

"Yeah. Maybe one day I'll listen."

That brought a laugh. "Well, you nailed it. You've refused to listen to anything I've said about God for five years. But it's true. He's the only way to get rid of the ache. To fill up the hole."

"Easy to say. It's like a nice little script all good Christians rehearse. But it's not that easy. It was when I *had* faith that everything fell apart around me. My parents became the ugliest and meanest people I knew. I still hate having conversations with my own mom because of the negativity. Faith in God is what tanked my life. Let me climb a mountain or fly into a blizzard any day."

"And *that* makes you feel better?" Kyle crossed his arms and hiked an eyebrow.

If he were honest? Not really. But it did fill his time and his thoughts.

"Yeah. That's what I thought." Kyle leaned his elbows on his knees. "Look, I'm far from perfect. I have a temper. I struggle with all kinds of temptations. But the Bible never told me that when I became a Christian, I'd be a saint overnight, or that my life would be easy and smooth sailing. What I did learn was that life would be filled with trials, and my *faith* would help me grow through those trials to be a better man."

Zack stared him down.

"Your faith didn't ruin your life, pal." He paused to take a deep breath. "You let go when you should've held on tighter."

"So it's *my* fault my life tanked?"

"If the crampon fits. . ." Kyle tempered the remark with a smile.

A short laugh escaped his lips.

"Think about it. If you were climbing and let go of the rope—you'd take a nasty, if not life-ending fall, right? Would you blame the *rope* for your fall?"

Ouch. Was that what'd he done? Zack leaned back and laced his fingers behind his head. "You just cut to the chase, don't you? I'm almost afraid to admit that you're making sense." What would happen if he quit his daredevil ways and lived the way *normal* people lived? Let God take over and fill the hole?

"Good, 'cause I'm hungry. This isn't rocket science, my friend. Promise me you'll think about it."

"Deal." He leaned forward. His chest already felt a thousand pounds lighter. "As long as you don't nag me." Maybe he was on the right track. He could even call his mom just because. But then again, maybe he was rushing things.

"No guarantees, man. I'm great at nagging." Kyle tossed a menu on the table. "But I'll buy your lunch to make up for it."

"You're on."

Chapter 8

A cclimatization will be one of the most important aspects of this trip. That's why it's so important to maintain the schedule we've laid out, carry high, sleep low, and rest on rest days. We've also got to take weather into consideration, so be prepared for some storms. Denali is unpredictable." Their guide for the next twenty-eight days, Lionel, was a wealth of information. Even with all the climbing experience Karon had racked up the past year, she'd learned a notebook full more today.

He handed them each a sheet of paper. "Let's go through this quick." He spoke with a British accent that clipped at a pace her little Southern brain already couldn't keep up with. Oh boy. "We're almost at sea level right now, day one. We'll fly into Base Camp on the Kahiltna Glacier at 7,200 feet. We'll stay there day two to get used to the altitude before we begin our ascent. Day three we'll climb to Ski Hill at 7,900 feet. Day four, the Upper Kahiltna at 9,600 feet. Day five, we'll rest and acclimate. Day six, we'll climb to 11,000 feet. Day seven, we'll rest. Day eight, we'll carry to Basin Camp and sleep low back at 11,000. Day nine, we'll move to Basin Camp. Once we get there, we'll be at 14,200 feet. We'll take days ten and eleven to rest and acclimate again. Days twelve and thirteen we carry to Ridge Camp and sleep at Basin Camp. Day fourteen, we'll move to Ridge Camp at 16,200 feet. Day fifteen, High Camp at 17,200 feet. Day sixteen, we'll rest, and day seventeen will be our first possible day to summit."

Karon wrote in shorthand to keep up with the guide. "And the rest of the days are in case we have to deal with weather?"

"Yes. Many of our climbers make it to High Camp but never see the summit because of weather." He smiled. "But since you've taken extra time for this expedition, the chances are higher that we'll be able to wait out a storm or multiple storms and still summit in time for your return."

Clint flicked her in the arm. "Good, because I'd hate to take a month off work and sit in a tent the whole time freezing my toes off."

Karon rolled her eyes. "Excuse my brother, Lionel. Please continue."

Lionel gave Clint a scolding look any teacher would be proud of—and Clint even squirmed. Karon liked this guy already. "All your gear has been checked and double-checked. AMS has prepared everything else on our end. Any questions?"

Clint looked to her and, with wisdom beyond his years, kept his mouth shut.

She rubbed her hands together. "Nope. I'm just ready to get up there."

Lionel shut his notebook with a snap and smiled. "Then let's load up."

❧

The small plane that flew them to the glacier gave them a spectacular view, but Karon preferred Deline's Otter since they'd flown around each of the peaks. This ride was closer to the ground and Karon loved it. Her adrenaline pumped. She couldn't believe Lionel could sit in the noisy plane and snore.

Denali stood tall, its massive structure covered in snow and ice. No wonder the mountain was named by the native people as the *High One*, Sultana, the *Wife*, and Begguya, the *Child*.

The regal family were the crown jewels of the Alaska Range. And just as a family should, they stood firm together.

Her mouth dropped as she watched an enormous avalanche on the steep slopes of Sultana. Whispering a prayer that there weren't any climbers in the area, Karon kept her eyes glued to the beautiful devastation.

As the plane banked to land on the thirty-six-mile-long glacier, she prayed for their safety. The magnitude of what they were about to embark on sent chills up her arms. Excitement and a touch of fear caused her to giggle.

Clint leaned closer. "Nervous?"

"A little."

"You'll do great. Besides, you've got me, and I've never failed at anything." He smirked.

"Pride goeth before the fall, little brother." She pushed him back into his seat.

"Only on Tuesdays."

Lionel opened his eyes from his nap. "Are you two chums going to be like this the whole trip?"

"Worse!" they shouted at the same time.

"Oh good." Lionel shut his eyes again. "Entertainment."

The pilot shook his head, lowered the plane, and flew the final approach.

One soft bounce and they were skidding along the glacier's surface.

Even with her sunglasses on, the glare burned her eyes. Karon took off her favorite aviators and replaced them with her glacier glasses. Much better. At least she could see now. Her eyes would have to adjust to the brightness over the next month.

As they unpacked the plane, Karon couldn't wait to meet other climbers and explore the Base Camp. Her excitement only grew as they said good-bye to the AMS pilot.

Lionel directed them to haul all their equipment and sleds to where they would camp. Each of them would be responsible for a large amount of supplies. Clint teased Karon before they left that the frame pack was bigger than her. And he was almost correct. But during the months of training, she'd grown strong and could carry the required amount of weight, just like him.

Her excitement propelled her forward, and pulling a sled, she raced Clint to the camp.

She tripped the last three feet and flew headlong into a snowbank. Even face-first, she couldn't contain her laughter. She smacked at the arms pulling her out. Clint always had to baby her. But as she wiped the thick layer of snow out of her hair and face, she realized the strong arms that held her weren't her brother's.

They belonged to a very tall, incredibly cute ranger named Zack.

Chapter 9

Zack was a goner.

Even before her flop into the snowbank, he'd watched Karon's antics. Her laughter was contagious. From the moment he heard it, he wanted to feel that same joy. And after his talk with Kyle, he felt a glimmer of hope. Maybe he really could come back from the pit he'd lived in all these years.

Karon wiped snow off her face and stared at him. Then she busted out laughing again. "I'm sorry. Guess I don't make the best first impression."

Her brother walked up behind her. "Oh, you make an impression all right. Just ask that snowdrift over there."

She swatted at him. "Guess I'll never live that one down, will I?"

"Nope." He held up a tiny camera. "And I got a great picture of it, too." Clint brought the view screen over to Zack. "It's a great shot, isn't it, Ranger Taylor?"

Karon grabbed for the camera. "You're asking for it, Clint." For a moment she looked embarrassed, and then the laughter started again.

Zack adjusted his goggles. "I think I should plead the fifth." The picture was hilarious. Arms and legs splayed with the snow exploding around her as she hit. But Karon probably wouldn't appreciate hearing that.

Brother razzed sister a little more. "This would make a great post on Facebook, don't you think?"

Karon finished brushing off snow and stood straight, not missing a beat. "Only if you want the picture of you as a baby with your bare little hiney exposed to the world."

"Oh, you play dirty."

"I learned from the best."

Zack watched the interchange. He'd never had siblings, so the banter was new to him. Sarcasm and Southern accents flew across the snow, but the warmth that radiated from the two made him yearn for more.

Clint smiled. "Thank you, thank you very much."

"For what?" She placed her hands on her hips.

"For saying I'm the best." He took a bow.

She smacked him. "Pfft. I didn't learn anything from you, baby brother. I was talking about my kindergartners."

Zack laughed out loud at that one.

Lionel walked up to him and held out his hand. "Ranger Taylor. How're you this fine day?"

"Good, Lionel. Good." The guide's presence reminded him to focus on the task at hand. "You all set?"

"Yes, indeed," the guide answered. "We'll be here tonight and tomorrow night to acclimate before we ascend."

"All right. I have to check with the others. Let me know if you need something." Zack hesitated. He wanted a reason to come back and check on this party.

Karon and Lionel pulled sleds and gear away. She waved to him as she left.

Clint stepped closer to Zack. "Excuse me, Ranger Taylor?"

Zack stopped. "Yep?"

"Do you like to read?"

He narrowed his eyebrows. "Read?"

"Yes, read. As in books."

"Um, sure. I guess." Where was this going?

"My sister is a book buff."

Zack scratched his head. "A book buff."

Clint let out a sigh. "As in, she loves books. Inhales books."

He still didn't get it. "Okay. And I need to know this, because. . ."

"Are all rangers this dense?"

If it hadn't been so funny, Zack might've been offended. "I sure hope so." Otherwise, he really was an idiot.

Clint laughed at that one. "I'm trying to help you out."

"What do you mean?"

"With my sister. Karon." Clint crossed his arms. "You like her. I saw how you were looking at her in the briefing. . .your reaction when she said I was her brother."

Whoa. Zack held up his hands.

"Don't deny it. You already stuck your foot in your mouth, and if you looked at her much longer today, I guarantee there'd be drool frozen to your chin." He turned to walk away. "If you want to talk to her again, ask for a book. That's all I'm sayin'."

❧

Karon couldn't believe it. Her first night sleeping in a tent on the side of Denali and she threw off the sleeping bag because she was hot. Maybe she wore too many layers. Or maybe the fact that the sun still shone played tricks on her mind. Her brother snored on the other side of the small tent, his long arms extended. That man needed a king-sized bed just for himself. Shoving him over, she smacked his arm. "You're snoring, you big lug. Be quiet."

A grunt and then a snort and then blessed silence. Karon peeled off her top layer and slid back into her bag. Tomorrow she might see Zack again. That alone made the delay in ascension worth it. At first, she hadn't been too happy with the schedule, but the need for her body to adjust to the altitude was imperative. She did *not* want to be one of the poor people who suffered from acute mountain sickness. Now that she knew Zack would be at camp all day, her impatience sputtered to a stop.

Never had she been so instantly attracted to a man. What drove him? His prickly exterior appeared to cover…something. Cover she knew all too well. But never in a million years did she think a man would be attracted to her after cancer.

A glance in the mirror earlier that morning had made her pause. For years, she'd avoided her reflection. Today, she'd run her fingers through her short curly locks, stared into the brown eyes, and wondered if a man could love a battle-worn woman like her.

Karon leaned back on her pillow and prayed. God loved her more than she could ever imagine. She'd leave her attraction to Zack Taylor in His hands.

A pillow in the face woke her up the next morning. "Rise and shine, sleeping beauty." Clint's hair spiked in several directions. "I'm hungry."

Grit filled her eyes. She cracked one open. "And what? You expect me to fix it?"

"Don't you want to?"

"No." She pulled the sleeping bag over her head. "It's my summer vacation."

Clint guffawed. "Like I'm going to believe that. You chose to spend your summer vacation climbing a mountain. What's a little breakfast?"

"Get it yourself."

"Wow, someone woke up on the wrong side of the slope." He tapped the top of her head. "It's okay, because I'm going to be gallant and make breakfast for *you* today."

She lowered the bag to below her nose. "Really?"

"Yep."

"This I gotta see." Karon flung off the sleeping bag and jumped to her feet.

❧

After her "sumptuous feast" as Clint called it of bagels, omelets, and a protein shake, Karon strolled through the Base Camp enjoying the sounds and activities. A *lot* of people were climbing this mountain. More than she imagined. But the thought comforted her rather than discouraged her. At least she wouldn't be alone if there were problems.

For some strange reason that she didn't want to admit, her gaze searched for a certain ranger. When she spotted him, she felt the smile all the way to her toes. He was so stinkin' cute. Rugged. And fierce. There really wasn't a good reason why his somber personality attracted her. But she was drawn. Like a moth to a flame.

Zack turned. Waved.

Karon's heart did a double flip. Man, he was downright gorgeous. Why would he be interested in her? Best not to get her hopes up.

Heading her way, Zack spoke to another ranger as he walked. Karon took several tentative steps toward him. If there was ever a time to start living her life—it was now. Her steps grew longer, more purpose filled her stride. And she allowed the smile that filled her to flood her face.

Snow crunched under her boots and in two more strides, she met Zack in the middle of the Kahiltna camp.

"Hi, Karon."

"Ranger Taylor."

"You can call me Zack." One side of his mouth curled up half an inch. "I hear you're a book buff."

Clint. She looked back toward her tent and saw her brother wave. The stinker. "I am." A laugh bubbled up. "And I can guess how you found that out."

Zack gave her a simple nod, started walking to the side,

and with a slight move of his hand invited her to join him. "So, do you have any recommended reading? Something a guy like me would enjoy?"

"Sure, I've got lots of ideas. But I only have two books with me because of the weight. I would've brought ten in case we got stranded in a blizzard, but AMS set me straight on the norm being two. That and the fact that everyone shares and trades on the mountain." She was rambling. Stinkin' nervous jitters. Always brought out the worst of her jabbering. Best to focus on his question. "You need something while you're on the mountain or for once you get back?"

"If you've got something now, that'd be great. I didn't bring anything to read with me this time."

Time to test the waters. "You okay with Christian fiction? Because that's all I read."

"Sure. . ."

An idea formed. Several titles ran through her brain. One of her favorites was the *Discarded Heroes* series by Ronie Kendig. She had *Nightshade*—the first book in the series— with her and wanted Clint to read it, but maybe Zack would be a better choice. "I have a military thriller with me that's one of my faves. I'd be willing to let you borrow it. On one condition."

"And that would be?"

"You have to discuss it with me when you're done." Maybe then she would find out where he stood in his faith.

He tilted his head for a second. "I think I can handle that. As long as there's not a test or a bunch of worksheets I have to fill out."

"Ah. So you've found out I'm a teacher." Her heart did another flip. How much did this man know about her? And did he find it out all on his own because he was interested? Or did the rangers have to know all this information in advance?

She hoped it was the first option.

"With tiny feet." He kept walking. Slow, long strides that allowed her to keep up with him.

He'd noticed her feet? Seriously? This guy was full of surprises. "Yep. Some of my kindergartners have feet almost as big as mine." She smiled. "So you don't have to worry about tests from me. But I might ask you to finger paint your book report or make a macaroni sculpture to represent a character from the book."

His eyebrows raised. "You have a great sense of humor."

Was that a good thing or a bad thing? He was so hard to read.

"I bet your students love you. Even if you do have the same sized feet as a five-year-old." That corner of his mouth turned up again. This time, a little higher.

She stopped and turned toward him. "I've got to know. What is it with the feet? Aren't most men completely unobservant? I know my brother is, and all my friends tell me their husbands are."

He halted, pulled up his glacier goggles, and looked down at her feet. "That's a secret, Miss Granger. But let me ask you a question."

"Okay. Shoot."

"Haven't you ever heard that a long time ago, the Chinese would bind the feet of the girl children so that their feet would remain tiny?"

Ah, she knew where he was going with it now. The Chinese believed that tiny feet were beautiful and attractive. "I did know that. I'd forgotten." So was he implying what she hoped?

Chapter 10

Did he just give too much away? Zack watched her face as she processed the information. Might as well go for broke. "Bet you don't have trouble finding footholds when you're climbing."

Her bell-like laughter split the air. "I never thought of it, but you're right. I've never had trouble because my feet fit on almost any little ledge, crack, or crevice."

Yep. The guys would never let him live it down if they saw him flirting.

She continued walking, seeming comfortable in the silence. Her questions about Christian books threw him a curve. After talking with Kyle, he still wasn't sure if he was ready to let God back in. But faith seemed important to Karon. What did that mean, that both of them had mentioned faith? That God was trying to get at him?

They walked a ways up the glacier before she spoke again. "So...tell me about your job. I know you're a mountaineering ranger, but you're also a rescue helicopter pilot. How do you do both?"

A safe topic. She wanted to get to know him, too. Good. "Well, during climbing season, I take rotations at Base Camp and High Camp like the other rangers. Just one of each, though, because High Camp rotation is thirty days. Right now, I'm on Base Camp rotation, then I'll return to the ranger station and be on call for rescue duty. There's another guy they call in for rescue when I'm on rotation. Then next month, I'll do my thirty days up at High Camp."

"Wow. You guys do that all winter, too?"

"No, we don't keep rangers up here during the winter months. It's too brutal. Although there are those who've tried to climb it."

Her mouth dropped open. "Seriously? Someone would attempt this in the winter?"

"Yep, last year, we had three guys try it in January."

"That's crazy." She shook her head. "Why would anyone do that?"

The question made him laugh. He'd wondered the same thing, but he'd been itching to go rescue them in one of the worst storms ever. "Because if they would have made it, they would've been able to say they summitted Denali in January, in the dark."

Her mouth made an O. "Gotcha. So it was totally a macho, conquering thing."

The comment caused him to bristle a little. "Maybe. But isn't that what you're doing?"

She bit her bottom lip. "Maybe. At least the conquering part. But it's more than that."

He waited. Hoping she would share the real reason she was attempting to climb this mountain.

"It's about living my life."

"Can't you live your life back down in Louisiana?"

"Well, sure. But. . ." Several moments passed. "I need to do this."

"Why?"

"I just do."

Should he tell her he knew about the cancer?

Too many thoughts jumbled in his brain and confused him. Kyle had nagged him, as promised, since their talk, and Zack couldn't decide what God wanted from him.

Karon's light voice broke through the moment. "Haven't you ever longed to live your life to the fullest? No one holding you back. No *thing* holding you back. Just living. . .to *live*." She paced with her hands on her hips. "Making the most of every day. Because every second is precious. Every person is precious. Every breath—"

"Precious." He smiled. "Yeah, I get it." He turned away. Had God answered him? She put his very thoughts into words—understood him. In a way no one else ever could. "We've got the same perspective, we just traveled different roads to get there."

"What do you mean?" She paused in her stride and watched him.

"You came here with a life wish. You want to summit this mountain as a symbol of your life—that you're living it." He put a hand on her shoulder.

No flinching. No pulling away. No confession. She just stood there, waiting for him to go on.

"I came here with a death wish. . .trying anything and everything to risk my life."

❧

Karon jolted at Zack's words but she also understood them. She considered blurting out everything about her cancer. But would that repulse him? Even though his words took her back, she really wanted to hear the rest of his story. Maybe it was too soon; from the increased pace she could tell he'd closed up. He walked on ahead. "Zack, wait. I want to ask you a question."

"Sure." His brows lowered.

"You said you *came* here with a death wish? Does that mean you've changed?"

A moment passed. "I hope so—that is, I'm trying. Although

it's too early for me to say the transformation is complete."

"I'm not sure I understand. . . ."

His steps slowed then stopped. A muscle in his jaw twitched. "I'm not good at this, sorry. But you're right, every moment counts." His shoulders rose as he took a long breath. "I turned away from God a long time ago when my life fell apart. I blamed Him." He started walking again, slow steady steps up the glacier. Karon was at his side. "A good friend of mine, another ranger, took me aside recently and asked me about it. I told him that of course it was *God's* fault because when I *had* faith my life took a turn for the worse." A sad chuckle reached Karon's ears. Zack shook his head. "But my friend asked me a great question."

She waited.

He stopped and looked straight at her. "He said, 'If you were climbing and let go of the rope, would you blame the *rope* for your fall?'" Zack shook his head again. "It was amazing. In that one simple moment, I understood. My faith in God—or even God Himself—hadn't caused my life to tank. Because He's the rope. I let go, when I should've been holding on tighter." Zack shrugged and continued walking.

Karon smiled. "So you're saying you're a believer?"

"Yep." He stared ahead. "Have been a long time. Just haven't been holding on to the rope like I should. But I'm changing that."

She tugged on his parka sleeve. "Zack, wait." A lump the size of Texas grew in her throat as he stopped a few feet below her and pulled his goggles up. "Thank you."

"For what?"

"For sharing that with me. I need the reminder to hold a little tighter to the rope, too."

They walked together in silence back down to the camp. Karon's thoughts ran a mile a minute. This man beside her was quite a conundrum. He both attracted and confused her.

"Can I come by your tent later to get the book? I've got some other duties to attend to. . . ." Back to business, Zack didn't wait for a response, just gave her a nod.

Karon admired his broad shoulders as he walked away. One minute they'd shared a pretty deep connection, and the next? He left.

With a sigh, she turned back to her tent and decided to focus on food. She already missed jambalaya, crawfish, and shrimp. Maybe she could grab another bagel if she made it back to the tent in time. After the first week, they would be eating more tortillas, so she wanted to eat bread now while she had the chance.

The afternoon was spent hiking and hydrating to help them adapt to the elevation change. Then they rechecked gear and prepared dinner. Tortellini was on the menu and she found herself starved. Hopefully Lionel would let her pile on the mozzarella cheese. She wanted extra cheese on pretty much everything. As their private guide, Lionel catered to most of their wishes, as long as they were within reason. Even with the hardships they'd face on the expedition, she was looking forward to the climb.

But not looking forward to saying good-bye to Zack.

Chapter 11

Tomorrow she'd be gone. Up the mountain, on the adventure of her life. Zack longed to spend every minute with her, but his job demanded his attention. He'd never had trouble focusing before.

But that was before he met Karon.

He looked at his watch. Eight p.m. They'd be going to bed soon, even though the sun still shone in the sky and would for hours to come. But they had to be ready for a long day of climbing, and they needed rest.

Clint popped his head out of the Grangers' tent. "Hey, wanna play a round of spades?"

"Sure, I was just heading your way."

Karon, Lionel, and Clint all smiled when he entered.

"We need a fourth, my good man." Lionel's accent seemed deeper. "You can be Karon's partner." He winked.

Great. Now there were two matchmakers. But Zack didn't mind. "Sure thing. Bags or no bags?"

"Bags." Clint and Karon spoke at the same time.

"Be forewarned, chap, they're brutal." Lionel leaned back. "I haven't won a trick yet."

Two hours and five rounds later, Karon excused herself and left the tent, while Zack enjoyed the camaraderie of the guys. It'd been a long time since he'd allowed himself to relax and have fun.

"Well, it's past bedtime," Lionel said. "And I've got to haul these dossers up the mountain tomorrow. So, out you go, Ranger."

Zack said his good-byes but missed getting to see Karon. Maybe he'd get the chance in the morning, but he doubted it.

As he hiked off to his own tent, Karon's voice followed him. "Zack! Ranger Taylor!"

He turned. Her cheeks were red from the cold.

"Hey, I brought you that book." She held a gallon Ziploc with a book inside. "I hope you enjoy it."

"Thanks. It's been a long time since I read a novel, so I'm looking forward to it." He reached out for the book. Didn't want to break the connection between them. Would he see her again?

She held out a hand. "It was really nice to spend time with you. Thanks."

Zack reached out and grasped her hand then wrapped his other around it. "I hope it's not the last time we see each other, Karon. . .in fact. . .I wanted to ask you something."

"Sure, go ahead." She didn't let go.

Her gloved hand felt warm even through the thick layers. "I'd like to know if you'd be willing to go out with me. Later. . . you know. . .when we're off the mountain. . .sometime." Idiot. Such an idiot. He almost wanted to roll his eyes at himself. What was he? Sixteen again?

She giggled. "You mean, there aren't any great restaurants up here on the mountain? I hear there's an incredible view."

The joke helped calm his racing heart. "Well, I was hoping to take you *out* someplace, not just *up*."

"But up is so beautiful."

"So are you, Karon."

She sucked in a breath.

"Is that a yes?" He waited. Like a kid. Seconds felt like hours.

A slow smile formed on her face. "I'd love to go out with you."

"So, it's a date?"

She shook her head. "No. I can't."

His heart lurched. He stared at her for several moments then squeezed the hand he still held between his.

"I'm sorry," she added.

"Good night, Karon. I hope you get your wish."

❧

Zack's words echoed through her brain as she trudged up the Kahiltna Glacier pulling a sled and her huge frame pack on her back. Of course, he'd been referencing her wish to summit Denali, which was why she was freezing her tuckus off at this very moment, but another wish was at the forefront of her mind. The wish to fall in love and get married. Hope sprouted inside her with thoughts of Zack, but how could she consider going out with him when she hadn't even told him the truth? What if he had no desire to date a woman who'd had cancer? No. She refused to say yes and then have him fulfill his obligation out of pity.

Even though the sun shone bright and there wasn't a cloud in the sky, the wind whipped around her like a tornado. Lionel kept telling her to be thankful, many people never had the chance to see all of Denali because it was shrouded in clouds most of the time, but she wondered how long the wind would batter and bruise her aching body.

All the training, all the practicing, all the books—none of it prepared her for the real climb up Denali. When she read that the weather in summer on Denali could be worse than the weather on Everest in the winter, she'd found it interesting. Now the bitter wind ripping through her drove the point home. And they weren't even to 8,000 feet yet.

"Come on, children," Lionel yelled back. "While we're still young."

Clint was too far behind her to hear, but Karon couldn't help but laugh. This expedition was her idea, and here they were. She'd better focus. The summit of Denali awaited.

Days three, four, and five passed much the same. On day six, the wind died down, and they climbed to 11,000 feet. As the sun beat down on them, Karon took off two of her outer layers. Clint had stopped fussing over her, which was a much-needed reprieve, and Lionel turned out to be quite the spades player—even with just the three of them playing.

Her body had done well getting used to the higher altitude so far, and she felt strong. Stronger than she'd felt in a long time. If only she'd been strong enough to tell Zack the truth about her cancer.

The sleeping bag confined her as she tossed and turned. Too late to go back and change her answer to Zack. It was best this way. Besides, she had a grueling climb ahead of her. But she was on her way. To the top of Denali.

❧

Zack paced in front of the radio, his thoughts pinging around. Why couldn't he get Karon out of his head? "Any news. . .um. . . ?"

"Dude, you're ridiculous." The new ranger—what's-his-name—shook his head and walked away.

"Can't even remember the new guy's name, huh?" David walked up and thumped Zack's shoulder. "You *are* ridiculous."

"Well. . ." He thought for a moment. "No, I have no idea what his name is. Can't we just call him 'rookie'?"

David's laughter rumbled. "It's okay. I don't remember his name either. *Dude*," his friend mimicked the new ranger. It cracked his nervous shell. "Normally takes me a while to get used to the new guys anyway."

"Yeah, but most of the time, we know 'em first. We've

worked side by side or climbed together." Zack took a long swig from his water bottle. "And it didn't help that I was distracted the guy's first few days."

Another punch in the arm. "So the great adventurer finally admits it? He's come down to the same level as us regular people and found out there's more to life than the great adrenaline rush?" David swept his arm wide and pretended he had an audience. "Hear ye, hear ye—"

"Oh, shut up." Zack couldn't help but laugh and pitched a snowball at David.

"But you admit you were checkin' up on your girl, huh?"

The words "your girl" had a nice ring to them. If only Karon hadn't turned him down. Yeah, he was pathetic. All these years he'd avoided women and relationships. Amazing how one week could change it all. "Haven't heard anything today. The wind's been howling really bad up there the past few days, so I was a little concerned."

"Aw. You're worried. How sweet."

Zack punched his friend in the arm. "Concerned. Not worried. I just wanted to know if they'd checked in."

"Uh-huh. Pa-the-tic. Just sayin'."

"Better watch it, David. Wait until you find someone. I'm gonna razz you even worse."

"I'm shakin' in my boots, pal." His friend cowered.

The hulk of David shaking in front of him made Zack bust out laughing. So maybe he *was* being a little ridiculous. Karon could take care of herself. She knew what she was doing. And she had Clint and Lionel. She'd be fine.

Really.

Chapter 12

The mountain glistened in the sunlight. The wind returned with a fury and severe cold dropped on them. Even with the sun shining almost around the clock every day, Karon felt the chill in her bones. The higher they climbed, the more water she drank. Food wasn't interesting anymore, but her thirst never seemed to be quenched.

Every now and then, a glimpse of another peak gave her pause. This was more of an undertaking than she'd imagined. The broadness of Denali stretched before her. Ice and snow as far as the eye could see.

Each step took her closer to the goal. And each night as she rubbed sore muscles, she thanked God for the opportunity. The chance to do something so extreme, so different.

They'd spent another day resting after making 11,000 feet. Then a day carrying to Basin Camp. Today, they were *moving* to Basin Camp at 14,200 feet. Even though she'd already climbed this path yesterday, she found the hike exhilarating. Always something new to thank God for—even Clint's complaining. Or his snoring. At least her brother loved her enough to do something like this with her.

Their pace had slowed. Karon caught up with Lionel and spoke through her mask. "Everything okay, Lionel?"

"Yes. I believe so. Had a dizzy spell. I'm all right now." Their guide looked tired.

Karon wondered if he'd been resting enough. Lionel was such a go-getter, and the staff at AMS said he never took any time off. They called him the "Energizer Bunny."

He pointed ahead. "Not too much longer and we'll make Basin Camp. I don't know about you chaps, but I'm looking forward to something warm for supper, and these climbs always make me miss teatime."

"Like hot soup?" Karon felt hunger pangs for the first time in a couple of days. "That sounds heavenly."

They trudged up the mountain, the steepest part of their climb done for the day. Karon tried to even her breathing. At this elevation, there was approximately 50 percent the amount of oxygen as sea level. Hopefully her body had been doing its job and acclimating. The bitter cold seeped into her boots. Maybe tomorrow would be a good day to try her overboots. She didn't want to seem like a wimp, but her toes were freezing.

By the time eight p.m. arrived, they'd eaten a hearty meal, and were all in bed. Karon looked at the ceiling of the tent. "Clint," she whispered. "You awake?"

"Barely." The wind that day had roughed up his voice. "But I won't last much longer. Whatcha need?"

"Nothing. I was just thinking." She tucked her chin farther into her bag.

"Might as well tell me." He rolled to face her. "You have a captive audience."

Karon got a brief glimpse of his eyes. Most of the time, they were all covered from head to toe in gear. Her brother looked tired. "What do you think of Zack?"

"As in, Ranger Taylor, Zack?"

"Yep."

He paused. "I think he's a hard worker, serious. . ."

"If I had an extra pillow, I'd throw it at you. You know I like him, don't you?"

"It's a tad bit obvious, yes. At least to me."

Karon laughed. "I know you told him about my love of books."

He stared at her.

"And you thought he needed a little shove."

More silence.

"So. . .I'm assuming that means you're okay with it?"

Clint raised himself up on an elbow. "Okay with Zack? Yes. Okay with you moving on with your life? Yes. Okay with you finding someone to cherish you? Even better." He lay back down and shut his eyes. "I just hope he knows how really special you are, Kare Bear."

The use of her nickname brought back a rush of old memories. "Thanks. But I feel like an idiot. I turned him down."

"You what?"

"He asked me out and I turned him down."

"Why?"

"He doesn't know about the cancer. What if he can't deal with it and pushes me away? I don't think I want to deal with that rejection."

Silence reigned again for several seconds. Clint cleared his throat. "I have a feeling Zack already knows. Didn't you say the rangers had to know?"

"Well, then, why didn't he say anything?"

"Maybe he was respecting your privacy."

"Oh. I hadn't thought of that."

Her brother reached a hand out and patted her hat-covered head. "I thought you were gonna stop worrying about what people thought? You're incredible, Karon, and if Zack is smart, he'll snatch you up."

"Thanks."

"You're welcome."

"And, Clint?"

"Yeah?"

"Thanks for doing this with me."

"Sure. Just don't tell me you want to do Everest next because my answer is no." He rolled over and within a few minutes the snoring began.

If only she could turn off her brain that easily. Karon tucked herself back inside the depths of her warm sleeping cocoon. For the first time in a long time, she allowed herself to dream of a future with a man by her side.

A blond, scruffy-faced, mountaineering ranger.

The call came in around 2:00 a.m.

Zack and David headed up to just below 11,000 feet to rescue a victim of acute mountain sickness. By the time they arrived, the climber was worse. Zack feared high altitude cerebral edema, and they began their descent immediately. The wind and bitter cold fought them the whole way, and exhaustion began to take its toll.

When Zack returned to Base Camp and the victim was flown out, he realized his rotation was done and he could get off the mountain and sleep in a real bed. His only other thought was of Karon.

Before climbing onto the helicopter that would take him back to the ranger station, Zack looked up to the mountain one more time. He prayed for her safety, and asked God to grant Karon's wish of reaching Denali's summit.

Zack awoke after twelve hours of dead sleep. He slid his feet to the floor and stretched. Thirty-eight straight hours of being awake just didn't cut it anymore at his age. Add in the climbing, rescue, and high altitude, and no wonder his body wanted to return to the bed. But he had too much to do. Besides, if he went back to bed, he'd probably dream about

Karon again, and he needed to focus. Not that focusing on Karon wasn't fun. He enjoyed it too much. And he hardly knew her.

And she lived in Louisiana.

He passed a globe on his desk and gave it a spin. Louisiana was a long way from Alaska. A very long way.

Zack ground some beans and made a fresh pot of coffee. He had reports that needed to be written, and the rescue helicopter needed a couple of safety checks today. Might as well hit the ground running.

After a long run on his treadmill and a shower, Zack headed out the door. His cell phone rang. It wouldn't be anyone from the station; they'd use the radio.

"Hello?"

"Hey, man, it's David."

"What's up?"

"Thought I'd give you a little news."

Zack's heart skipped a beat. "I'm listening."

"Your girl's on her way to High Camp." David clicked off before Zack even got to say thanks.

He shook his head. High Camp. That meant that if the weather held, she might get to summit in a couple of days and then she'd be on her way back down.

But not to him.

Chapter 13

Once they left Basin Camp at 14,200 feet, Karon felt the difference in her bones. She was wearing out. And Lionel didn't look like he was faring much better. Clint didn't say much, just kept up his pace behind her. The wind and cold tore through them. And now, clouds shrouded them in the top heights of Denali.

They stopped for a few minutes and Karon eased the heavy pack off her shoulders. Lionel sat very still twenty feet above her. As she approached, he lifted his goggles. "Do my eyes look all right to you?"

She wasn't sure what to look for, but the glassy appearance of his eyes scared her. "I don't know, Lionel. I'm not a doctor."

"Ten years I've been leading expeditions and guiding people on this mountain. I haven't been sick in all that time."

Wow. Ten years. She chuckled. "I work with five-year-olds. I'm lucky if I avoid their bugs every few weeks."

"I'm not trying to scare you. I just believe in being totally forthright. And, Karon, I don't feel well. The only symptom is a sore throat right now, but I don't feel well. Not at all." He replaced all his gear. "Let me get you to High Camp and I'll radio in. There's usually a doctor there as well."

Karon nodded. She couldn't imagine getting sick on the side of a mountain. Sick at home on a comfy couch or in bed was bad enough. Poor Lionel.

She walked over to Clint and told him what was going on. In a matter of minutes, they were back on the trail to

High Camp. Hopefully someone there could help their guide feel better.

An hour of torturous climbing passed in the wind and now blowing snow. The weather had changed from bad to worse in an instant. Lionel, Karon, and Clint were all tethered together with rope, and Karon could barely see the next step in front of her, the visibility was so bad.

So this was the horror all the books talked about. A blizzard on the side of the mountain in the middle of a climb. No wonder so many people never saw the summit.

She redirected her thoughts. Maybe singing a song in her head would help. Clint loved to call her *songbird* because he always caught her singing something. But up here? Too cold. And she had a hard time keeping a tune going.

What about her memory verses? She'd challenged the ladies in her Bible study class at church to memorize scripture with her. The thought of everyone arguing over which translation made her laugh. It had been one of the first times after her cancer that she stood up and made an executive decision. No one argued with her choice of the NASB because they were so shocked that Karon was back.

The laughter faded in the cold of her mask, but it felt good to think of something other than the agony of each step.

She started reciting at the beginning of Psalm 23. A perfect passage for the task before her.

The LORD is my shepherd, I shall not want. He makes me lie down in green pastures; He leads me beside quiet waters. He restores my soul; He guides me in the paths of righteousness for His name's sake.

Even though I walk through the valley of the shadow of death, I fear no evil, for You are with me; Your rod and Your staff, they comfort me. You prepare a table before me in the presence of my enemies; You have anointed my head with oil; my cup overflows.

Surely goodness and lovingkindness will follow me all the days of my life, and I will dwell in the house of the LORD forever.

There were days, not so long ago, that Karon thought for sure she was headed to the Lord's house sooner than later. As she focused on heaven and her Savior, she realized some very important things. If the Lord granted her any extra time on this planet, she would live it. Not wonder about all the what-ifs. Not worry about what people thought.

And here she stood. On the face of Denali, the tallest mountain in North America. Even if she didn't summit—she'd be okay. Proud of what she had accomplished. Pleased that she'd tried.

In the next step, her toe kicked something large and the momentum caused her to tumble over the obstruction in the path. When she righted herself, she tugged on the rope toward Clint to warn him.

But as Clint approached, Karon knelt in the storm to see what she'd tripped over.

Lionel! Covered in snow and unconscious.

❧

Clint unpacked one of the sleds while Karon tried to rouse Lionel. But it was no use. The man was out cold. She went to help Clint sort supplies, so they could hopefully make it to High Camp and help for Lionel. With this storm, she felt the urgency as surely as Clint did. The visibility had diminished as the day went on, and they'd now have to pull Lionel on a sled.

Clint yelled over the wind into her ear. "It can't be much farther to High Camp. Maybe an hour at most. I say we keep going in hopes we can make it to the doctor."

Karon nodded. "Have you tried the radio?" Her voice screeched.

"I just started warming up the batteries. But so far, nothing. That's why I think we should keep going. I haven't seen any other climbers in a while."

For the first time since they'd started, Karon was nervous. And indecisive. "Are we doing the right thing? Didn't you read the mountaineering guide? It said it took, what...twice as long to answer questions or make decisions at high altitudes. What if we go the wrong way?" Her breaths quickened as her voice raised in pitch. "What if the storm knocks us off the trail and no one can find us?"

Clint grabbed both her arms. "We don't have a lot of time, Karon. Let's move."

❧❧

Zack pushed against David's arms. "What?"

The other ranger let go. "We received a transmission that their guide collapsed. That's all we know. We haven't had any other communication."

"Where were they? Did you get coordinates?"

John headed toward Zack. "Son, you need to calm down." The lead ranger could keep a level head anywhere. "We'll get ready for a rescue once the weather cooperates. But right now, you know as well as I do that there's no way to fly into that."

Zack didn't want to admit anything. The other rangers in the room watched, the seriousness of the moment etched into each of their faces. These people were his family. They understood. Better than anyone.

"I'd like to be the one to fly in." He straightened his shoulders.

John paused and looked down. "When I clear the flight, you and Kyle will go in. But I want Kyle flying this one."

Zack clenched his fists.

"We all know, Zack. The Granger woman is special to

you. I don't want you pulling any of your crazy stunts to get in there, putting our people and equipment in jeopardy."

The anger burned. He needed to risk it all to save Karon. He had to. She had to live.

John strode closer to Zack and waved everyone else out of the room. "Don't get angry at me about this decision. I see it on your face—I know you're feeling desperate. You should be thankful I'm even letting you go out, but with weather as bad as this, I need another pilot in case Kyle has trouble. Besides, you can't fly the helo *and* go down to rescue her at the same time." The older man laid a hand on Zack's shoulder.

The heat fizzled out of his anger. John was right. "Yes, sir."

"Good. Now get some rest. We don't know how long this will take. There are several other groups that haven't made it to their next camp. This storm could have stranded or injured a lot of climbers."

Zack nodded and watched his boss walk out of the conference room. What would happen to Karon up there without a guide?

A hand on his shoulder made him jump. Kyle stood there with a stupid grin on his face.

"What?"

"You let go of the rope again?" His friend gave him a pat and left without waiting for him to answer.

As he walked to the window, Zack realized Kyle had been correct. Again. But how could he share all this with God? He'd always shouldered his own problems. He was the ranger. He was the rescuer. And even though she'd turned him down, he'd been hoping he could persuade her otherwise.

Then the words he'd spoken to Karon during their briefing came back to haunt him. He'd grilled her about being self-reliant and being able to self-rescue. Seriously? Was this how God was getting his attention?

In all his life, Zack realized how far self had gotten him. Nowhere.

Yep. He'd let go of the rope again. But he could rectify that problem.

Lord, You alone know what's really going on up there. Please protect all the climbers. And guide those of us who need to help them.

With that simple prayer, Zack grabbed hold of the rope.

Chapter 14

Thirty grueling minutes had passed since Karon and Clint loaded Lionel onto a sled and began dragging him up to High Camp.

She was out of energy and out of memory verses. Whatever possessed her to climb this stupid mountain in the first place? Had she totally lost her mind?

Images of a roaring fire and hot chocolate with marshmallows floated through her mind. She felt like one of the little puppies trudging through the snow in *101 Dalmatians*. Her nose was frozen. Her toes were frozen. And yes, even her tail was frozen.

Next time she watched that movie with one of the neighbor kids, she'd have a new appreciation for the little puppy's feelings.

She heard little B's voice in her head. *"You can't quit, Miss Karon. You gotta keep going."*

She'd never forget those words. He'd whispered them to her in the hospital. Then the children's choir she'd directed for umpteen years came and sang a song from an old Christmas musical.

"Take a step of faith. Take a step of faith. When you can't see your hand in front of your face, take a step of faith. . . ."

A smile split her chapped lips with the memories. And even with ice and snow covering her from head to toe, she knew she had to keep going. A resurgence of energy came from a well deep within. God was with her. He knew what was going on. He knew exactly where her little speck was on the side of this great big mountain.

And He was in control. No matter what.

A hard jerk on the rope brought her attention back to the task at hand.

Another long, hard jerk. And then she was sliding—no, being dragged—*up* the mountain. What on earth?

She grabbed her ice axe and tried to slow her ascent. Karon sat down hard, dug her boots in, and slammed the axe into the ground. A momentary halt and then another long jerk on the rope. What had happened to Clint? How could he be dragging her up the slope? Or had he found the camp and the other climbers were pulling? But that made no sense—she was out of control and the sleds were tumbling.

Her oxygen-deprived mind searched for answers as she slowed to a stop. "Clint!" The wind overpowered her voice. "Clint! Where are you?"

Nothing. Just the wind.

Karon surveyed her situation. The two sleds were overturned. Which meant poor Lionel was face-first in the snow. She anchored her rope with the axe and raced down the slope toward him. After righting his sled, she found him to be unconscious still. No blood or cuts that she could see. And he was still breathing. Hopefully all the layers protected him from any injuries. The supply sled was a little worse for the wear, but nothing major was damaged.

One horrible question remained.

What had happened to her brother?

❧

Zack checked his gear one final time as John approached. "I'm ready to go, sir."

His boss nodded. "Keep your head, Zack."

"Yes, sir."

The blades of the helo were already whirring as Zack ran to it and jumped in. The weather wasn't terrific, but at least it had calmed down some. Three other rangers were prepared to drop since a couple other expeditions had been caught in the blizzard. The goal was to get everyone who needed medical attention out, and get everyone else safely back on course.

Easier said than done, but Zack's attention was focused. He wouldn't be letting go of the rope again.

As they flew the forty-five-minute flight to Denali, Zack prayed for all the climbers. And he sent up an extra prayer for a tiny brunette.

❧

The wind calmed, and a break in the snow gave Karon a better sense of her bearings. She decided to take advantage of the weather and look for Clint. She checked on Lionel one more time and tugged on the rope to ensure her anchor held. Taking tentative steps away from her supplies, she called out for her brother, each time taking a moment to listen for any reply. She followed the rope she hoped was still attached to him for several steps and almost followed it into a hole.

Every climber's nightmare. To fall into a crevasse covered by a snow bridge.

Karon lay on her stomach and crawled to the edge, hoping not to follow in her brother's footsteps. As she peeked over, she spotted him lying in a heap at the bottom. She was a terrible judge of distance, but it seemed a long way away. No wonder she'd felt dragged up the mountain. As his weight fell into the crevasse, the rope had pulled her along. His leg looked crumpled underneath him. She swallowed the bile threatening to rise in her throat. "Clint!" Her voice was hoarse and strained. "Clint! Wake up!"

He moaned.

"Clint!"

Nothing.

Karon tugged on the rope. It was still attached to his harness. She glanced up at the sky. It didn't look as ominous as before. How long before they were hit with another storm?

Lord, I need help. And strength would be nice. Superhero strength.

Another moan came from below. "My leg. It's broken, Karon."

"Other than that, are you okay?"

"I think so, but the pain's pretty bad. I'll probably black out again. So don't do anything stu—"

She looked down. He was passed out again. And without his leg, how would he ever be able to climb out? The crevasse was a sheer drop of ice.

A glance around gave her an idea. If she could just get enough leverage, maybe she could get Clint out of the crevasse herself. But then what? She was still alone, with two unconscious men.

Men! They were all worried about *her* climbing Denali, and look at who was unconscious. She laughed out loud at the thought. Bunch of wimps.

At least her sense of humor was intact. God was with her. Her adrenaline surged. She could do this. Karon Granger. Cancer survivor. Denali climber. And add guide and brother rescuer to the list.

Bracing her legs against a large rock ledge, Karon pulled with everything in her. "Clint!" she yelled into the crevasse. "You lazy bum. Wake. Up."

She pushed with her feet, and pulled on the rope. Inch by inch. "Clint, so help me, you are going on a diet when this is over." Each word oozed through gritted teeth. Didn't some statistic say that grunting or yelling improved your strength by 30 percent? Well, she would yell at her brother the whole way if she had to.

"No more cookies." She yanked.

"And no more homemade pies." This time a grunt.

"Until you lose five hundred pounds. . ." she huffed, "and apologize three million times. . ."

"Ahhhhh!" she screamed in the frigid air. Every muscle burned, but if she let go now, her brother would crash back to the bottom of the crevasse.

"You owe me!" Another huge pull and she saw what she hoped to be part of Clint's parka. She had no idea how to get him up over the edge. Her lungs burned. Not enough oxygen for her muscles. Or her brain. Spots danced in front of her eyes.

Lord, I need some help here. Please. . .

Karon closed her eyes and breathed deep. She tugged again. But lifting him over the edge would be a feat. She took stock of her situation. If she could wedge her feet in that crack in the ledge, maybe she could put all her body weight into pulling Clint up and out.

She jammed her size five boots into the crack and tested her leverage. She could lean back, which would be down-slope, and use her body as a counterweight. A giggle erupted at the thought. Her brother better appreciate the fact that she was strong, because her little frame probably weighed half of his. She'd just have to use every ounce she had left. Clint's life was at stake.

Karon prayed again. Not even understanding all her requests, but God knew. She bent her knees a few times and tested her foot positioning. Her little boots wedged perfectly in the crack. She wouldn't slip.

Leaning back, Karon tugged and yanked and pulled with everything in her. Her legs pushed against the ledge. Hand over hand, she inched the rope upward.

Chapter 15

Zack scanned the mountain below. So far, two rangers had been dropped to help other climbers who'd been hurt seriously in the storm. But no sign of Karon. Yet.

His heart plummeted. The negative voice inside him tried to remind him that was where faith got him every time. Zack shook his head. He. Would. Not. Let. Go. Of. The. Rope.

The voice quieted.

Kyle spoke into his headset. "We'll find her. Don't worry."

Zack nodded. He closed his eyes and sent up another silent prayer.

When he looked down, he laughed. There she was. Waving at him.

Kyle flew close enough for him to drop about a hundred yards away. Zack threw on his backpack and clipped his harness to the line.

Kyle shot him a look and two-finger salute. "See ya soon."

"Thanks." Zack dropped out of the helicopter.

As soon as his feet touched the ground, he unclipped his gear and his line and waved Kyle on. Zack used his radio to call High Camp. They weren't far. And since visibility was better, he could use their help.

Karon's laughter echoed down to him. Her arm was still raised, waving to him. But as he approached, he noticed she lay upside down, with a crumpled form about ten feet away, and what he assumed to be Lionel strapped to a sled about twenty feet away.

Zack hiked to her and shook his head. "Now, Miss Granger. What seems to be the problem?" He tried to hide his pleasure in seeing her again.

She laughed even harder, hiccuped, and struggled to catch her breath.

He squatted downhill from her so she could see him.

"Long story short—Lionel's been unconscious for a couple of hours. Clint and I were hauling him up to High Camp, or so we thought, in the storm, then Clint fell into the crevasse and was unconscious, too. After pulling him out, I felt like Jell-O and had no energy left, but my feet were wedged in that crack, so I've been lying here upside down laughing myself silly and then I heard the helicopter and just knew—"

He glanced at her boots. "Wait a minute—I'm sorry to interrupt—but you pulled your brother out of that crevasse? All by yourself?"

She grunted at that one. "Well, me and God. And a little yelling and hollering."

"But he must weigh—"

"It's my turn to interrupt, Zack. But all the blood's rushing to my head and it's beginning to hurt. Do you think you could get my boots unwedged so I could get up? I'm worried about that big lump that I just dragged up out of that hole."

Clint groaned. "I heard that."

Zack helped her sit upright, went to her feet, and kicked her boots out of their shackles.

Karon didn't miss a beat and shouted back to Clint, "I know you heard that, you lazy bum. I had to haul your sorry self up while you pretended to be unconscious—"

"I wasn't pretending to be unconscious—"

"Oh good. So in other words, I just saved your life."

"I don't know if I'd go that far, but did I hear you threaten me with no more cookies? Not even your special cookies?"

Zack shook his head. His radio crackled. The doctor and another ranger, Dawson, from High Camp were coming to help.

Within the hour, Zack helped set Clint's broken leg and strap him to a sled, while the doctor attended to Lionel.

The doctor headed over to check out Clint's splint as Dawson explained to Zack and Karon, "Apparently, good ol' Lionel has broken his streak of not being sick for over a decade. He has a virus, a sinus infection, and acute bronchitis all at the same time. It's amazing he lasted this long at this elevation."

Karon piped in. "But he didn't even have any symptoms until earlier today."

"Well, it must have hit him really fast. Poor guy. I wouldn't want to have that at home, much less up here." Dawson patted Zack. "Want to introduce us?"

"Karon Granger, I'd like you to meet Ranger Dawson."

"Nice to meet you, Ranger." Karon shook the outstretched hand.

"That was quite a piece of work, lady. You pulling your brother up all by yourself." Dawson nodded.

Karon turned to Zack but spoke to Dawson. "Yeah, well, I had quite a lecture from another ranger about holding on to a rope. And that helped. A lot."

❧

Karon packed up her gear and her brother's in the snow while she waited for Zack. He stood quite a ways away with the other ranger and doctor talking on the radio. Her brother would be picked up by helicopter with Lionel and the other injured climbers. There wasn't room for her, so she assumed she would just trek down the mountain with another group.

She wasn't sure how she would haul all their gear down herself, but after their adventure, she knew she'd find a way. Somehow.

Zack walked closer to her. A few words of his conversation floated over. "Thank you, sir. I appreciate that."

He approached and squatted next to her. "So, Karon."

"Zack." Her heart fluttered. Good grief, she wasn't a kid anymore. But this sure was fun.

"I just got clearance from my boss to be your guide the rest of the way."

"What do you mean?"

"Well, you're only a few hundred yards from High Camp. You can set up your tent there, I can stay with the rangers, and then hopefully the next day, I can take you to the summit."

She blinked. Did he really just say what she thought he said?

"Karon?"

"Don't you need to acclimate?"

"I just spent some time on a rescue at higher altitudes, and I've been at Kahiltna for over a week. If I hydrate well tonight and tomorrow, I should be okay."

"Are you sure?"

"The outlook looks good for tomorrow, and if we head straight down, it should be okay." He reached out for her hand. "Besides, I'd like to be there when you get your wish."

Her heart thundered. Was it selfish to finish without Clint? Without Lionel? Or was God granting her wish in more ways than one?

"Well? John and all the rangers want you to be able to do this, Karon. Everyone is behind you."

She smiled up into his goggles, even though he wouldn't be able to see it through her mask. "Let's do it."

Chapter 16

The sea of clouds below separated Karon from the rest of the mountain. Sultana stood to the southwest, her peak appearing like a lonely island amidst the fluffy white swirls. It wouldn't be long now before they would stand on the summit.

No time like the present to come clean.

"Zack, I need to tell you something."

He turned toward her. "But we're almost there. You want to stop now?"

"Yes, I do. I'm sorry." She fiddled with the zipper at her neck. At least his face was hidden by all the gear. It'd be easier this way. "I told you I really wanted to go on a date with you."

"But you turned me down."

She took it back—she wished she *could* see his eyes. This was harder than she thought. "Yeah, but it's because I hadn't told you something really important." Deep breath. "I had cancer. I'm in remission, but there's no guarantee it won't come back."

"So you're afraid I won't want anything to do with you?"

"I *was* afraid. Afraid you wouldn't think I was whole. Afraid you wouldn't want—"

"I already knew, Karon."

"You did?"

"Yep."

"And you don't mind?"

"Nope."

"And I turned you down!" She placed both gloved hands over her face.

"Well, we can rectify that." He took both of her hands in his. "Karon, would you like to go out on a date with me?"

"I'd love to."

"How about now?"

"You're on."

❧

The day couldn't have been more perfect. Clear skies, calm wind—well, for the top of Denali it was calm—and Karon at his side.

The sun beat down on them as he led her to the summit. Her wish granted.

As they stood on the tip of Denali's peak, Karon took pictures with a tiny digital camera. She turned toward him. "It's breathtaking."

"It sure is."

"Zack?"

"Yeah?"

"Thank you."

He followed his instincts and wrapped an arm around her shoulders. "You're welcome."

"Not just for this. But for everything."

"I don't know what everything is, but you're welcome."

She leaned in to him. He'd been missing out all these years, chasing a thrill that never lasted. He was thankful God had saved him and prepared him for Karon.

"I'll always remember our first date, Zack."

He looked down at her. She didn't have any trouble balancing since her tiny feet found footing just about any-where. His massive size twelves wobbled next to her. He squeezed her tighter. She wrapped her arm around his middle.

"This is the best date ever."

Taking in the view around him, Zack agreed. God knew what it would take to bring him around, and then He brought Karon into his life.

Zack turned to face her. "I'm hoping you'll agree to share a few more dates with me, Karon Granger."

"Oh really? Like how many?"

"However many we can fit in for the rest of our lives."

"It's a deal. But on one condition." She poked him in the chest.

"You and your conditions. I still haven't followed through on the last one."

She poked him again.

"Okay, okay. . .I'm almost afraid to ask."

"You have to seal the deal right here, on the top of Denali."

Zack grinned. "I think I can handle that. . ." He reached out, took off her goggles and mask, and peeled off his own. Their chapped lips and cheeks met for the first time in the icy, thin air at 20,320 feet. And nothing had ever tasted sweeter. A gust of wind sucked the air off the mountain as Zack pulled back, but he couldn't contain his grin.

He replaced her gear and his own as they each inhaled the thin air. "I promise I'll do it right when we're not risking our lips to frostbite."

She giggled and took his hand. "But won't it be a story to tell? I'll always be able to say, you took my breath away."

Kimberley Woodhouse is a wife, mother, author, and musician who lives, writes, and homeschools in Colorado with her husband and two children.

DARING
HEIGHTS

by Ronie Kendig

Dedication

To the Talkeetna mountaineering rangers who risk everything on the High One to protect the mountains and the
climbers. Through my research, I gained an incredible
respect for you.

Chapter 1

Embraced by volumes of leather-bound books, collegiate hardbacks, the occasional paperback, and a wealth of loneliness, Jolie Decoteau drew her legs up to her chest on the chaise lounge. She hugged tight the frame that held heartache and bittersweet memories.

Her gaze rose to the cross-and-beam ceiling, aching. Her father's death had widened the hole that existed after Gael's death. From the second-story library loft of her father's home office, she could almost pretend Daddy was still here. Still working. Still on endless phone calls. She could see his wavy silver hair and hear his deep voice booming through the room that gobbled the entire northern wall of the estate.

"I'm going to marry her, Jolie."

"Seriously? What does she have that you could want?"

"Everything I don't already have—freedom, perspective, joy, love—"

"Love? Your family loves you!"

His long fingers traced her cheek. "You loved me, Jolie. Dad loved his work, and Mother loved being rich, being provided for. Dad doted on you, but he only knew how to push me."

"Don't be crazy." She swatted away his hand, but when he turned to leave, she caught his arm. "You can't leave me, Gael."

But Gael had left. Permanently. He'd been her strength since childhood. Now, her father and her brother, the only people who really understood her, who supported her, were gone. And with that emptiness a massive responsibility surged to the surface of her grief.

Leaning back, Jolie closed her eyes. "Why did you do this, Daddy?" She rubbed the knotted ridge above her eyebrow where a headache threatened. With a shuddering sigh, she slid her gaze beyond the rolled spindle casing to the massive L-shaped desk that hogged the bank of windows. Daddy would often slip out onto the terrace on a phone call, but his voice carried through the air, into the office and back up to Jolie.

If only his voice would come to her now. Give her wisdom. Explain *why* he'd left her in charge of Decoteau Industries. Why would he usurp the power, the expertise of his right hand, from his own friend—Baron Schmidt? It didn't make sense. And yet, Baron had been nothing but gracious and guiding since her father's death three months ago.

"Jolie!" the shrill pitch of her mother's voice carried through the house faster than a sonic boom.

Blowing air out and vibrating her lips, making the annoying noise her mother hated so much, Jolie sat cross-legged. *Young ladies don't sit like that, Jolie.*

Purposefully, she stayed in place. *Really, Jolie. Sit up straight. Show some pride, darling.*

"Daddy, Daddy, Daddy, how did you ever put up with her for thirty years?"

But her father had seen the sun, moon, and stars in her mother's eyes. The only thing Jolie saw was a black hole of antagonism.

Below, the creak of the office doors preceded the *click-click* of her mother's heels.

Maybe if Jolie lay flat, her mother wouldn't see her.

"Jolie, are you up there again?"

She rolled to the side and slid the volume back in place. Tracing its spine, she tucked her heartache away, something her mother expected. "Just reading," Jolie called.

A huff. She stood in the doorway. "Baron is here to see you." Another puff of air. "Although I'm not sure what you two need to discuss. James said he'd take care of everything. You don't have to worry, Jolie."

James Sheppard. Her father's best friend. The man who probably should've taken power at D. I., or even Baron. Anyone but her.

"Nobody's worrying. We're just doing our best to honor Daddy's legacy." Jolie pushed to her feet and made her way to the spiral staircase. As she descended, she saw the man who would be her right hand at Decoteau Industries. "Hello, Baron."

Her mother sparkled in a tailored silk pantsuit and heels, thanks to the diamond necklace, earrings, and rings. Hair perfectly highlighted and coiffed, she could grace the cover of any magazine and be mistaken for a forty-something rather than a sixtyish woman. *Au natural*, at that. Jolie had inherited her mother's fine bone structure and thin build, but she'd reflected her father's quick mind, blond hair, and tall height.

A gong resounded through the house.

"Now, I wonder who that could be."

"It's probably James and Aidan Sheppard, Mother." Jolie motioned Baron to the leather seating that separated her father's desk from the wall of books. Stepping onto the carpeted area, she drew in her courage. "They're picking me up for the trip, remember?"

Touching her fingertips to her forehead, her mother feigned light-headedness. "Oh, Jolie." She placed a hand on her chest, her chin puckering. "I keep telling James I don't want you on that trip. Please, darling, don't go."

"I've already told you—"

"Why on earth would you go there? After. . . What if you die like Gael?" Her eyes glossed, threatening her perfectly applied makeup. She cast a look to Baron then composed herself. "If you'll excuse me."

Her quick steps warned Jolie of the panic chasing her mother through the doors, which Baron, trailing her mother, closed.

Jolie eyed the doors as Baron returned to the hand-carved Persian rug and leather seating appointment. "Is everything okay?"

"Please," he said as he motioned to the sofa while he took the wingback chair. "I wanted to talk with you privately." Tugging up his slacks, he perched on the edge of the leather seat. His gray eyes bore the weight of whatever was coming. Quite honestly, it made Jolie want to squirm. Instead, this was one of the times her mother's insistence on "saying less" could be worked to an advantage, though Jolie had always struggled with that rule of Marceline Decoteau Etiquette Rules.

Coiling her anticipation and anxiety in her hands, Jolie placed them in her lap.

"Look, there's no easy way to say this, and you know I don't say things lightly."

Jolie laughed. "No, Daddy always lamented that you were as silent as a monk most of the time." Her smile faded. "Unless it was important."

"It is." He swallowed. "Jolie, I don't believe your father's death was accidental."

Heat splashed down her spine and numbed her mind. "But the reports. . ."

"I know." He motioned his hands in a placating manner. "It's quite an accusation, but there are a number of things bothering me." He scooted forward. "I'm glad you're going on this trip because it will get you out of harm's way while I sort through this. . . ." He paused, meeting her eyes. "I've hired a private investigator."

Heart thumping a little faster, Jolie crossed her legs. "Do you think I'm in danger?"

He dropped his gaze. "You're the CEO of Decoteau Industries, and I won't lie to you—that decision flew in the face of a lot of influential and powerful people."

"Including you."

He shrugged. "No, not really." In his late forties, Baron had always taken things in stride. But being overlooked in favor of a midtwenties girl?

How insane! "Baron, you were my father's confidant. You and James knew everything. You both advised him in every single decision."

"Including the one that named you as CEO." His genuine smile warded off a plethora of concerns. "Trust me, Jolie, I agreed with your father. You're young, yes, but you're fresh. You have a new perspective, and you have years of sitting under your father's tutelage to guide you."

"Two." She thrust her hands into her hair. "Two years, Baron! That's all."

"Two, officially, but all your life unofficially." A lengthy sigh eased a smile from his face. "Do you know what I did for Amaury?"

"Advised him."

He snorted. "Well, yes, but I also handled all his data encryption and secured his files." Alert, keen eyes peered at her, burrowing deep. "A side. . .benefit, is that I knew when to invest. . . . So, while I do not hold the fortune your father— and now *you*—held, I am not lacking for money." He stuffed his hands into his pockets. "In addition, I became well versed in monitoring traffic."

"Hacking." Jolie couldn't help but smile. "You're the one who taught Gael to hack."

He laughed. "Guilty." He nodded then shook his head. No

doubt the same grief clutching him as it did Jolie. "Anyway." He swiped a finger across his upper lip. "Your father had me watch the network surreptitiously. And since he died, I've kept the same regimen." Sorrow lined his forty-something face. "It's my own fault. I should've noticed it—might've saved Amaury. . ."

"Baron, don't." Jolie yanked hard against the anchor-like weight of guilt. "Don't blame yourself. Please. He never would. And I never will."

She heard a commotion of voices from the grand foyer. No doubt her mother arguing with Mr. Sheppard and his son, Aidan, about the trip, about the lunacy of taking her "only remaining blood relative back to *that* mountain." Losing Gael had been hard on everyone, but it seemed to pluck the last thread of strength from her mother. For Jolie, not having her brother here to tease and pester left a huge hole, but there were far too many pieces to pick up to sit and mope the way her mother had.

Hands fisted, eyes darting back and forth over the carpet, Baron said nothing. Finally, his shoulders drooped. "Okay. You're right. I can't save him, but I can save you."

"Me?"

"I believe someone is trying to take Decoteau Industries out from under you. And I have a suspicion of who."

"But they can't!" Her voice squawked. "Who? Who is doing this?"

"I'd rather not say till I have firm proof. It's part of why I asked James Sheppard to take you on a trip."

"You asked?" Jolie hesitated. Here she thought it'd been Aidan's idea. They'd talked through high school of making the trip, but after Gael's death. . .they hadn't spoken of it again. She pushed to her feet and moved to the windows, where her father so often did his thinking. "It's so crazy. Daddy should not have put me in charge." Turning back to him, she felt a chill of dread pour over her thoughts.

"He talked many long hours, weighing the cons and pros about you taking over." Baron joined her. "He believed in you, Jolie." Passion filled his voice. "He saw how seriously you took your education. He knew you sat up there, pretending to read, but you captured everything. You listened to him, learned from him." He motioned to the loft. "Why do you think he started taking you on trips, including you in board meetings?"

Jolie shook her head and looked out over the stunning landscape. "Mother always said those trips were to help me find a husband."

"Bah!" Baron threw his hands up and growled. "Your father wanted you to see what the corporation was about. Do you honestly think he asked your opinions because he *needed* them?"

She drew up straight and considered the man before her, the man so like an uncle. "He was testing me."

"You bet your leather boots." His wide grin crinkled the corners of his eyes. "You passed, Jolie. You're a natural."

Heat infused her cheeks. "I'm not—"

Clicking, like a woodpecker, severed her response. Her mother's shoes on the wood floors, hurrying from the foyer where the others waited.

"Jolie!" Her mother flung open the doors. "Please. Please tell me you won't do this."

Though Jolie hated the angst her decision caused her mom, this trip had significant meaning. It would cut down to size the mountain that killed her brother.

❧

"Why are you here, son?"

David Whiteeagle looked into the wizened features of

his father, who sat in the bustling café with him, grilling him. Again. He glanced down at the plate of eggs, sausage, and biscuits. Hearty helpings. It'd be his last homemade meal for a good while. "Eating?" He lifted one shoulder.

"You're not fooling me."

David breathed a laugh. "I'm not trying to fool you."

"You sit up there"—his father stabbed a finger toward front door—"and waste away."

Ah. This again. David set down his fork. "Dad, we've been through this." He lifted the cup of strong, black coffee and took a gulp.

"No, *I've* been through it. You've been *around* it." His father waved his big, thick hands, the same ones he'd passed to David. "You ignore."

Irritation clawed its way up David's spine. "I have a *job*. I'm not wasting away." Why he even voiced those words he didn't know. He'd said them a hundred times since returning to Talkeetna four years ago.

"She's gone, David. Gone!"

A loud bang reverberated through the small, packed café. Only as pain spiked up his arm did David realize he'd slammed his fist on the table. Swallowing his anger, he drew his arm back. "I have to get to the station." He plucked a ten from his wallet, laid it on the table, and pushed to his feet.

A vise clamped around his wrist. "She was my daughter. Don't think I don't miss her, too. But it's time—I want you to move on." Craggy lines marked brown eyes with wisdom, and David remembered all too well the feeling of utter exposure when those dark orbs set on him.

"Move on to what, Dad?" He slumped back down in the chair. "I've got a job. You and Mom are here."

"But your heart isn't."

Each breath felt as if he were trapped beneath a glacier.

David clamped his jaw and ground his teeth, staring at his half-eaten breakfast. "Dad, please. . .don't—"

"You're a good man. Find a wife. Get on with your life. Don't waste it trying to save what can't be saved."

"*Lives* are saved." Breathing hurt. "Every time I'm up there."

Lips taut, his father stared at him, hard. David felt he'd committed some great crime as those penetrating eyes unraveled his secrets. "When will it be enough?" His father rapped his knuckles on the table. "How many will it take to appease your guilt? To help you stop punishing yourself?"

"You've got it wrong. I'm—"

"Do I?" Challenge pulsed through the dark brown irises that were so like his own.

"How we doing over here, Mr. Whiteeagle?" Deline Tsosie, the café owner's daughter and manager, cut through the thick tension with her buttery-sweet voice. Her smile had little welcome and plenty of warning. "David?"

"Just fine."

Deline, the only true Aleutian beauty in the shadow of the High One, smiled at him. And. . .it was fake, which meant she agreed with his dad. No surprise there. It wasn't the first time he was the odd man out.

Back-stepping over the chair, he grabbed his jacket. "I need to get to the station."

Stoic, jaw set in resolve, his father stared at the table.

David shook his head and started for the door.

"David."

Between two tables, he hesitated. Glanced back.

As if the clouds parted and the sun shone through, his father's face changed, relaxed. "May God keep you in His hand. . ."

Three heaving breaths later, David finally completed

the saying. ". . .but never close His fist too tight." The words nearly choked him. He wasn't in the mood for platitudes or feel-good mantras. But it'd been a tradition long held in his family to not part without it, and despite his objections to his father's words, any venture up into Denali could be a climber's last.

A slow nod was his father's only reply. And it shoved David around. He punched open the door and stepped into the gloomy day. Why did his dad have to start that? And on the day when David would head up for his patrol. Why'd he have to remind David of Mariah, of Denali exerting her power over the weak humans who dared trespass her rugged beauty?

He started for his truck—

A horn blared. Deafening. Terrifying. A blur of black whizzed past.

David shielded himself with his arm.

Thump! Side-view mirror smacked his bicep. Pain reverberated through his arm. He jerked back, adrenaline spiking as the driver of the shiny Escalade tore off without so much as slowing to apologize.

"Slow down!" As he watched the vehicle barrel up Main, he took in the equipment plastered to the roof. Skis, packs, tents. Heading to the ranger station no doubt. He waited. . . watching as they banked left onto B Street. "Great. Rich kids," he muttered. Going up into his mountain. Would they never learn?

No. They'd keep forking over dough—which helped Talkeetna, he had to admit—for their climbing registration. Though they'd often claim experience in climbing, David invariably had to dive in and save someone.

And if they'd just messed up his arm. . . He tugged the long sleeve of the thermal shirt up, grimacing at the throbbing pain emanating around his elbow.

"Hey, Grizzly. What's eating your lunch today?"

David glanced up and found Deline on the top step of the café, smirking. "Not in the mood today."

"Are you ever?"

He eyed the large red welt ballooning around his humerus. "Stupid. . .self-absorbed—"

"Really shouldn't be so hard on yourself."

He shot her a glare. "Not me—those stupid rich kids." He jabbed a finger down the road. "That Escalade."

"I saw." Too much amusement lurked in her words.

Tugging his sleeve back down, David stepped aside as tourists poured in and out of Tsosie's Café. "What d'you want? Speak your piece. I gotta get moving."

Hands in her jeans pockets, Deline came down a step. "Your dad—"

"No." David shook his head. "Don't go there."

Somber brown eyes held his. "He just wants you to come home, wants to see you happy. So do I."

"Yeah, what do you know about happy, Deline? Have you told your pop you want to leave the café and fly full-time?"

Her eyes blazed. "I told you that in confidence," she bit out through clenched teeth.

She'd been like a little sister to him since first grade. They'd dated in high school but their personalities slipped and collided like ice in glaciers. Resolved to be friends, they'd been close ever since.

"You don't have to always be the hero."

Drawing out his truck keys, he eyed Denali, the memories too fresh of carrying his sister's body down the brutal landscape. He would never let himself forget. "Yes, I do."

Chapter 2

Denali sacrificed her brother. Haunted by the thought, Jolie endured the two-hour orientation by the mountaineering ranger, complete with the dangers of climbing, things to watch for, things to avoid. Then more and more droning until the ranger with electric blue eyes came to the proper disposal of human excrement.

Resisting the groan climbing her throat, Jolie let her gaze travel the memorial plaques of rangers who'd died on the mountain. Of course Gael wasn't up there—he wasn't a ranger—but it still pricked at her that he was among those who'd lost their lives.

Depressed thinking about those who'd died, she pushed her gaze through the door, past the reception desk with its waist-high counter, to the door. Though from this angle, she couldn't see the forbidding mountain, she felt its call. Having climbed it once before with Gael, and many other mountains beside, she had the experience and knowledge of the etiquette and safety measures the ranger spoke of. But what hung in the back of her mind was entering the landscape that had made a sacrifice of her brother.

Gael died doing what he loved, with the woman he loved. She missed him, missed his laugh, missed his big-brother advice, guidance, and proverbial kick in the backside when she wanted to give up or slack off.

"You're a Decoteau—you can't afford to slack because the world is watching, waiting for you to fail or screw up."

And yet, she'd done both of those for many years. Until Gael was gone. Sobered by his death, she swung in the other direction to get her life back on track, to make him proud. Even though he could never again say that her halo was on crooked.

The old tease pried a smile from her lips.

"You're watching him, too, huh?"

Jolie blinked and looked at her longtime friend Nikki deSanto. "What?"

A bubble of laughter erupted in the reception area and pulled Jolie's attention in the very direction Nikki nodded. Leaning against a back wall in the open sitting area, a brawny guy stood talking with the laughing ranger station manager. She swatted at him, and he ducked his shoulder away, which turned him in Jolie's direction.

Jolie's breath backed into her throat as familiar dark, brooding eyes met hers. But what filled her with warmth was not his good looks or his powerful presence but the memory of his angry, hateful words the day of his sister's funeral.

"You rich people think you can buy anything, including forgiveness. Forget it! My sister is gone because of your brother. He cost my family everything!"

How could he blame Gael for what happened? It was like David Whiteeagle didn't realize her family had suffered in the tragedy, too. But his grief-borne anger hadn't stopped the crush she'd had on him since she was fourteen. His native Athabascan heritage made girls like her swoon with his jet-black hair, high cheekbones, square jaw, and mysterious eyes. But then there were his ears she'd always thought too small. And his temper that was too big. Mercy, she would do anything to avoid being on the wrong side of his anger again.

A jab in her side jarred her out of her thoughts and into Nikki's giggles. "He's got it going on in all the right places, don't you think?" She jabbed her again. "He's staring at you."

When the memories faded and the heat of embarrassment filled her once again from his contemptuous glare, Jolie returned her focus to the ranger giving the presentation. Was he glaring because he recognized her? She'd like to think she'd grown up a lot since their last encounter, enough that he *wouldn't* recognize her. Funny how she'd been the life of many parties as a teen, flirting and freely dating, confident and carefree as the daughter of an oil tycoon. But David. . .he made her feel ashamed of that wealth and upbringing.

Jolie couldn't stop her gaze from traveling back to him. Tension formed knots in her shoulders as he snatched a clipboard from the desk. The very clipboard she and the others had used to sign in. He muttered something then wagged the board at the manager, who yanked it from his hands.

"There are ranger Base Camps at various levels," the ranger at the front of her group said. "On patrol during your climb will be myself and David Whiteeagle. That grizzly right there is David." He pointed. "Trust me when I say don't cross him. And the way you cross him is to go up on *his* mountain unprepared or without care."

The others laughed as they considered David. Too much truth hung in Ranger Knox's statement for Jolie to find any humor in it. Must be sad to be known as a grouch. And yet, she couldn't stop staring.

"There will also be a doctor ranger and two others at Base Camp," Ranger Knox continued. "Outside, we'll do an equipment check. If you fail that, you don't climb." Groans bounced around the room, but he shrugged. "Sorry. We'd rather you be ticked and alive, than ill prepared and dead. Just remember, even though you paid good money to climb the High One, it's not worth it if it's your last."

Like Gael. Had he known it'd be his last? He proposed to Mariah Whiteeagle at the peak. At least, she assumed it'd happened. Gael had told her the whole plan before the fateful trip. Jolie's fingers dug beneath the collar of her turtleneck to find the necklace. She slipped her pointer finger through the gold ring dangling there. On their descent, neither made it back alive.

"He's still staring," Nikki said under her breath.

Jolie refused to look. Refused to give him another chance to hurt her. But in her periphery, she saw him pivot and stomp out of the building. *Keep walking, David. Nobody needs your attitude.* She'd come to Denali to make peace so she could move on after her father's death.

"Okay, if you'll head with me out front, we'll do the equipment check," Ranger Knox said as he tromped toward the entrance.

As they stepped into the heavily clouded morning, a commotion sprang up to their left. Heading down the steps, Jolie saw David arguing with an older man.

"I'm fine," David with a snarl.

"If you don't want me to bench you, let me examine it."

David huffed, his jaw muscle popping under the tension. Finally, he yanked up his black thermal sleeve, up over the elbow, and tucked it above his bicep.

"With muscles like that, I think I might need his services," Nikki said under her breath.

A large red spot around his elbow stilled her.

"Whoa," Nikki said. "Looks like he got whacked."

"Yeah, by a side-view mirror."

Nikki gasped. "He's the one Derrick hit coming up here."

"He hit *me*," Derrick said with a snicker as he and Aidan Sheppard bumped fists. "Not my fault he stepped into the road without looking."

Compunction pulled Jolie toward David. If they'd hurt him. . .

She had tried to get Derrick to stop, but he'd argued they were already late and would lose their registration and right to climb. Then he went on about how the guy should've been paying attention. That David wasn't laid out in the road gave Derrick's conscience a carte blanche from guilt.

"How'd this happen again?"

"Big black Escalade."

The man, apparently the ranger doctor, glanced toward Derrick's vehicle. "You and rich people."

David snorted and nodded, looking around. "Tell me about it." His gaze rammed into hers.

Fire bolted through her stomach. At first she couldn't move. Which was insane. She met with dignitaries, presidents, princes. . . But David Whiteeagle? Where was the barf bag? "Hey, um, I. . ." She pointed to his arm. "Derrick should've stopped. We tried to make him."

David's jaw muscle rippled again as his lips pulled taut.

"I'm sorry." Her stomach squirmed under his narrowed gaze.

He jerked around with a hiss and yanked his arm free. "Hey!"

Touches of gray at the doc's temples matched the snow-blotted front lawn. "The bone is bruised, but I don't think it's broken. You'd need an X-ray to be sure."

"It's not broken. I'm fine." David yanked the sleeve down. "I have an equipment check to do."

❧

David brushed past the girl who wasn't a girl anymore. He remembered the sixteen-year-old version, the petulant partier who'd ended up in the news more often than climbers summitted. Even then, drop-dead gorgeous. But now—she could wipe a guy's good sense from his head.

That was, if she hadn't been born a Decoteau. If she wasn't the sister of the man who'd killed Mariah. No way would he give her an inch of anything.

"You haven't changed much."

Her words drew him up short. "Excuse me?"

Jaw jutted, she folded her arms over her raspberry-colored North Face jacket. "We apologized. But you held it over my dad like a boulder." She stretched her arms out wide. "It was an accident, or don't you know what that is?"

David's pulse pounded. He stepped closer. "Accidents happen when people aren't prepared."

Her eyes enlivened. "And they happen when experienced climbers *are* prepared. It's the whole point—nobody's at fault."

"All he had to do—"

"He did everything he could. It was an avalanche!" Her eyebrows winged up. "How can you blame that on my brother? What, did he have power over the wind and snow?"

"No, but if he was so experienced—"

"Don't make accusations you can't back up."

"Oh, I'll back them up all right."

"Hey. *Hey!*" Ranger Logan Knox wedged in between them, palms on David's chest as he gave his fellow ranger a nudge. "Dude, c'mon. Get a grip."

Teeth grinding, David severed the emotional tie those caramel eyes held over him. He took a step back, and humiliation flooded in as he felt the shocked stares of those around him.

"What is with you, man?" Logan asked in a low tone, guiding him away.

"She's a Decoteau."

Logan hesitated and looked back, and that little hesitation gave David the affirmation he needed—someone to understand what riled him. Holding David's arm—right at the tender bruise—Logan stopped. "Look, man. I get your anger, but you gotta wind down your temper."

"Why do you think I'm heading to Base Camp?" David stretched his neck. "Days alone with nothing but wind, ice, and snow."

"And a Base Camp manager, a ranger doctor, and another ranger."

"Yeah, but there's nearly forty miles of glacier to give me the space I need."

Logan laughed. "Dude, I don't know if *Denali* has enough space for you. Listen, seriously, man." He sighed. "You need to get over this. It's eating you up. Mariah wouldn't—"

"Don't."

"I will because Mariah was your sister—she loved you. But as an experienced climber, she knew what—"

The *whoosh* of each heartbeat clogged David's hearing. He swallowed in an attempt to clear it.

No-go.

"All right," he called out to the others loud and strong, cutting off Logan's lecture. "Get your gear and lay it out for inspection."

David stalked away from Logan, away from the mountain of pressure building at the base of his neck. As he and Logan checked the Decoteau team's equipment, he tried to scratch the look of shock and hurt lingering in his mind along with the memory of a pair of caramel eyes. It bugged him that he'd hurt her feelings. But he stretched his neck and dug into the check.

Though he'd hoped to find their equipment faulty or to discover vital pieces missing, each check confirmed they'd followed protocol and smart climbing measures to a T. To boot, their gear was top-notch quality.

"Everything should be here," said a stocky-built guy who

was ranked as the senior climber. James Sheppard. His son, Aidan, repacked their gear as David finished checking it. "I'm very careful about my climbs. It's an adrenaline rush, but I realize who has the power."

David straightened and considered the man with salt-and-pepper hair. "Yeah? Who's that?"

He thumbed toward the mountain. "Denali."

With a nod, David moved to the next spread of equipment and crouched to inspect. He hesitated when someone in brown insulated overpants came into view. Jolie. He pinched the bridge of his nose. Why hadn't Logan checked her stuff? She was thin and pretty. And blond. Probably had just enough skill to make the climb. But what if she got into trouble up there? Would he be hauling her dead body off the mountain the way he had Mariah's?

Something in him clenched at the thought. He leaned on her ice axe with his knee, begging it to snap. If it snapped, he could deem her unprepared. Send her packing. A twinge of guilt hardened—just like the axe. It didn't give.

He stood and stared at the equipment. Everything in pristine order. And just like Sheppard's—the best available. No surprise for the rich, spoiled daughter of an Alaskan oilman. Yet the gear wasn't new. Not even gently used. It had enough wear to prove it'd roughed mountains.

"Was this Gael's?"

Jolie frowned. "No. Why would you ask that?"

"It's seen some good use, but it's taken care of, too."

She turned toward him, shock in her expression. "I—"

"Jolie's an expert climber," a guy with too much goop in his hair said as he joined them.

"Not true, Derrick," Jolie said.

Derrick. The guy she'd said was driving the truck when they hit him. This was the type of guy she wanted to climb with? Someone who would run another person down, then not even stop to check on them? He grunted. That told him how things would go up there.

"I'm not rated." Voice soft as a light dusting of snow, she leveled her gaze on David. "But I've done enough climbing to be experienced."

David wasn't going to listen to her go on about how she could conquer this mountain. *You know, on second thought. . .* "It wasn't enough that your brother died out there? What, you have a death wish, going up with guys like him?"

She drew back. "Who do you think you are? What gives you the right to talk to me like that?"

"Forget it." He waved her off with another *forget it* then trudged to Logan. "When they get stuck or hurt up there, I am not hauling these rich kids off my mountain."

Chapter 3

Coddled on three sides by the high peaks of the Alaska Range—Mt. Foraker, Mt. Hunter, and Mt. McKinley—Base Camp welcomed the DeHavilland Otter that ferried Jolie and her team to the southeast fork of the Kahiltna Glacier with a stiff wind. The thirty-minute flight numbed her mind as she wrestled with the haunting knowledge that this rugged range had taken her brother's life. Ironic that Baron had sent her here for safety.

As the pilot and Mr. Sheppard lugged the gear from the plane, Jolie drew her pack and sled off to the side.

"Being that gorgeous, I think I can forgive him for the rich kids comment."

"What?"

Nikki nodded in the direction of the Base Camp structure jutting out of a mound of fresh snow. There, in his thermal shirt and overpants, stood David.

Mountain lion. Rippling with tension, waiting to pounce from his crouched position. Expression as cold and forbidding as the mountain he guarded. And yet, a lion seemed too small, too paltry. He definitely had the grizzly bear presence—large and powerful.

His comment had cut deep. Why? It wasn't any less venom filled than his heated words on the day of the funeral. But. . .maybe she'd hoped that he'd see her now, see that she wasn't sixteen or spoiled anymore, and he'd. . .

What, Jolie? Beg for a date? Say he was wrong?

111

Hurt clogged her mind as Jolie and her team grouped under his all-too-scrutinizing gaze. She wasn't sure she could stand another day beneath his withering glare. After all, they would spend tomorrow here with logistics and crevasse rescue practice before setting out on Tuesday.

Mr. Sheppard and Aidan staged the equipment and set up tents, and Jolie busied herself with helping Nikki set up the last of their equipment for the night. Derrick banged his iPhone against his palm, cursing.

"No reception, Derrick." Jolie rolled her eyes and lifted Nikki's pack onto her back. "Did you pay attention to anything at the ranger station?"

Sporting a knit skullcap and expensive jacket, he grinned. "Yeah, you."

Ignoring his flirtatious comment, Jolie glanced around the Base Camp. To think, Gael had been here a week before he died doing what he loved, with the girl he loved. She'd ached for what they had, that special something. Not even their parents had the kind of love Gael and Mariah shared. Would she ever? Becoming managing partner of Decoteau Industries pretty much stripped those chances—she'd be immersed in all things D. I. for the next twelve months—at least—getting up to speed on all things D. I. if she wanted to honor her father and carry on his legacy with excellence.

A chill that had nothing to do with the thirty-degree temperature cloaked her in its icy embrace. Bitter whispers on the wind reminded her that she was alone.

Staring at the jagged mountains jutting up from the glacier, she shuddered, remembering Baron's words. ". . .*someone is trying to take Decoteau Industries out from under you.*"

Her father possibly murdered? Too insane to think about. It bordered on the ridiculous. But what if Baron was right? She'd thought about the possibility the whole trip to

Talkeetna, then a little more on the flight up to here.

She twisted and appraised the landscape with a long sigh. At least, out here, she was safe from whatever or whoever.

"He's watching you again," Nikki said in a nonchalant voice as she unrolled her bedding.

"Huh?" Jolie looked up from her arctic sleeping bag.

"Ranger Grizzly." She nodded toward the Base Camp shelter.

Jolie spotted the back of David as he stepped into the inverted U-shaped building, still wearing only his thermal shirt and overpants. Had he really been watching her? What, to see if she was doing something wrong? "Probably wants to point more fingers or find fault."

Nikki's green eyes probed her. "What's the story between you two?"

"He's Mariah's brother."

Gaping, Nikki froze. "Gael's Mariah?"

Swallowing hard at the way her friend put that, Jolie gave a quick nod. She pushed onto her haunches then stood. "I think I'm going to take a walk before I bed down."

"A walk?" Nikki looked around, her face puckered with confusion. "Where?"

With a shrug, Jolie said, "Around."

Tromping the perimeter of the 7200 Base Camp pumped heat through Jolie's body and afforded her the physical and mental room to think. Why, of all places and times, did David have to be here, to remind her, to reprimand for a perceived wrong? She came to Denali to release her brother and father one last time. To move into the role her father had named her to. A role she accepted with honor but. . .

She hunched her shoulders and let her gaze travel the forbidding mountain. As if it stared down on her, daring her, warning her. *You're not good enough. Never have been. You'll regret invading me just as your brother did.*

But Jolie did not believe her brother had one regret.

Well, maybe one—that he didn't get to spend his life with Mariah the way he'd wanted. They'd had a long talk before the proposal, and he shared how he wanted to show Mariah the world, lavish love and gifts on her like she'd never known. And even then, Gael worried that he couldn't make her happy. She had a close-knit family. She'd known a type of stability she and Gael hadn't despite their parents still being alive and married—well, until Daddy died. Jolie always guessed Gael's love for Mariah was more about the girl being the antithesis to Mother, a rich socialite. Used to wealth. Arrogance. Entitlement. Women had jockeyed to be her friend. Few wanted to be friends—real friends. Most didn't. And her mom never cared about anything but having the life she wanted, regardless of leaving her family empty emotionally.

I never want to be like her.

"Can I help you?"

Startled by the question, Jolie blinked. Found herself standing just inside the Base Camp store that sported a couple of tables with necessities. Ranger Knox held a thermos, steam spiraling out of the top.

She indicated his steaming drink. "I. . .do you have any more of that?"

Ranger Knox grinned. "Right here." He turned to a steel carafe sitting atop a stack of supply boxes. "Do you have a thermos?"

"Oh. Yeah." She felt the blush rise to her cheeks. The rangers were very protective of the environment, which meant they didn't hand out Styrofoam cups for hot drinks. "Let me grab it."

A snort from the side surprised her. Sitting in a camping

chair, David shook his head. She could just hear his thoughts, *Stupid rich girl.* Wouldn't be the first time. And probably not the last. Would he ever see her as anything else?

Did she care?

Jolie stomped into the darkening day. He could keep his foul attitude and gorgeous looks. She groaned as she dug through her pack and retrieved the thermos.

"What's got you riled?" Nikki asked.

"That grizzly bear."

"Ran into him again, did you?" Nikki's words held way too much amusement.

Shooting a glare at her friend, Jolie pushed out of the tent and returned. Inside the Base Camp store, she handed the double-insulated thermos to the ranger.

What David lacked in manners and personality, this ranger made up for in spades. Electric blue eyes. Enough sense to have at least a lightweight jacket, overpants, and boots. "What makes you come up here into the maw of the High One?" He handed the filled thermos back to her.

She sensed a challenge in his question and cut a glance to David. Had they talked about her while she was gone? "What? You think I can't climb?"

"Whoa." Ranger Knox held up his hands then tucked them under his arms. "Just small talk, Miss Decoteau. I've seen some women best men twice their size on this mountain." He leaned back against the counter. "Patience goes a long way up here."

"Sorry." Steam swirled up from her thermos, tingling her senses with its sweet scent. "Apple cider?"

"Special family recipe." He poked a finger toward the grizzly bear in the corner. "When he's in the house, it's always available."

Jolie considered the brawny guy and he her, as if waiting

for her say something. "What's in it, poison?"

The left side of his mouth quirked. "Special brand, just for you."

Her heart pounded. Whether in anger or what, she didn't know. "What, no extra charge because I'm rich?"

"Hey, we always can use the money if you're donating." He studied her, his gaze sweeping over her boots, overpants, and jacket. "I'll just put it toward the rescue costs."

She knew he meant to insult her. "Why? Will you need rescuing?"

Logan sniggered, lowering his gaze toward his mug, but the smirk was there and Jolie soaked in his pleasure. That was, till she met David's scowl. His nostrils flared.

In the back of her mind, she saw the toothy snarl of a grizzly.

ॐ

David jolted awake. Light pervaded his tent. But that wasn't what woke him—light reigned in Alaska. Roughing a hand over his face, he pulled himself upright. Glanced at his watch. Two a.m.

Grabbing his jacket as he climbed out of the sleeping bag, he tried to shake the mental fog. Shake the weight that seemed to press on him. Urgency sped through his veins, and he made his way to the Base Camp manager. "Hey, Maggie."

She looked up from her perpetual cup of tea.

"What's happening?"

"You tell me. Why are you up? You've got a few more hours."

"Dunno." He shrugged. "Just woke up. Where's Logan?"

"Climber went missing in a crevasse shy of 7800."

David nodded as he peered out at the Base Camp. Lazy light oozed over the horizon as the sun hid behind the peaks.

No real full nighttime. Thanks to a bout of decent weather, the Base Camp looked moderately empty. Climbers headed out at midnight when the mountain was colder, thus reducing the chances of finding one of those crevasses. So, at this hour, most were gone.

Across the way, he saw the marker for the familiar Decoteau cache. A black banner with a lion. The Decoteau Industries symbol. Jolie. When Deline deposited the expedition here, Jolie had gone to work with her team, setting up their Base Camp, burying their cache, then quickly bedding down so they could get out early. Well, that was, after they had the exchange. The one in which she'd accused him of trying to poison her.

David huffed. The forty-eight hours since her departure had not been enough time to cleanse his mind of the annoyance that was Jolie Decoteau—and it hit him. The flurry of frantic images from his dream. The scream. *Her* scream. Seeing her reach for him as she slid down the side of Motorcycle Hill. *"Help me, Daaaaaavid!"* He squelched the howl against his soul.

"You okay?"

Snapped out of the memory, David looked at Maggie, her brown hair askew the way it always was. "Yeah. Sure." David stalked around Base Camp, inspecting the antennas, talking with climbers who'd made it to the peak, reminding others who weren't as careful in their environmental attentiveness. He kept moving to escape the images of Jolie falling to her death.

Why should it haunt him? He didn't care about her. She was a rich girl who had life handed to her. His thoughts turned to his sister. Mariah had pined after Gael Decoteau, thrilled that a rich guy would want her. That she'd have a chance to leave Talkeetna, to escape being "trapped." Well, he didn't need a rich girl to rescue him. He was fine here. The people, the mountain, suited him just fine.

He gave his head a shake. "Word from Logan?"

"He'll be okay," Maggie said from a stool near the back. "Why don't you get some more shut-eye. If something happens before he gets back, you'll need to be rested."

She was right. He knew she was. But something in him thrummed. "Anyone heard chatter from the Decoteau expedition?"

Silence met his question, and he looked over at Maggie. Arched, amused eyes met his.

"What?"

"Nothing."

"Then why are you smiling?"

Tilting her colored-brown hair, the forty-something woman narrowed her eyes at him. "In all the years you've worked Base Camp with me, I can't recall a single time you've asked about an expedition."

David shrugged. "Just got this feeling. . ."

Though he'd teased Jolie about having to rescue her, David held little doubt that she would make it to the top and back. The way she'd moved around Base Camp showed she had experience. More so than the dork with slick hair and slicker words. What was his name? Darryl? Darrin? Aw, who cared?

How was she faring? She'd probably make the top and come back fine. Without needing help. Without needing him.

David punched to his feet.

❧

Roped together, Jolie and her team had left Base Camp two days ago, having to descend four hundred feet down Heartbreak Hill then rising a thousand feet to where Camp 1 huddled just below Ski Hill at roughly 7,800 feet. While climbing with the sixty-pound pack on her back, the sled dragging behind with the evenly split gear, and digging her poles into the icy terrain, Jolie expected the trek to leave her tired. But *this* tired?

True, twenty thousand feet on Denali felt like twenty-three on the Himalayas, but still... They weren't even halfway up. She'd made it to Camp 3 with Gael last time. Crazy to be this exhausted. And nauseated.

When they slunk into the camp, though relief sped through her veins at seeing the rangers' tent, her hopes were short lived for two reasons. One, somehow her mind leapfrogged from "ranger tent" to David Whiteeagle, an annoying and unrealistic jump. Two, being here didn't mean a break. It meant two or three days of lugging supplies up to the camp at 10,000 feet. The thought plied a groan from her exhausted limbs.

"You don't look so hot," Nikki said as she passed a plastic bowl of food, cooked up, compliments of Aidan Sheppard.

Though Jolie took the food, the thick scent wafting up from it made her stomach churn. She set it to the side on the ice bench in the kitchen tent. "Just getting used to the altitude, I guess."

Nikki eyed her and the bowl. "Then you need to eat to keep up your strength."

Without thinking, Jolie took the bowl, scooped some stew, then lifted the spoon to her mouth. If they were at a lodge or something, she was sure this would taste great. But here, with her churning stomach, cold sweats, and a headache, it tasted like lead.

"It's going to be a long day tomorrow," James Sheppard said as he and Aidan joined them. "Jolie, how you holding up?"

She managed a reassuring smile. "Just need to rest. It's been a long day."

"Thinking about Gael?" Aidan, blond locks peeking out of his knit cap, smiled. "I haven't stopped since we entered the town."

Jolie nodded as her heart plunked against her own heavy thoughts. "Every turn reminds me of him." She sighed. "But I'm going to do this. For him. To make peace with his death, and my father's."

Aidan nodded. "Same here—well, about Gael." His gray eyes shifted to Nikki, then came a quirk of his lips in a slow smile.

Stealing a look at her best friend gave Jolie the information she needed. Nikki offered him a smile in return then tucked her head. Whoa. Since when had these two been into each other? And why did it make Jolie ache as if a fire were in her chest?

"Hey, where is every—" Derrick trudged into the kitchen tent and plopped down next to Jolie, draping an arm around her. "Man, this air is trippin'."

If there ever was a rich kid who expected life to be handed to him, it was Derrick. Why he'd wanted to come, she didn't know. Well, yes she did. He'd been competing with Aidan since the day Derrick and his parents moved to Fairbanks, his father taking over as COO of Decoteau Industries. The only one not directly connected to her father's empire was Jim Sheppard. He'd been her father's best friend since middle school. Played football and baseball with him. Went into the Marines with him.

Tummy churning, Jolie took a sip of water from her insulated water bottle. Flavored with electrolytes, it went down cool. She felt it splash against her insides. A throb started at the base of her skull.

"Tomorrow, we'll start moving supplies," Sheppard said.

On his feet, Aidan ladled some more stew from the pot. Then he eased himself onto the ice bench next to Nikki.

Lifting a steaming spoonful, he blew on it. "We'll need to catch the weather report."

His father lifted the long-range radio. "Eight o'clock."

Eight? That was another two hours. "I think I'm going to bed down." She stood and the world shifted on its axis.

Sheppard lunged to his feet, his hands steadying. "You okay, Jolie?"

Fingers to her forehead, she pushed through the mental fog and the ringing in her ears. "Yeah. Just stood up too fast."

"She's feeling sick, too," Nikki added.

Jolie frowned at her friend.

"Hey," Sheppard said, a finger lightly lifting her chin. "Jolie, you've climbed enough—is this AMS?"

"No." Though the symptoms seemed right-on, she wasn't convinced this was mountain sickness. She'd had it before—it was why she'd never made the summit with Gael. No way was she going back down, not without conquering the beast of the mountain that had taken her brother. Besides. . .going down, alone. . .Baron's warning hovered just outside the rim of her consciousness. "No, I think I just need to rest. I'll be fine by morning."

"If it's AMS, Jolie—don't take chances with it. You and I both know it can be fatal." Sheppard's words were fatherly and protective. "I know how much this climb means to you, but I really don't want to have to deliver you deathly sick or dead to your mother."

She smiled. "That wouldn't go over well."

"I think if she just hangs in there, she'll be great." Derrick's words were supportive and Jolie appreciated it.

"Just stay hydrated—several liters a day." Sheppard nudged her water bottle. "You need to refill that and guzzle."

"Guess you're sleeping with your pee bottle." Aidan snickered.

Great. Such polite conversation. "I'll be fine. Just need to lie down for a while." Jolie glanced to Nikki, whose wide green eyes begged her *not* to invite her along—obviously so she could stay with a certain heartthrob.

Jolie slept fitfully, shivering the whole time. Granted, it was twenty-something degrees up here, but with the pad and the inflatable mattress beneath her arctic sleeping bag, she normally didn't tremble so much.

She woke, drenched. Aching. Head throbbing. Hands trembling. She grabbed her water and guzzled, anything to rid herself of the thickness of her tongue. Groaning, she squinted toward the form next to her. Nikki. And beside her, Aidan and Sheppard. And Derrick behind her. How long had she slept? She grabbed her watch and eyed its face. Whoa.

Dragging herself from the sleeping bag without waking the others proved arduous. Limbs weak, she barely supported herself. Tripped. Tumbled. Crashed into someone's pack. Something hard banged against her forearm. She bit through the pain, trying not to wake the others. But her practically drunken clambering should've woken them already. Maybe they were this tired, too.

She pushed out of the tent and stumbled toward the open toilet. Propriety was lost to environmental concerns and necessity. After emptying her bladder, she trudged to the kitchen tent and sat down. Something was wrong. Way more wrong than altitude sickness. She'd had AMS. This felt nothing like it, even though the symptoms were crazy-similar.

Had she caught a virus?

Or had Baron been right? Was she in danger?

Jolie wanted to laugh. In danger from whom? Derrick, her best friend of ten years? The squirrely guy who only knew how to flirt and be loud, though a really nice guy. Or the man she'd practically called brother—Aidan—and his father who'd been her father's best. . .friend?

Jim? Had Jim killed her father?

Her stomach heaved.

Jolie bolted out of the kitchen tent and pitched herself into the snow. Bile launched up her throat. She retched once. Twice. Three times. Stinging, acidic. Vile.

What else could cause her to feel so sick? *Water. I need some more water.* She grimaced, realizing she'd left her bottle in the sleeping tent with the others. Great. She'd probably fall all over them again trying to get to it. Hit herself again on—

Jolie's breath backed into her throat and collided with the memory of banging her arm in the tent. Instinctively, she touched the still-sore spot. Remembered the feel, the glint of black. Small, compact. L-shaped. A. . .gun?

But who would have a gun?

There was only one way she'd be this sick this quick on the mountain. Someone had poisoned her.

That's. . .insane!

Then why the gun?

Jolie's pulse sped.

But that could be AMS as well.

Her gaze rose to the thousands of feet more she wanted to scale. Gael. . .

I wanted to break its power. But it seemed the High One exerted too much influence. If she had AMS and went up, the sickness would turn into high altitude cerebral edema. And she'd die. But if she stayed with the team, if someone was trying to kill her, she'd die.

She only had one choice, regardless of whatever was true. She had to get out of here. Right now.

Chapter 4

C amp 1 reported a missing climber." Logan appeared in the afternoon sunshine.

David turned from the sled-cum-minibathtub and snatched a towel, drying off his head, chest, and arms. "Delayed descent?"

Maggie held up the cards she used to monitor the timing of the various expeditions on the mountain. "No, we're good. Nobody's late."

He stuffed his hands into the sleeves of his thermal and pulled the shirt over his head, then grabbed his jacket following the Base Camp manager and Logan. "Who's missing?"

Logan turned, his eyes weighted.

David felt something inside him shift. And in that split second, he knew. "Decoteau."

With a sigh, Logan nodded. "Her expedition guide, Sheppard, called in. Jolie—"

David's pulse careened. "Jolie?"

Hands on the mapping table, Logan pointed to Camp 1. "He bedded down at about one. When he got up at three, she was gone."

"Whoa. Hold up." David ran a hand over his damp hair. "What do you mean, gone?"

"Sheppard said she wasn't feeling well, so he encouraged her to return to Base Camp, afraid it might be AMS, but she said she wouldn't, that she was just tired. Then—he wakes up, and she and her gear are gone."

Maggie held the radio. "Do you think she went solo?"

Logan hesitated then shook his head. "No, she's a good climber. She knows Denali can't be done alone. And if she wasn't feeling well. . ."

David's gaze fell in the direction of Heartbreak Hill. "Radio Camp 1. Tell them to watch for her." He steeled himself. This was good. She deserved this, thinking she could come up on his mountain and tame it.

"You're not worried?"

"No." The lie burned like battery acid around his thundering heart. "And I'm sick of rescuing rich kids off this mountain."

"Then why are you here? Because most people who can afford to do this aren't exactly low income." Challenge hardened Logan's words. He tossed down a pen. "I'm going to gear up and head up the trail."

"You were gone all night with that family," David fumed. "You're in no shape for another rescue."

"I don't care. This feels off to me. And if you're going to sit there and say it doesn't, then I'm the only one left to go after her."

"She'll be fine. You're the one who said she's experienced."

"And I'm also the one who said she was sick. Then she vanished."

"What about the news?" Maggie's question quieted both of them.

"What news?" Logan asked.

"Just what I heard on TV before I came back up—rumor has it, her father was killed."

"Amaury Decoteau?"

Maggie nodded, her face pale. "What if whoever killed her father is up there with her now?"

"That's crazy—in fact, you both are." David squashed the

primal instinct in him to protect. Within that instinct existed a flurry of emotions. First, strangled grief for Jolie—losing her brother *and* her father? That had to hurt. Then guilt for the way he'd treated her, shoved her around with his rough words. Then back to the agitation that he was worrying about her. "I'm not going after some rich girl who wanted to prove she was bigger than the mountain that killed her brother."

"What? You mean like you?"

David stilled.

"That's what you're doing, right? Being out here, protecting—protecting whom from what? You can't be everywhere. Deaths will happen, David. But this one—you have a chance to do something, to protect someone you know, someone who already lost to the High One."

"Stop. Just. . .leave it alone." His hollow words fell against the cold snow as his dreams—no, nightmares—rushed back at him.

Snow crunched as he trudged toward the Edge of the World. Wind blasted him. Light vanished. Dark reigned. Icy drops needled his face.

Sound carried on the howling wind.

David slowed, tugging his hood closer as he peered over his shoulder. What had he heard?

"Daaaavid!!"

He spun, feet partially stuck in the snowdrift. Squinted against the whiteout.

"David, help me!"

Plunging through the knee-deep powder, he got nowhere fast. "Jolie?"

"David, help!"

Something *was* wrong. Very wrong.

Logan came to his side. "Dave, what's wrong?"

"I. . ." No no no. He promised himself he wouldn't rush to her rescue.

But he wasn't a coldhearted jerk.

He stared out at the frozen tundra. He'd never forgive himself if he had the chance to do something and didn't. What if a ranger had the chance to save Mariah—? "I think I'm about to eat my words." He backed out of the tent. "Notify Camp 1. Give them her description. Notify next of kin."

"I know what my job is," Maggie said, only a little annoyed. "And you better know what yours is."

David's gut ignited as he pointed to Maggie. "Notify Camp 1. Send out her description," he said, his mind and heart buzzing. "Beautiful blond. Raspberry North Face jacket, brown overpants, black boots."

Maggie held his gaze. "Eye color?"

"Honey—brown."

"Birthmarks?"

David scowled. "What? How would I know?"

"Well, you seem to know everything else about this *beautiful* blond."

Heat stamped his face. "Just do it." Her laughter trailed him into the icy terrain, along with a crunch of boots from behind.

"You sure you want to do this?" Logan asked.

David grabbed his gear and shouldered his pack. "Why wouldn't I?"

"I don't know, maybe something about never rescuing rich kids off *your* mountain. . ."

His friend would never let him live this down. And trying to explain why he felt he had to do this would only make things worse. "If I tried to explain, you'd just mock me."

"I'm already doing that."

"Exactly." David grabbed a radio then started through

127

Base Camp, navigating the huddle of climbers waiting for the next Otter out.

"David."

He hesitated and glanced back.

"Are you sure. . . ?"

The question bore the implications of what he could find—or not find. It warned of losing yet someone else, and with Jolie's connection to Mariah's death. . .

"I have to."

"No, you don't."

David smirked. "Yeah, actually, I think I do." Sunglasses on, he looked toward the glaciers. "I had dreams about her screaming for help, *my* help." He glanced back to his friend. "I couldn't live with myself if something happened and I didn't try."

Logan seemed to understand. "Keep us posted and Godspeed."

He gave a two-fingered salute then headed toward Heartbreak Hill. This was his problem—always knowing when things weren't right. It got him in the middle of too many messes. And in the heart of this situation, his first instinct was to teach her a lesson for leaving her team. Let her eat snow. Have a cold burial. But that would make him a jerk. Each step down the four-hundred-foot descent pounded against his anger.

Even if she was sick, even if—in the remote possibility— she was in danger, what possessed her to take off alone? Solo climbs were restricted to the most experienced climbers. Now, not only had she put herself in danger against the elements and the mountain, but she also put his life in danger. When would rich people get it through their thick skulls that there was more to life than them? Well, he'd help her understand once he found her.

If he found her.

Despite his irritation that told him to stop hurrying, let her feel some of the trouble she'd created, one thought pushed him: the thought of her broken body lying at the bottom of a crevasse.

God, help! Everything hurts.

It even hurt to think. But she must think in order to make it down the mountain alive, down to David.

No, not David. He hated her. Despised her. She could expect no help from him. Still, Base Camp would get her help. She'd avoid the normal routes, use her ski stick to check for crevasses as she went, but first. . .

Swallowing against what felt like wool in her mouth, Jolie slumped against a jagged outcropping. She tugged her water bottle from her pack and held it in her mouth, swished to wet her mouth, then gulped. With a heaving sigh, she squinted against the sun, which made her feel like she was walking through a sauna. Crazy since it was cold up here. But with her pack and whatever made her sick, her sweaty clothes clung to her body. Tempted to remove her jacket, she shook off the thought, knowing her body temp was too low. Fever. . .that was why she was hot.

Or was it?

Using her arm, she swiped the perspiration from her forehead. Squinted across the glaring white of the forbidding beauty. She understood why Gael loved it here. Why he'd chosen this place to propose. Though at the moment all she wanted to do was puke all over it.

Jolie took another swig of water then stored the bottle in her pack again. Her limbs felt like anchors and her brain like buried cache. Eyes fluttering as she took in a labored breath, she knew she needed to rest.

But what if. . .what if someone really was after her? To come after her now, they'd have to give a good explanation to the others about their departure. It would take some convincing.

Unless they said they were worried about her.

A groan escaped her lips again. She pushed onto her feet and swayed. Jolie swung out her hands. Rest, she needed rest. A stiff wind whipped around her, swirling and taunting, tugging her to go on. A little farther. In her mind's eye, a cleft beckoned her to its shadowed space where she could tuck herself in and rest.

She gripped her forehead and plodded onward. Stumbled. Fell to a knee but kept moving. Urgency and fear hauling her down the mountain like prey. Reaching back, she rifled through her pack and caught her water bottle again. Sipping as she went, Jolie's mind tangled. Or was it her feet that tangled?

Jolie shoved a hand through her long blond hair and grimaced. *I'm going crazy.* That was part of mountain sickness, wasn't it—confusion? What if she couldn't tell friend from foe? She hurried, glad she'd already placed the crampons on her boots.

What if they were closer? She glanced back. Pristine white snow glared at her. A dark spot stopped her, stopped her heart. Was that someone following her? Jolie swallowed. How would she protect herself out here?

She whipped around, plunged onward, heart thudding against the questions she could not answer. *Oh, Daddy. Where are you?*

Dead. She knew he was dead, but he'd always been there for her. Held her close when Gael died. Her mother vanished into the void of her own pain.

Jolie.

The voice whispered on the wind, pulling at her. Taunting her.

I am losing my good mind.

Jolie!

Certain she'd heard something that time, she glanced back. Though she saw nothing at first, a shape shifted up around the pass. There, near the jagged rock she'd slumped on. Had she really come that far? Or...was that another rock? Again, her mind tangled. As did her legs. She stumbled. But not before a blur froze her. She looked back.

Movement!

Her breath backed into her throat. Someone *was* following her!

❧

He'd throttle her.

"Hey, Tony," David said as he dragged the sled the last few feet to the Camp 1 Base Camp ranger's tent, narrowly avoiding a cluster of tents.

"David?" He came out of his chair. "What're you doing up here?"

"Missing climber. Blond, reddish coat, early twenties. Seen her?" He removed his jacket and stuffed it into the pack, the heat of the sun beating on him.

"No," Tony said, looking around as if he might spot Jolie now that she'd been mentioned. The sun bronzed the guy's skin like a surfer's. "It's been pretty quiet for the last couple of days, thanks to the good weather. Seen a few groups descend, but no loners today."

"Yeah?" David panted as he squinted around the half-dozen groups gathered for rest and acclimatization. "Well, keep an eye out. Might have AMS."

"You got it."

David trudged up the incline, checking any place that might pose even the slightest shelter. "Where are you?" he muttered as he rounded a corner. Wove through Camp 1, double-checking with climbers and the rangers there to see if anyone had come across Jolie. Of course not. That would be too easy. And since she was out to make his life miserable, to put him in jeopardy, being here where it would make sense would defeat that purpose.

Trudging on, he determined in his heart to really let her have it. Enough was enough. He'd had it. And he had to admit, he was disappointed. She seemed to have a decent brain behind that pretty face.

He should just go back.

The dream.

But those too foolish to heed common sense weren't his problem.

Then why was he still climbing up?

David!

Oh great. Now he was hearing things. And her voice. Soft, like the soft, waxy touch of a flower petal. *Man, you are losing it.*

"David!"

A whisper of a cry on the wind drew him 'round. He looked up the pass. Pure white. To the side. Rocks. A crack that marked the dangerous maw of a crevasse.

Directly above it—

"Jolie, no! Stop!" He cast off his pack as he saw Jolie practically throwing herself down the mountain—straight toward the crevasse. "No!" He waved his arms. "Stop!"

"Help!" she cried out. "David, help!"

Jolie lunged forward.

And tumbled.

Slid down. . .down. . .straight into the crevasse.

Noooo!" Heart in his throat, David threw himself the last three yards. "Jolie!" He went to his knees, moving as quickly as safely possible and using his ski stick to probe for more fissures that could send him to his death. "Jolie, are you okay?" Iciness bled through his overpants, numbing but not saturating. "Jolie."

Why wasn't she responding?

"Jolie! Can you hear me?" Panic streaked through him, his breathing shallow and painful. *Calm down. You'll find her.*

A low moan that yanked on his heart pulled David closer.

Snow dropped away, his hand slid downward. He jerked himself up, pulse thundering. He scooted back and continued around, searching, calling. "Jolie, where are you?"

He peeked over the edge. The deep, vertical fissure in the mountain ran at least twenty feet deep, if not more. Where one ledge cut back, another jutted, barring him from a clean line of sight. Several chunks were broken. . .and another farther down. He angled trying to see around the jagged lips. She had to be—

A boot! He saw a boot. "Jolie! Jolie, can you hear me?"

Nothing save the bitter wind.

He'd have to rappel. David spun, dug his ice axe into the snow to use it as an anchor, then moved to pound in an ice screw as a secondary anchor. He donned his leg prusiks and prepped the mechanical ascender. At the lip of the crevasse, he padded the lip of the anchor to prevent the rope from digging into the snow and ice.

He used another rope and carabiner to lower his pack down into the crevasse. Once it was down, he went to work lowering himself into the icy gorge. Though it took only minutes to get set up at the bottom of this inverted pyramid, he felt like it'd been an hour.

David lowered himself onto his buttocks then rolled onto his belly, holding the rope as he eased over the edge, mentally chewing her out for not staying with her team and roped up. A team rescue would be so much easier.

He rappelled down the fifteen feet to where she lay. He unhooked himself, then using his stick again, he probed the area, praying he wouldn't discover another crevasse.

"Jolie!" David scrabbled to her side, pressed two fingers to her carotid, and visually probed the rest of her for injuries. Nothing bent at an unnatural angle. No blood. Her pulse was there but rapid.

"Jolie," he said, smoothing his hands over her limbs, assessing more firmly whether she had broken bones.

She moaned.

"Jolie, c'mon. I need you to wake up."

Yes, definitely needed her awake. Eyes open. Fighting back. Anything to reassure him he wouldn't have to attend another funeral.

"Hey." He patted her cheeks.

Her eyes fluttered open, squinted, then locked on him. "Oh no."

"Is that any—"

A demonic growl erupted—right along with her vomit. It struck his overpants, his boots, and jacket. Splatted his face.

David pushed back onto his haunches. "You have *got* to be kidding me!" His stomach roiled at the stench. He pressed the back of his hand to his nose and groaned as he stood, staring at the mess on his clothes. "Unbelievable. Of all the. . ."

"I'm sorry." Looking miserable, Jolie bent in half, gloved fingers digging into the snow, sniffling. She peeked up at him, whispering another apology. Face blanched, lips not their sultry pink—

David gritted his teeth. He grabbed a handful of snow and rubbed off as much of the mess as he could. "Are you hurt?"

Surprise skated off her blanched face as she considered him, slowly shook her head, then pressed her fingers to her forehead. "No. . . I—I don't think so." Her weak, defeated voice depleted what little was left of his irritation.

With a huff, he dropped to his knees. "You're pale. Let me check you over before we prusik back up."

After an almost imperceptible nod, Jolie lowered herself to the crevasse floor and closed her eyes. David gently touched her side, probing for internal injuries. "Let me know if something hurts."

She let out a sigh and draped an arm over her eyes.

"It was stupid to leave your team." He smoothed his hands over her right leg, then the other, working his way up her left side till he positioned his fingers against her carotid again. Rapid, consistent pulse. "Rope up, stay with them— you wouldn't have fallen."

Her arm dropped away and she glowered.

He waited for her snarky comment, her witty comeback. Instead, she swallowed and shook her head quickly, as if warding off something.

"Your guide said you weren't feeling well." He crouched and ducked his head to look into her eyes. "What's going on?"

"Nothing," she said, her words thick with exhaustion as she hauled herself upright. "Can we get going?"

"First things first. I need to know what condition you're in. Dizziness?"

She shook her head.

"Nosebleeds, drowsiness, shortness of breath, pins and needles?"

"Weak and sick." As if that should sum it all up. "And my head hurts."

"Probably hit it when you tried to do an aerial and ended up down here." He meant it to be funny, but something weighted her features. She wasn't talking back or fighting. And that worried him. "Jolie." He touched her cheek, drawing her gaze back to his. "Why'd you leave your team?"

Something skittered through her expression but vanished as fast as it came. She squeezed her eyes shut.

"Dizziness?"

"No, everything is blurry." She dropped her hands against her lap and squinted up at him. "Do you have anything to eat?"

"You're hungry?"

She shrugged.

"Guess since you emptied your stomach all over me. . ." But it was weird. People with AMS usually had a *loss* of appetite. He retrieved a protein bar from his pack and her water bottle from hers then returned and crouched in front of her. David held them out. "Eat up." He wasn't sure she could make it. "We have a lot of area to cover."

She studied him then took the proffered items. He hadn't seen AMS or HACE like this. She seemed to have a severe case and yet, not. The headache was weird. Dizziness, yes. But the increase in appetite, the shaking fingers. . .

David readied the harness and prusiks, trying not to pay too much attention to Jolie, to her sluggish movements as she rinsed her mouth and tore open the bar. "Drink," he ordered as he roped up. "Stay hydrated."

She glared at him. Then her gaze rose to the height of the crevasse. "I'm not sure this is a good idea." Jolie lumbered to her feet. "I'm sick. And tired."

"And what, staying down here to freeze to death or wait for a snowdrift or avalanche to bury us is a better option?" He smirked, trying to rouse her from the stupor that had fogged in her strong spirit. "Sorry." He cocked his head as he hooked the rope into the carabiner. "I like my toes nice and pink, not black with frostbite. Speaking of. . ."

He shifted a couple of feet and lifted her hand.

"What're you doing?" she asked, surprise coloring her words.

He tugged off her thick glove, then the insulator. Warm in his hands, her fingers showed only the slightest tinge of the frigid temperatures. He stuffed her glove into his mouth as he removed the other and checked her digits one by one.

"How. . .how'd you find me so fast?"

The vulnerability in her question drew his gaze up, surprised to see the pale face filled with rosiness. . .and yet still pale. What was this?

Insanity, that's what. Why was his mind even trying to go *there*? She was a Decoteau. A rich girl. He'd vowed to never deal with her or her family again.

He stuffed her hands into her gloves. "I'm a mountaineering ranger. I know where to look for *trouble*."

Instead of striking back with one of her lightning-fast comebacks, Jolie just dropped her gaze and drew on the gloves. "I didn't. . ."

Standing over her, he couldn't tear his gaze from the soft lines of her cheekbones, the straight nose, the delicate eyebrows. Even sick and roughed up by Denali, she had a beauty that any guy with eyes couldn't miss.

She looked up at him, her lips parted as if to say something, then she stilled.

Then at once all the indicators registered: her quickened

pulse when he touched her, her red cheeks. As if she climbed a mountain. But she hadn't. She'd fallen off one, sort of.

Blushing? His gaze rose to hers. She didn't falter but seemed to shrink.

❦

The headache, the blurry vision, the nausea were all swept away by the brown eyes boring into her soul. Jolie willed herself to step away, to slap him with some snarky comment, but she stood spellbound. How long had she hoped David Whiteeagle would look at her like this?

No doubt he saw the crimson in her cheeks. She could certainly feel it, even around the fever and nausea. Her heart sped. Had he finally figured out she had a crush on him?

Okay, that sounded entirely too middle school. No, she admired David. Not only was he handsome and commanding, but he was smart and loyal. Mariah had bragged about David's 4.0 and his college scholarship.

The way he looked at her lips, then her eyes, sent a buzzing through her head and down her chest, straight into her heart, which rapid-fired. "What?"

He swallowed. Blinked. Looked at the rope. Went to work looping it and attaching it to a carabiner. "You feeling strong enough to prusik?"

Jolie peeked up at the ledge twenty feet above them. "I. . .I guess." She could barely stand and he wanted her to haul herself up that? But what were her options? Stay down here or get up there. She finished the last of the protein bar, wishing there was more—like ten more.

"You're sick and weak."

Something about the way he said that ignited a fire in her. "I'm *not* weak."

He scowled. Why did he always have to scowl? "It's not

an insult. Your body is down with mountain sickness. It can depress your ability to function." He quirked an eyebrow. "Is that better?"

Jolie lowered her head and swallowed, feeling stupid.

"This climb won't be easy."

"Can we get on with this?"

He snapped back to harness rigging, and Jolie couldn't help but notice his muscles. Grizzly in more than his attitude, apparently. Standing beside her five-ten height, he was several inches taller, and broad. Very broad.

He stuffed his foot in the prusik. "I'll go first so I can help belay for you."

Jolie grabbed his arm. "No." Her head pounded with the fear of being alone, of being where whoever had meant to kill her could finish the job. "Please—don't leave me."

David frowned. "Jolie, it's not like I'm leaving you. It's logistics."

"You don't understand—"

Another frown, this one deeper.

"Look, I know you don't think I can do this. I know you think I'm weak and silly—"

"Jolie."

"And that I'm a spoiled rich girl, who tries to buy her way and everything—"

"Jolie." He released the rope and turned to her, still hooked in, as he cupped her face, silencing her torrent of words.

Tears burned her eyes.

Her pulse whooshed in her ears. Even though he wore gloves and she couldn't feel his touch against her cold cheeks, he was here. Close. Staring into her eyes and turning her spine to jelly, her belly to a pit of molten lava.

She gripped his arm. "I'm not that girl. I can do this."

"Jolie—"

"My dad believed in me. He said—"

"Jolie, stop. It's okay."

"No, it's not. Something's wrong—"

He pressed his lips to hers.

The moment froze but Jolie ignited. The icy edges of her heart melted, warming beneath the strength of David, of his capable touch, and his woodsy-outdoorsman smell and charm. She lifted her arm to wrap around his neck, elated at her teen fantasy coming to life, and melted into him as she kissed him back.

David broke off like an arctic wind. With wide eyes, he stepped back. Swallowed. Cleared his throat. "Okay."

Okay? *Okay?!?* He'd kissed her and that was all he could say?

"Now that you're not talking. . ." Though sarcasm tinged his words, something about his comment fell short of its mark. In fact, he looked shaken. "I'm going up."

Horror washed through her. "You kissed me to shut me up." The kiss that had shot through her like a bolt of lightning.

Not looking at her, David grabbed the rope. "I'll lower the rope for you. Hook in and I'll belay." He hesitated then hauled himself up with those powerful muscles and that thick head.

She could kill him. Kill him and never regret it.

She watched him ascend. Two feet. Three. . .

He was really going to leave her. Right down here. What if he got to the top and decided to do that and head to Base Camp? Probably would—just for that kiss. She'd reacted too strongly. He'd think she was *that* kind of girl.

But his leaving her would make it very easy for whoever wanted her dead. They could make it look like a very convincing accident.

She should tell David. Tell him why she left the team. But he wouldn't believe her. Especially now that she'd thrown up all over him, gone hysterical on him, then kissed him like the stupid, spoiled rich girl he thought her to be.

Four feet. He made it look effortless. "Your ears are too small for your head."

David huffed. Belayed. "Your mouth is too big."

Smart aleck. "You should know—you kissed me."

Crackk!

In a surreal, nothing-could-prepare-you-for-this-nightmare sort of way, Jolie saw a clump of snow dropping toward them. Below it. . .David tumbled. "Augh!" He flipped, the harness no longer taut against his weight, and dropped hard.

Chapter 6

D avid!" Jolie darted to him as he rolled onto his side and groaned, cradling his shoulder. Kneeling, she helped him as he climbed to his knees. "Are you okay?"

He held up a hand, his face a mixture of pain and pride. "Stay back. I don't want you to throw up on me again."

Arrogant, prideful grizzly bear. "Are. You. Hurt?"

He rotated his arm and growled. "A little. But I can make it."

"No. You can't."

His face lit with indignation.

Before he could mouth off again, she pointed to the top of the crevasse. "The anchor's gone."

His gaze shot upward, then to the rope in a heap a dozen feet away. Defeat pushed him to the ground. David roughed a hand over his face then climbed to his feet. He trudged away.

"What're you doing?"

Holding the arm he'd injured close, he rummaged through his pack then pulled out a radio phone. "I am never going to live this down," he growled. With that, he crouched and did something to the phone before he lifted it to his face.

"No!" Jolie lunged toward him, the world spiraling with the move. She tumbled into the snow.

David spun. "What are you doing?"

She clambered to her knees. "Don't call."

Anger sparked in his eyes. "If I don't call, we die."

142

Jolie licked her lips. "Sorry. Just. . .don't mention my name."

"Why?"

He wouldn't understand. Or believe her. In fact, she wasn't sure herself.

"Afraid someone will find out the oil heiress got herself stuck in a hole on the same mountain her brother died on?" He grinned. "Imagine what they'll say."

His words felt like a slap in the face. Why she'd let herself kiss him she'd never know. "Just. . .please." If whoever wanted to kill her had a radiophone, they'd know she was alive and know her location. She couldn't—*wouldn't* risk that.

"Base camp, this is Whiteeagle."

"David." A woman's voice broke through the swirling wind. "Where are you?"

"South of 7200, in a crevasse."

Silence hung in the cold seconds. "*In* it?"

"Yeah."

"What about your climber?"

Jolie breathed a silent prayer of thanks that her name wasn't mentioned.

"We're both fine. No injuries. The anchor broke loose."

"Okay. Hang tight. We'll get help your way."

"Thanks." He pressed the radiophone to his forehead and closed his eyes as he let out a long sigh.

A sudden rush of craziness overcame Jolie. Dizzy and sick, she dropped to her knees. Her stomach heaved but nothing came up. An ever-widening red circle grew directly beneath her. She stared at the sphere, confused. Another red circle. Several more. Blood? From what?

❧

David saw the blood dripping onto the snow and scrambled to Jolie's side. With the altitude, nosebleeds were common, especially for those with acute mountain sickness. "Hey." Hand resting on her back and one on her shoulder, he nudged her shoulders up. "Your nose is bleeding. Sit back."

Jolie's eyes fluttered as she moved under his guidance.

Using his teeth, David pried off his glove and pinched her nostrils. "Thought I told you to drink."

"I did."

"Not enough, obviously."

"I downed the water." Jolie propped against the wall, her head tilted back a little, and took over holding her nose. The blush in her face was gone, replaced too quickly by a white sheen. "I think. . .I think something's. . .wrong."

Using the loose snow to clean his hand, David smirked, trying to keep things light so she wouldn't panic again. "Ya think?" Nothing like seeing that look in her eyes. It was why he'd kissed her. Stupid-fool thing to do, but she wouldn't listen. And now. . .now he couldn't stop thinking about the way she'd reacted. Or how he reacted to her reaction.

"No, no. . ." Jolie muttered. "I think. . .someone—"

"If you wanted to be alone with her, all you had to do was ask."

David spun at the taunting voice just in time to see a rope snake down the wall of ice and snow. It thumped against the ground. At the top, a familiar pair of blue eyes peeked down at him. "Logan," David said with a laugh. "Am I glad to see you."

"Yeah, yeah. That's what they all say."

"How'd you get here so fast?"

"Already en route on patrol. I was heading up when Maggie radioed your position." He nudged his chin toward Jolie. "Can you get her hooked up?"

"Yeah. I need to rig a torso harness. Hang on." David worked the rope, watching Jolie. He quickly tied the gear to it and gave a quick tug, signaling its readiness. As it rose to the top, David rigged the harness. "Jo, how ya holding up?"

Arching an eyebrow at him, she let her eyes close.

On his haunches before her, he slipped the harness over Jolie and tightened it. She lifted herself up with a wince.

"No throwing up," he ordered.

A glimmer of a smile came with her soft snort and shake of her head.

"All right. On your feet." He took her hands and tugged her up.

"David," she said, her words thick but clear. "I am not crazy."

He smirked as he hooked the carabiners into place. "No, just spoiled."

"Listen—"

"Okay to go," David shouted to Logan and braced Jolie as her body tugged upward. She poured those honey eyes over him as she ascended. He watched, grateful for the physical distance between them. Too much of that girl could be his undoing.

Then it struck him—how had she descended so fast and so deep into the crevasse that held all that was sacred to him?

That kiss. . .it'd felt like he'd stuck his finger in a socket. Electricity shot through him at the softness of her lips, the quick intake of breath, the way she clung to him. . . . It took every ounce of willpower he had to break off that connection. He'd never had an experience like that. And it scared the willies out of him. He didn't want to feel those kind of things for the girl whose brother got Mariah killed.

Yeah, definitely needed distance.

The rope lowered and David hooked up. Prusiking up tugged at his banged-up arm and shoulder, but it also allowed him to work off some of the frustration and claustrophobia Jolie had created.

Once he hauled himself over the ledge, David breathed a sigh of relief. But a short-lived one when he saw Logan tending Jolie. He lifted the cord and roped up as he made his way over to them.

"What's going on?"

Logan glanced up at him, and though he didn't say anything, his expression told David a lot. "Here." After drawing a bottled water from Jolie's pack, Logan handed it to her then stood. "We'll be right back."

Logan pushed to his feet and pointed a few feet away. "Let's talk."

"Shouldn't we get moving?"

"In a second." Logan trudged to the sled. "What happened?"

David shrugged. "Anchored in, then lowered myself to her. She was unconscious on the crevasse floor. When I tried to come back up, the rope gave."

Logan lifted his pack and handed something to David.

His ice axe. *Correction: half the axe.*

"It didn't give," Logan said. "Someone cut it."

"I don't get it." Studying the grooves in the wood handle, David felt an ominous chill trace its icy finger down his spine. "It looks like it was hacked off."

"With an ice axe." Logan's blue eyes sparkled as he took in the terrain, as if looking for someone or something. "Did you hear anything down there?"

Just white, forbidding Denali.

"Only the wind, Jolie throwing up, and. . ." The howl of his heart as they kissed. Jolted by the thoughts, he shifted away so Logan wouldn't see his embarrassment. "Who would do this? Why?"

"Remember what Maggie said?"

"Dude, c'mon. There are easier ways to kill an oil heiress."

"Sure, but easier ways to get rid of the body and hide the

evidence? Up here, with snowdrifts and storms burying man and vegetation alike?"

"But drifts are unpredictable and storms come and go as they please."

"So, this person decided to help it along. . .only she got away. You came to help. So, this person"—again, his gaze skated the mountain—"has to get rid of both of you now."

David swallowed.

"Out here, they could get rid of her and nobody would find her decomposed body for months, if ever. You know that better than me."

Hands on his belt, David stared up the incline. Then his gaze rose to the sky. He noted several factors: the warmer, moist air and the wind loft speed. "Logan."

His friend straightened, taking in the surroundings, the elements. "Oh no."

"Tell me that's not what I think it is."

"I would but then I'd be a liar."

"Why—*why* can't I get a break?"

Logan hesitated. "Think we can make it to Camp 1?"

"No way. We need to dig in *now*." Together, they grabbed a tent from the sled, chose a spot with an incline at its back, and set up.

"What's going on?" Jolie asked as she stumbled toward them, her lips bluish.

David didn't pause in cutting blocks to form an ice wall around the tent. "Storm coming."

"Are you sure? There wasn't a report of storms—"

"Lenticular clouds form swiftly. Little to no warning." David swung and heaved, placed, then did it again. And again. "Get inside. Guzzle that water."

"How long will this last?"

"A few hours at most." David felt the sweat trickling

down his back. The aches in his shoulder and arm screamed at him. He yanked off his jacket and tossed it inside. "It'll be gone by nightfall when the temperature drops."

"Is that supposed to be reassuring?" Jolie slid her pack into the tent but didn't enter.

"Absolutely," Logan said with a laugh. "If you've seen a lenticular—trust me, you'll be very glad it lasts only till nightfall. It's a beast."

"Let's just hope we survive till then." David tucked himself into the tent.

"Actually, more like four days."

David paused. "Come again?"

"That's why I came up after you," Logan said. "Maggie got a storm warning. In twenty-four hours, we're going to get slammed hard." Meaning coated his expression. "It's bad."

Chapter 7

Something dug into her shoulder. Jolie shifted, then shivered. Frigid temperature and the howling wind pulled her from a fitful rest. Her eyelids felt like weights, but she pushed them open all the same. A loud roar nudged her from a fitful sleep. Jolie forced her heavy eyes open. Startled to find someone lying within inches of her, she steeled her response as her brain caught up with the sight. Caught in a storm on Denali's West Buttress. In a tent. With David.

Laid out on his back, one arm over his head, he seemed perfectly at home.

Curled on her side, Jolie shivered, the jerky movements exhausting her muscles. She tried to swallow against her parched throat but it felt like gulping rocks. Peeking around her sleeping bag, she scanned the semidarkened interior for her water bottle—and found Logan in his bag behind her. They'd sandwiched her. At least the gesture gave the illusion of safety and warmth.

If someone was after her the way she believed, would a storm be enough to hold them off? Trying to push through in a whiteout like this would get them killed.

Ah, there. Her bottle lay near the zipped tent opening with the packs. All blocked by David. Great. Could she reach across him? She had to. Her tongue felt three sizes too big.

"Your mouth is too big."

David's taunt annoyed and amused her. But stretching

over him to reach her water tempted her to get back at him. Chewing the inside of her lip, she peered down at him.

Whoa. The guy looked tense, even asleep. Tight corded bicep over his head. The too-small ears...the dark Athabascan skin, black hair in a short crop, strong but chapped lips.

It'd been a wonderful, warm kiss. His outdoors scent tantalizing. She'd never felt so drawn to a guy. And as a Decoteau, she'd had her choice of bachelors. So why on earth had she been so attracted to a man who hated her just for existing?

"You stuck?"

Jolie sucked in a sharp breath, her gaze darting to David's. "You're awake."

"Always knew you were smart."

Did she really say that? *Good grief!* No wonder he thought she was an idiot. "I—I mean. . ." Oh, forget what she meant. No way could she dig herself out of that hole. She plastered on a frustrated expression. "I was trying to get my water. You're in the way."

With a smirk and eyes never leaving hers, David drew his other arm out of the bag, reached over, and grabbed her bottle. "This?"

She snatched it from him and settled back into the bed. He'd caught her staring at him, lost in her fantasy world, where she'd long ago imagined dating him, marrying him, and having perfect children.

Was it hot in here?

Stuffed back in her bag, she propped herself up and flipped the nozzle. Ignoring David's eyes, which had never left her, she lifted the bottle to her lips.

"Wait." David yanked it out of her hand.

"Hey!"

He sat up, closing the valve and staring at the insulated bottle.

"What are you doing? Give it back."

He angled it toward her. "You're sick, but the symptoms don't match AMS or HACE. So, what if"—he bounced the water bottle—"what if someone's tampering with your water?"

His words shoved her onto her backside. A chill spread through her chest. *I was right.* . . . Someone wanted to kill her. But. . .why?

"What's going on, Jolie?"

She met David's concerned stare. "What?"

"Don't play dumb. I saw it in your eyes."

Would he believe her? This was proof, wasn't it? What if he just accused her, again, of being a spoiled rich girl who thought everyone wanted her money? Okay, that wasn't entirely rational.

He scowled.

Her heart sped at the look on his face. "Okay." She held up a hand. "I. . .my father's confidant told me he thought someone had killed my father." Guilt chugged through her veins. Why hadn't she seen it? "He thought I might be in danger, so he was glad I was getting away for a while."

"I'd say trouble came with you."

"That's impossible. They're my friends! I know them."

"Apparently, not as well as you think." David held up the bottle. "If they messed with your water supply. . . It makes sense that you aren't getting better though you've descended."

It couldn't be true. Though she'd had thoughts along the same line, hearing him voice them gave her fears credence. And scared her more. "How exactly did they give me mountain sickness?"

"It's not mountain sickness. The symptoms seem the same, but there are a couple that have nothing to do with AMS."

"That's insane."

"Maybe, but then how do you explain that someone broke my ice axe?"

Jolie widened her eyes. "*What?*"

He tugged it over and held it out. "These are gouges from a sharp object. I test my equipment just like everyone else's before every climb. I tested it before I came after you. It was solid. No weak points." David leaned over and dug into his pack. He pulled out another insulated water bottle. "Drink from this—and a lot. Let's test my theory."

"How?"

"Well, if you start feeling better, then we're flushing whatever they poisoned you with." His expression turned grim. "Let's just hope we figured it out soon enough."

Holding his navy and black bottle, Jolie stared at it. Had someone really put something in her water? Tried to *poison* her? Panic banged on the door of her heart. She wouldn't let it in. Couldn't. Not with a killer or would-be killer out there, trying to bury her on this mountain.

Oh, Daddy. . .

But he wasn't there anymore. Neither was Gael.

Heaviness anchored her heart against the depths of despair.

"Hey," David said, his voice low and near. "You okay?"

She snorted a laugh. "No." Her voice cracked. "I can't believe this. I mean, yeah, sure—I've had people hate me because my father was an oil baron."

"Hey, it was different. There was more to it than that."

Jolie smiled through her blurring vision.

"Besides, I didn't *hate* you. . .not really."

"Really?"

David hesitated then looked down. "I thought I did." He sat on his bedroll, hugging one knee, his gaze down. When he spoke again, his words surprised her. "I miss her—Mariah."

She could relate. A lot. "I understand."

His gaze bounced to hers and he studied her for a moment, then lowered his eyes again. "Mariah was amazing. She...she kept me on track. Believed in me when I didn't believe in myself. She was incredible that way, ya know?"

"Gael was the same. So strong, always pushing me to be more responsible." She scrunched her shoulders. "I sort of did the rebellious teen thing."

"No—"

She shot him a look.

"You rocked it." He laughed. "Every tabloid had you on its cover for a year or two."

She groaned and sat cross-legged, nursing the water bottle he'd loaned her. "Don't remind me. I thought I owned the world. I felt *entitled* to just about anything and everything I wanted." She shook her head, embarrassed to confess to that.

"What changed you?"

"Gael." Jolie chewed her lower lip as she dragged her gaze back to David. "His death, actually. Not having him around, I felt like a spinning compass with no direction. I didn't know how to navigate life without him. I was angry and terrified." Her throat burned with the truth of her words. "Everyone expected me to turn into trouble, collapse."

"You don't seem the type to really care what people think."

"Normally, I don't." She took another sip, unwilling to look into those rich, dark irises and be exposed. "But there was this one guy I had a huge crush on—well, he pretty much shattered my world."

"Yeah? How so?"

Twisting the neck brace of the bottle, Jolie toyed with the truth. Tell him, and she might very well humiliate herself.

Ah, but she'd already done that. A lot. What was there to lose?

"He yelled at me, right in front of my brother's casket."

She braved his expression.

Still and stunned, David watched her.

Wind gusted into the tent through a sliver of an opening and tossed her hair into her face. But she didn't care. Her focus was trained on Ranger Grizzly, who suddenly didn't seem so grizzlyish anymore. "Told me he hated me."

❦

"Me?" His voice pitched. "You had a crush—" *She had a crush on me?*

And he'd shattered her world.

"Crazy, huh?" Soft and nervous, her voice betrayed her.

The most beautiful heiress in the world and she'd had a crush on him? Why couldn't he get his mind to wrap around that? She had a crush on him. The words played over and over in his mind. Right along with the revelation of the wound he'd inflicted on her.

He needed to man up. "Jolie. . ." What could he say—assuming he could push his brain past the fact that this drop-dead gorgeous woman had liked him? How did one make something like that better? "I'm sorry. I. . .I don't know what to say. . . ." What a jerk! "I was drowning in my own grief." And that gave him the right to hurt her?

Her smile rose then twisted to the side as she gave a one-shouldered shrug. "We live in different worlds. I guess I should've expected it."

"But you didn't." Man, could he reverse time, take back his hatred?

"Nobody had ever spoken to me—or anyone else in my family—like that."

"I was completely out of line."

"Yes." Jolie laughed. "Yes, you most definitely were."

Though he was slow in coming to the conclusion, he did

get to it: "But you never hated me."

She ducked her head and gave a halfhearted shrug. "Why?"

Because she still likes me. His mind flashed to the kiss, to the way she fell into his arms, responded with one of her own kisses.

David let out a quick puff of air and looked away. *What do I do with this?*

"I guess I deserved it."

That comment came out of left field. "Deserved what?"

"Your anger, the figurative slap on the face."

His gut cinched at the way she'd taken his rebuke, his tirade that had humiliated even his parents. "No, I don't think anyone deserved that. Especially not you. We were both buried in our grief."

Her gaze rose to his. "But you still hate me."

His pulse thumped against her words. "No." It was his turn to duck. But for him, it was shame that bent his head. "I hated the world. . .because I hated myself."

Whoa. He'd never said that out loud. Never admitted it to himself, either.

"Mariah invited me on the climb with her and Gael, but I blew her off. I think even then, I was jealous of what she and Gael had found. It was so much like what my parents had, and being three years older than her, I hated that I was still alone."

Why on earth was he spilling his guts like this? He verified Logan was sleeping. No way did he want that guy hearing all this. He'd never let David live it down.

"He really did love her." She reached around her collar and fingered something, then tugged. "He went to the 'Edge of the World' with her."

Noting her reference to a jagged portion of Denali near the

peak, David eyed the ring dangling on a necklace. "What. . . ?"

"It's the engagement ring." She craned her neck closer so he could see it better. "The jeweler messed up so it wasn't ready when they left for the climb. I'd promised to fly out and meet them once they returned to Talkeetna, so he could give it to her then. But. . ."

"They never returned."

Slowly, she shook her head.

David took the gold piece between his fingers and eyed the diamond. "Quite a rock."

"He said it didn't compare to her. See the engraving?"

"Easy to say when you have millions to toss around." David smirked as he angled it to read the inscription. *Love Conquers All.*

Except death. It hadn't conquered that.

"A girl would wait a long time to get something like that from me—and only life insurance would cover the rest."

"Well," Jolie said, her voice soft as silk, "for the right guy, a girl doesn't need extravagance. Just sincerity."

Beautiful words, but it didn't ease the ache he felt at remembering that she was way out of his league. At the same time, he couldn't help but wonder if she meant more with those words than she said. He traced her face, searching for any indication. . .

Who was he kidding? She'd said she *had* a crush on him. Past tense.

But she kissed me back.

He had to know. "For the right guy, huh?"

Jolie's breathing slowed as those soft honey eyes rose. "Only the right guy."

"Have you found him yet?"

"I don't know. It depends." Coy had a middle name: Jolie.

"On what?"

"Whether this guy is willing to start over, *tabula rasa.*"

"Huh?"

Jolie smiled—man, she had a great smile. "Blank slate. We'd have to start over. No more calling me a rich, spoiled girl."

"Wow, that's asking a lot. A man who'd lie for you."

Her mouth gaped. She slapped his shoulder.

David laughed, glad that the suffocating moment had passed. Taunting, teasing, and confrontation—he knew what to do with those. But this. . .this mushy, softhearted stuff did strange things to him. And to Jolie, obviously. He wanted the feisty, no-holds-barred woman back.

David noticed movement behind Jolie and stilled. "You're awake?"

Eyes closed, Logan didn't move. "Never went to sleep."

Chapter 8

Once a grizzly, always a grizzly. Should've known she couldn't tame the beast, or even draw him in to civility. Heart thundered with each pulse. Did he *really* think of her as spoiled? Or was it a tease? And look at how quickly he changed gears. He must be embarrassed that Logan overheard.

"We need your opinion," David said as he dug through his pack.

"What's that?" Logan said, still not moving.

Why couldn't she fall for guys like Logan? Guys who were calm, steady, and not easily ruffled. Was she a magnet for aggressors?

"On whether Jolie is a spoiled rich girl."

Humiliation spiked. Tears sprang to her eyes. Her chin quivered.

It's exhaustion. That's all.

Rustling to her left erupted as Logan came into view. "David, you have to be one of the biggest jerks I know."

"What?" David said with a laugh.

"You just crushed her."

David's face swung toward her.

Jolie ducked her head—which freed a tear. Curse those things. "No," she said weakly as she tried to look at him, but more tears escaped. "I'm fine."

His expression, even though she only saw it through blurry, tear-filled eyes, went slack. He touched her shoulder. "Jolie? Seriously?"

She blinked. Hardened. Anything to get rid of the stupid tears. "Just—don't worry about me. I know what you think of me now." The hurt, the anger, bubbled to the surface. "Forget it."

"Look, it was a joke."

"See?" Logan said. "You're a jerk." He angled in closer to her.

And that only plucked more tears. *Stupid, stupid, tears!* She was stronger than this. And what angered her was that she was proving him right—bawling over a guy who'd just called her a name. Didn't it mean she *was* a spoiled rich girl?

Always had money. Always had the things she wanted. As a teen she demanded her own way. But she'd changed. Even if he couldn't see it.

She could never be good enough, domestic enough for David.

"You just never know when to stop, David." Logan's reprimand tightened the stale, icy air in the tent. "And when you start feeling trapped, you fight. You bring out all your guns and start blazing till there's nobody left. And that's what's going to happen—you're going to die a lonely, miserable old man if you don't grow up and let go of this anger."

Tears stemmed, Jolie looked between the two, surprised the quiet ranger had unleashed on the grizzly.

"You don't know what you're talking about." The words David spoke held his infamous growl.

Oddly enough, Jolie found comfort in it. The raw power. But it was killing him, wasn't it?

"Actually, as your best friend, I *do* know what I'm talking about."

"Have you forgotten these people"—he stabbed a finger at Jolie, and the sensation speared straight to her heart—"killed Mariah."

"You know better. Mariah got herself killed."

"Liar!" His roar matched the storm raging outside.

Logan's face twisted in grief. "God forgive me, but she did, David. She went up there. She wanted to be with Gael. She loved him. But you—you won't stop blaming everyone else. What this is really about is that you didn't save her. Have you ever thought that if you had you'd be dead, too?"

Deep, deep pain radiated off David.

"Jolie isn't to blame. Gael and Mariah knew the dangers of climbing Denali. Everyone does because we brief them. They bear the blame of their deaths, if blame must be applied, which you seem to think it does. But if you don't get over yourself, you're going to lose Jolie, too."

Sucking in a breath drew both of their gazes to her.

Logan looked down. "I'm sorry. That wasn't mine to say."

But Jolie's gaze locked on David. Though he looked like a bomb ready to detonate, there also emanated surprise. Fear.

Wait—fear? In David Whiteeagle? The man born of this mountain?

Yes. Yes, it was fear. Penetrating, terrifying fear. Fists balled, lips tight, and shoulders bunched, he looked like a caged animal. Cornered. Frightened.

He spun around and dove for the tent's zipper. He yanked it up.

"David—"

Wind and snow barreled into the tent as David shoved himself out into the storm.

"David," Jolie shouted, but the ravaging elements tore away the sound.

"Leave him."

"But the storm—"

"He's been in worse."

Jolie spun on him. "Why did you do that? What if something happens? What if—"

"He needed it." Resignation hung miserably on Logan's face as he retrieved his water bottle. "It's been a long time coming."

Panic clutched her in its icy talons. Jolie watched, numb, as Logan zipped the tent closed then dug into one of the packs and drew out two bars. He handed her one.

Jolie drew away.

"He's changed, for the worse." Logan sat down, slumped. "We met at a camp when we were ten. He was always intense, drew the girls like flies." He stared down, seemingly at nothing, then shook his head. "But since Mariah's death—he's been unbearable. Everyone's afraid of crossing him, upsetting him."

Jolie swallowed, her gaze flitting to the opening, begging David to return.

"He became a ranger to make up for what he didn't do for Mariah. And now with you in danger, I think all his old defense mechanisms are exploding." Forlorn, he looked at her. "I know you think I'm horrible for yelling at him like that, but...we've tried the nice routes. And I think...I think God's using this time—*you*—to force David to face something."

"What?"

"Himself." Logan balanced the bar on her crossed legs. "Just. . .don't think the David you've encountered here is the real him. Okay?" He jammed his hands back into his gloves. "And I'm sorry for dragging you into this, but if I'm right, then it was worth it."

"Right about what?"

"About how you feel about him."

Jolie refused to look away, even as heat seared her cheeks.

Logan smiled. "Good. Because I haven't seen him so riled up around anyone else, so I am pretty sure the feelings are mutual."

David felt the same way about her? Fluttering tickled her belly. Though she loved his intensity, which reminded her of Gael and her father, she wasn't going to step into a relationship prepped for abuse. She'd seen two friends go through that already. He'd have to do some serious changing.

"I hope you're right—" Jolie froze. "Not about David's feelings but that your words help, not hurt him."

"You and me both. I've never done anything like that before, but I was ready to *push* him into a crevasse." Logan munched his bar for several long minutes.

Jolie watched the tent, strained against the cacophony of wind and snow beating against the nylon tent, burrowed in between ice walls, searching for sounds of David's return.

"Your crush never ended, did it?"

"He's bigger than life."

"Maybe what you feel for him is more than a crush."

Warily, she eyed Logan.

He shrugged. "By definition, a crush is an infatuation that is usually short lived. Is that how you would describe what you feel for him?"

Jolie fingered the pattern on the water bottle and whispered, "I don't know what I feel for him."

"Does it feel like infatuation?"

Maybe as a teen, it'd been that. . . .

"You seem more mature than a girl with an infatuation. And you withstood his taunting and his anger pretty stiffly. I can't tell you how many girls he's scared off with that."

"A lot, huh?"

"Yes, and I'm pretty sure that's how he wanted it. But you aren't scared."

"I was." Which was why she'd never come back to Talkeetna, though she dreamed often of seeing him. "He gets under your skin. . . ."

Logan laughed. "That he does."

"And. . .I realized today, that his anger—it's not really anger."

Logan eyed her.

"It's grief." She swallowed the lump in her throat. "He and I have that in common."

❧

Firelike fury fueled his anger. So much that David wondered why the snow around him hadn't melted. Stuffed above the hastily erected walls that embraced the tent, David sat on his haunches, hard rock pressing into his back. The storm's whiteout reduced visibility to just a few feet. But over the last few minutes, during lulls in the wind speed, Logan's laughter catapulted. So did David's anger. Mad that his friend had pushed him. Mad that his friend had been right. Furious that his friend was in that tent with Jolie right now.

"And if you don't get over yourself, you're going to lose her, too."

How could he lose something he never had?

And yet, the thought wrapped around him like a straitjacket. Jolie was too good for him. Too rich. Too beautiful. Too sweet. Too. . .everything.

David held his head and tucked his chin. The thought of being alone, being. . . Oh, he just couldn't fight it—*not* having a chance with Jolie suddenly seemed like the worst thing in his world.

While he'd teased her about being spoiled, it was true in a way. She had everything she wanted and needed. He had a job that kept him on his mountain for weeks at a time. What woman in her right mind would accept that?

I'm not good enough, God! I don't deserve her.

"You didn't deserve My love either, but I gave it."

Heady and powerful, the reply warmed David with

conviction. How many times had his mother told him love wasn't earned? It was a gift.

"Kind of jumping ahead here," David whispered to the wind. Who was talking love? He'd just been measuring the facts of life. She was rich. He wasn't, not by any stretch of the imagination. He couldn't give her the life she was used to.

A life? There he went again, getting the sled before the dogs. He hadn't even taken her on a date. What if they went out—and there again, was the money thing. No doubt she'd want to go to a steak house or some other expensive place. Living in Talkeetna all his life, he didn't even like the city. She'd been born and bred in it.

"We're a bad match, God." David thudded his head against the rock wall behind him.

"Then why are you out here arguing with Me?"

"You ambushed me," David said with a laugh. "That wasn't fair."

"True."

Okay, that didn't help except to push his foul mood a meter below the frozen landscape. If he even wanted a chance with Jolie—and he did—then he needed to square some things. Starting with letting go of his little sister.

But how did one do that and still honor her memory? Was letting go the same as not caring?

No, even he didn't believe that. But it felt that way—that he didn't care if he wasn't angry. And honestly, he knew that Mariah would've slapped him into next week if she'd been here and had seen how he'd acted. She might've been younger and smaller, but that girl had ruled the roost.

Much like Jolie.

He ached, thinking of the pain and hurt he'd inflicted yet again. Which in the heat of the argument had angered him more. Not at her or Logan, which was where he'd aimed his anger, but at himself. For hurting her. She might be feisty and strong, but there was a soft, tender spot in her. And. . . somehow, in some crazy way, it had his name on it.

She *did* like him. So much that she wanted them to start over. A blank slate, she'd said.

It blew him away that she'd be willing to do that. . .so they'd have a chance.

What a. . .sacrifice.

Whoa. God was right.

He imagined God was laughing at that statement. "Sure that was a blinding flash of the obvious to You."

"*So. . .what will you sacrifice?*"

"My anger."

Was that enough? It was a start, but once he worked that out, once he let go of what was churning up within him, what then?

David sat in the blistering cold, his mind and limbs agitated. He stood and stretched his legs, wishing he could do something about the burning in his mind. But that was the point, right? Sacrifice—never intended to be fun or pain-free.

No pain, no gain.

And going in there, apologizing to Jolie. . .that was some kind of pain.

Why?

Because. . .because he would have to admit he was wrong. That he didn't mind so much. He could man up and own his mistakes. No, what really ate at him. . .was the fact that she'd seen him at his worst. Been the brunt of his anger. Could she forgive him?

What if he went back in there and she told him to take a flying leap off the Edge of the World?

Only one way to find out. . .

God, I have no right to ask, but please. . .

As he worked his way down the small cluster of rocks to the tent, David's heart rate doubled at the thought of the conversation he had in mind. What would he say? Maybe he should plan something. That way he'd sound intelligent. Around women, he stuck to smart-aleck comments or no comments at all to keep them at a distance. He didn't want that with Jolie. So, how—

As he rounded the corner, David's heart backed into his throat.

A dark shape moved near the tent.

Chapter 9

Braving heights and bitter memories, Jolie had trekked into the untamed territory of Alaska's forbidding mountain—and also into David's life. The peace she'd come to make wasn't the peace she'd found. In fact, she wasn't sure she'd found any peace at all.

Having become sick—*poisoned*—she hadn't reached the summit. Hadn't conquered what had defeated Gael. And in being sick, she'd encountered yet another forbidding element—David Whiteeagle's heart.

She wasn't sure which hurt more.

"How are you feeling?" Logan's voice rose above the wind tugging on their tent.

Pulled from her thoughts, Jolie searched her body. "I. . ." She hadn't felt the urge to retch in hours—not since David had given her his bottle and disappeared. "Better. A lot better, actually."

Logan nodded. "Good. Keep hydrating."

Obediently, she took another swig. "Don't you think we should check on David?"

"If he doesn't have enough sense to come out of the cold. . ." He snickered. "I'll give him ten more minutes."

"He's been out there awhile."

With a smirk, Logan gave another nod. "He's a ranger, Jolie. And no matter how ticked he is, he won't get stupid."

The tent flap zipped up.

Jolie's heart leapt at the thought of David returning—

though she wanted to cram his hurtful words down his throat. "Da—"

Logan lunged at her. "Get down!" He barreled into her.

Face colliding with the nylon tent bottom and the hardened ground beneath, Jolie hauled in a breath.

A crack resounded, distant yet close.

Thud!

Smothering, the tent collapsed, wrapping Jolie and Logan in its cocoon. A weight dropped on them. Wrestling. Writhing.

She peered over her shoulder but saw only orange-and-white material.

"Stay down," Logan shouted as he pinned her.

Frenetic and hard movements continued. A fight. Another loud pop ensued. A dark color ballooned over the tent, widening slowly and. . .dripping.

"Blood!" Jolie whispered.

"That way," Logan said, pointing to a small opening. "Go!"

Wrangling her legs free, Jolie crawled into the raging storm. Wind yanked at her jacket and limbs, her hair loose beneath her hat. They scrambled into the tangle of rocks that had acted as a partial barrier between the tent and the storm. She climbed up and glanced back.

David threw a hard punch into the face of—

Jolie froze.

Aidan Sheppard.

Face contorted in rage, Aidan twisted—and produced a gun. He aimed it at David.

"No!" Jolie's shout sailed through a lull in the wind.

Aidan jerked. Redirected his aim.

Directly at her.

Her pulse shallowed out. Her legs grew leaden.

Something pushed at her.

But all she could see, all that impacted her, was the guy she had almost considered a brother.

Behind him, a flash of movement, David dove at him, arms wrapping around Aidan and shoving him into the snow.

They wrestled again. Threw punches.

Jolie couldn't watch. Blood marred the pristine white snow. "He's going to kill him."

"Stay here." Logan worked his way back to them, leaving her alone.

How had Aidan gotten away from the others? What about Derrick and James?

In the fight, Aidan broke free. Amid the tent, the broken ice chunks and debris, Jolie searched for David and Logan. The tent writhed, with them in it.

Aidan! Where'd he go? She scooted down a half-dozen feet, searching the rugged outcropping. "Aidan!" He wasn't going to get away with this, with trying to kill her. A realization shoved her forward. He killed her father! "Aidan!" No, he would not.

She rounded a bend and stopped short. Pulled back to use the rock face as a shield.

Skis on, Aidan stood smiling at her down the barrel of his gun. "You nearly got away."

"So did you."

His smile faltered. "Ah, but see? I will get away."

"Why? Why do you want me dead?"

His face went grim. "Your father. . ." He bunched his lips. "My father worked his rear end off for twenty years. . .and your father gives the whole kingdom to you! You, a twenty-three-year-old spoiled rich girl. My father deserved to be made CEO, not you!"

"You're right. You're right—I even asked Baron why I'd been put in charge."

Aidan hesitated and hope surged that he'd give up this quest to wrest power at D. I. from her fingers—her dead fingers.

"Well, nobody will have to worry now. My father will be named CEO—right after your funeral."

"Jolie!" David's shout thudded into her.

She turned just in time to see a puff of smoke at the end of Aidan's handgun. In the space of an eyeblink, the wall beside her erupted.

So did the mountain—a resounding crack boomed above.

Aidan's gaze rose. His eyes widened.

"Jolie, get back!" David's words pushed her a step back, just in time to see a blanket of white whoosh over the lip and hurl itself at Aidan.

A weight shoved into her from the side. Threw her backward. Her head rammed into something. The world went black.

❧

Adrenaline still poured through his veins as he stared at her unconscious form. A red knot above her temple glistened beneath the rising sun.

David knelt beside Jolie as she lay unconscious against the rocks. Her head had hit the boulder, but she was alive. The avalanche that had swept over the gunman also opened a crevasse that swallowed him.

Though Logan went to check if they could rescue Aidan, David knew the chances were slim to none. The area was unstable after the snowdrift and with the crevasse. . .

"Jolie?" He touched the side of her face with his gloved hand.

A moan worked its way up her throat as she shifted.

"Jolie, you okay?"

Her eyes blinked open and he couldn't help the smile.

Then she shot up and groaned, hand going to her forehead. "Aidan."

"Logan's looking for him."

She looked around. "The avalanche. . . How did we not. . .?"

David eyed the ledge above. "You were far enough under for protection." He sat back on his haunches. "Let's worry about you, getting you off my mountain."

Her eyebrow arched. "*Your* mountain?" She sat up with a small grunt then allowed him to pull her upright.

"It's as mean as I am."

"You got that right."

The words dented his hope that they could start over like she'd said—well, she'd said that before he got stupid and mouthy. "I deserved that."

Jolie hesitated, her honey eyes on him, which made each beat of his pulse feel like a jackhammer. "Wow." Her lips almost quirked into that. "So. . .guess that makes you a spoiled mountain boy."

David grinned. "Only if that's what you like."

Again, Jolie stilled. "Did you get hit on the head, too?"

The laugh felt freeing. "I guess you could say that."

"David," Logan called as he worked his way back to them. "It's no good." He squinted against the glare of the sun on the snow. "It's a mess. I can't see anything and can't get down. It's too unstable."

"Expected as much." Though he roiled at the thought of leaving someone down there, he didn't have the equipment to dig. And with—

"David!" Jolie gasped. "You're shot!"

He winced. "Yeah, it's not bad." Actually, it was. Pain radiated through his shoulder but at least the blood wasn't gushing. He'd packed it with snow and stemmed the flow before rushing to Jolie.

171

"Not bad? You're shot!" Jolie repeated.

"Jo." David turned to her and cupped her face. "I'll be okay. Our priority is getting you to the hospital to make sure whatever he put in that drink didn't do anything permanent. Okay?"

"You called me Jo."

Did he? He hadn't really noticed.

"My dad used to call me that."

"I'm. . .sorry."

She gripped the sides of his jacket. "No, I like it."

David homed in on her mouth. Bent closer—

Logan cleared his throat.

Heat bolted through David. Embarrassment and agitation. He glowered at Logan.

"Sorry." But Logan wasn't really. "You've got a bleeding gunshot wound, she's been poisoned, and for some bizarre reason, the storm has given us an opening to get out of here. We need to move." He glanced at both of them. "Now."

After gearing up, they did a radio check and made contact with Maggie, reporting they were on their way down. They roped up with Logan in the lead, Jolie behind, then David bringing up the rear.

The four-hour hike to Base Camp took the last vestiges of David's strength. Each step felt heavier and more painful than the previous. A couple of times the rope pulled taut, alerting him to the fact that he'd dropped behind. He'd shuffled forward on his skis and pushed himself a little harder as they crossed the glacier back toward Base Camp.

Up the last pass, he saw the Otter waiting, along with three rangers and the ranger doctor. *Thank the merciful Lord!*

David unroped, dropped to his knees even as feet hurried around him. Ferried to the plane, David didn't want to look at Jolie. Didn't want her to see him weak, nor did he want her pity or fear. He'd be fine.

The forty-minute trip lumbered until David could not fight the fatigue any longer and gave in to its powerful embrace.

৪৯

Sitting on the edge of the hospital bed, Jolie stared out the window at her beloved Alaska. Though she hadn't been born here, she'd lived 80 percent of her life here. And she loved it. Especially since it had David Whiteeagle.

Who hadn't come to visit her in the two days since they'd been delivered to the hospital, even though he'd been released yesterday.

"Now, dear," her mother said, moving around the room, gathering belongings. "You get dressed because I am going to find that doctor and get you released to Dr. Hanley's care."

"I'm fine here, Mom. They've taken good care of me."

"You have frostbite—you were poisoned!" The injuries had mortified her mom.

"Neither of which are the fault of the doctors here. I'm fine. Really." And not ready to leave. Not yet. Not till. . .

"Nonsense. There are far better doctors in Fairbanks than out here in the middle of nowhere." Her mother lifted her purse and started for the door, tugging hard to open it. "Get ready. I'll be back soon."

Jolie pushed off the bed, her feet snug in the silly pink thermal socks the doctors insisted she keep. She shuffled to the window and peered out at Mt. McKinley, remembering David. His raw power. His anger. That drastic change in him right before Aidan—

Jolie tipped her head, touching her fingers to her forehead. She'd thought of him as a brother. And he'd wanted to kill her. Because her father believed in her, believed she had the wherewithal to run the company.

The door whooshed behind her followed by a soft thud.

"Sorry, dear. I left my ID in here when I called the insurance company a while ago." Her mother retrieved it. "Baron called from the parking lot. He's on his way up."

"Mom, you haven't told me—did they find Aidan?"

Her mother's face fell. "I guess I can't hide it from you. Yes, they found him. His neck. . .it was broken. He died instantly."

Jolie trembled. "I'm glad he didn't suffer. . . ."

"You have a bigger heart than me because I wanted him to suffer for what he did to you." Her mother shuddered. "And your father. Police went through his things and his father cooperated. They've found chemicals in Aidan's room. And e-mail exchanges with someone named Rameau, who apparently masterminded your father's accident."

Jolie turned away, choked by the news.

"Ah, Baron, so glad you could join us."

In the glass reflection, Jolie saw Baron's ghostly image. She turned back and offered him a halfhearted smile.

"The nurse said she was ready for you."

"Oh. Yes. Thank you. I'll be right back, Jolie."

Alone with Baron, Jolie braced herself, once again tracing the mountains with her gaze. "Did you bring them, Baron?"

"I did."

She turned and retrieved a pen from the table where her mother had scribbled notes from the insurance company. "Then let's do this."

❧

David slunk through the halls, hating hospitals, hating the smells, hating the false hope that lurked there. Though his shoulder still ached, his heart hurt more. After they'd stitched him up, he'd headed home. Sat in his room thinking and praying.

Somehow, he ended up at the hospital. On the fourth floor.

Standing in front of room 4218.

He swallowed hard then reached—

The door swung open.

A man in his late forties exited, a file in hand and a frown on his face. He scowled at David, who moved past the door, nerves jangled.

No, he wasn't going to be deterred. He turned back and slipped into the room.

His breath caught as he eased the door to. Jolie stood at the window in dark jeans and a soft white sweater. Her white-blond hair cascaded down her back.

Oh man. How had he ever convinced himself she would want him? She was out of his league.

"Your ears are still too little." Jolie's voice coiled around his heart as she peeked over her shoulder at him, those golden brown eyes melting his cold heart.

"And your mouth is still too big." He grinned, drawn in once again by her feistiness. Stretching his neck beneath the arm sling, he crossed the room as she turned to him. "Who was that guy?"

"Baron Schmidt, D. I.'s new CEO."

David hesitated. Yeah...she would go back to her people, to her father's business and leave him. "Right."

She burrowed into her folded arms. "I signed over control to him."

If she'd punched him in the gut, she wouldn't have surprised him more. "Seriously?" He shook his head. "That makes no sense. You'd give up..." His mind chugged to a stop. "Everything." What...what did this mean?

Jolie gave a slow, crooked nod. "I'm going to be the new COO, office out of another location, and remain on the board."

David scratched the back of his head. "What does this mean? Why?" He blinked and looked at her. "Wait—another location? You're leaving?"

"I knew you were smart," she said, throwing his words from the mountain right back at him. She seemed amused. "I don't belong in Anchorage." She seemed amused as she nodded at him. "How's your shoulder?"

"Healing." Who cared about his shoulder after what she just said. He stood a few feet back, nervous, his mind grinding on the gears of her words. "So, you're leaving."

She gave a quiet snort and shot him a look.

"Leaving Anchorage? Or Alaska?" He wasn't sure he could handle the latter.

But she didn't answer. Just watched him. Frowning.

Was she mad? Did she want him to leave? "What's. . . happening here, Jo?"

"Oh, David. . ."

She was in his arms before he could think twice. He wrapped her tight, burying his face in her neck. She smelled exotic yet sweet. Her arm around his shoulders and holding the back of his head proved intoxicating. "I wasn't sure I'd see you again," she whispered.

Her face was warm beneath his touch as he brushed a few strands back. "I wasn't sure myself."

"What convinced you?"

He stepped back, relinquishing her. "This." He lifted the small box from his pocket.

She paled and drew back.

"It's not a ring," he added quickly as he held it out. "At least. . .not yet. Maybe."

She opened the box then her wide eyes came to him. As if she didn't know what it was.

"It's a—"

She gasped. Melt-his-soul eyes rose to his. "Tabula rasa."

David grinned. "A clean slate."

She lifted it from the box and put it on, fingering the tiny chalkboard charm that hung below the hollow of her throat. "It's beautiful."

He tucked a strand of her hair back then slid his hand behind her neck. "No, *you're* beautiful." David slid his other hand around her waist and tugged her closer. "I'm sorry for unleashing my anger on you, for lashing out at you. I want that clean start you offered on the High One."

"Me, too."

He eased into a kiss that held the promise of a clean slate and love's daring heights.

Ronie Kendig grew up an Army brat, married a veteran, and they now have four children and a golden retriever. She has a BS in psychology, speaks to various groups, volunteers with the American Christian Fiction Writers (ACFW), and mentors new writers.

TAKING FLIGHT

FLIGHT

by Ronie Kendig

Dedication

To my amazingly beautiful friend, Kimberley Woodhouse—
thank you for inviting me to write this collection with you.
It's an honor and privilege to craft stories that are set in a
place that is so dear to you. You are such a gem! I love you,
lady!

Chapter 1

My soul is in the sky.
WILLIAM SHAKESPEARE, *A MIDSUMMER NIGHT'S DREAM*

I f one more guy taunted her, called her darlin', or otherwise
flirted with or demeaned her, she'd dump his burger and
fries right in his lap.

After I add lots of ketchup!

With a breath for courage, Deline Tsosie bumped her hip
against the swinging half door and stepped into the crowded
café. The breakfast rush was the worst. She navigated around
the wooden tables, chairs, ski coats. . .ignored the comments,
the stares, the whispers. The only thing in season right now
were tourists. Annoying, presumptive tourists.

"Hey, darlin'," a masculine voice called. "Care to hurry?
We've got to get up to the ranger station."

Deline stuffed her retort, flashed her best smile, and
said, "Sure thing. I'll be there as soon as I can." She delivered
the entrées to Mrs. Cole and her daughter, who gave her an
apologetic glance. "Okay, here you go." Wiping her hands on
her apron, she let out a breath. "Anything I forget?"

"You never do, sweetie," Mrs. Cole said. "Thank you."

"Deline," the daughter, Caroline, said, "do you think we
could start flying lessons?"

Deline's heart warmed, but she knew the girl's mother
insisted on Caroline waiting till she turned sixteen. "As soon

181

as you have your Sweet Sixteen."

Caroline deflated.

"How's your father, dear?" Mrs. Cole shared the concern that filled Deline's mind. "Is he still in the hospital?"

"Yeah, docs wanted to run a few more tests." Nobody needed to know the awful truth. And wearing it on her shoulder didn't help anyone. Not even herself. "He'll be home in a week or so, I think. Maybe I can call in backup, see if Lydia will come back for a while since she still hasn't found a job." Which reminded Deline that escaping Talkeetna didn't guarantee anything except distance from this place.

"I'll keep praying for you and your family," Mrs. Cole said as she patted Deline's hand.

"Thank—"

"Darlin'!"

Steeling herself, Deline lifted her chin and her good manners. She smiled at Mrs. Cole. "Thank you. I'll let Daddy know." She straightened.

"If they just knew your father kept a loaded weapon back there. . ."

But he's not here. I am.

In two more hours, she'd be sailing over the glaciers, soaring up into the maw of the High One with nothing but tingling Alaskan air and at least ten thousand feet between her and the suffocating—

"Morning, Mr. Bender."

Deline's blood ran cold. She slowly swung her gaze to the right where Roger Bender entered, his pocked face set like stone. She jerked away before he made eye contact.

"Deline!"

Shoot! Too late. "I'll be right there," she called over her shoulder.

"Sorry, I'm short on time."

And patience.

"You thought about that deal some more?" He motioned around the café with his cap. "Seems you're mighty busy. Maybe this is God's way of saying you should stay here—help your pa out, help the Tsosie legacy live on."

"My dad will be fine. And this café is his pride and joy, Mr. Bender. You trying to steal that from him?" Her heart rapid-fired against his passive-aggressive bullying. "Now, if you'll excuse me, I have to get these orders in because I have a *very* busy flight schedule."

He caught her arm. Gripped hard.

She scowled at him. "Hey—"

"Just be careful." He sneered. "It's dangerous up there, Deline. Wouldn't want to see you get hurt."

"Hey, fella," the demanding customer cut in. "Wait your turn. She's helping me next."

Yanking free from Roger Bender, Deline turned toward the other man. "I'll be right there, sir."

Roger stormed out.

Letting out a shaky breath, she rubbed her temple. The door chime tinkled again.

A square of light erupted on the far wall, glinting against photos of celebrities who had stopped in before heading into the High One. The glare reached its bright fingers farther into the café. Would it be too much to hope that the rude customer had left, too? Deline turned in that direction.

" 'Bout time, darlin'."

Sure enough.

If her father hadn't had a stroke and her mother skipped this earth for a better place, Deline would so walk out the door, get in her Otter, and take to the skies. And never set foot in Tsosie's Café again.

"Excuse me, miss? Is our order coming?" a woman asked,

frustration in her voice but not rudeness. Unlike the guy in front of her.

"The cook is working on it right now," Deline reassured her.

"Hey!" Grouch-man snapped. "Don't worry about her. I've been waiting—"

"Thanks for coming in." Deline sucked in a breath and smiled down at them. "Would you like today's special—"

"No, I don't want no special where you charge me an arm and a leg."

Deline gathered the tattered edges of her nerves.

"Deline, honey," Shana said. "Cook needs you. Question on another order." She nudged her toward the kitchen.

"Now wait a minute!"

"Darlin'," Shana said as smooth as honey. "I am waiting. What would you like?"

Hurrying out of sight before the man could break the power Shana's sweet charms held over him, Deline slipped into the back. She slumped against the wall and looked at Trent. "What's up?"

He glanced up from the professional cooking station. "What?"

Peeling herself off the wall, Deline filled herself a glass of water. "Shana said you wanted me."

His gaze skidded around the kitchen, as if he couldn't remember. "I. . .not sure why she said that. I'm doing fine, besides scrambling to keep up." He grinned as he looked down at the eggs on his cooktop.

"Ha. Ha." Deline guzzled the water. Sweet, dear old Shana. Looking out for her again.

Marji came out from the office. "Deline, Hilary just called in sick."

"Great." Deline pressed her hair away from her face. "Okay, I'll give Gen a call. Ask her to—"

"Gen's in Washington for the next two weeks, remember?"

Slumped once more against the wall, Deline thumped the back of her head against it. "Why is everything going wrong? I have flights this afternoon. I can't do both!" *Oh, Lord, help.* Staying on top of things, keeping her business up and running was key to the merger with Talkeetna Flightseeing and Air Taxi. Curt had worked the flightseeing tour into one of the best in the area, servicing more tours than any other business. He'd helped her get her pilot's license, guided her in building her own business. When cancer stole his wife then his kidney failed, he came to her, offered to partner up so TFAT could keep her wings.

"What about Emma?" Trent asked as he set a meal on a tray, snatched the ticket from the lineup, and set it beside the plate. "Order up."

He only mentioned his daughter because she couldn't get a job anywhere else. And there was a reason for that. Everyone but Trent seemed to know it, too.

"I'll keep that in mind, but it's too late for today." She dropped onto a stool and rubbed her face. It felt like the frozen tundra sat on her shoulders. What should she do? "Okay, let me call TFAT."

"No!" Marji rounded the door from the pantry. "No, you're not canceling flights. I'll stay."

"But you have Colin and the baby to think about."

"Well, he can bring Efraim up here and have dinner."

Despite the smile Marji sent her way, Deline knew Colin wouldn't be happy. He had looks and money but fell short in attitude and manners. How he ever convinced her friend to marry him was beyond Deline.

"I'm not sure. . . ."

"Well," Marji said. "I am. So finish up and get out of here. Get up into that plane and kill yourself."

Deline laughed. "You have to come up with me—"

"Oh no." Hands up, Marji shook her head. The short, red crop flipped like a saucer around her oval face. "You know very well I'll never do that. I'm fine working. Things are a bit weird right now. But once your dad's recovered, I know things will get back to normal. I don't mind pitching in till then."

"If you're sure. . ." Wow, would it really be this simple? Well, she had prayed, hadn't she?

The doors swung open again and delivered Shana into the kitchen. She raised her eyebrows and shook her head. "Lunchtime can't come too soon."

The joke couldn't be missed. One of their busiest times, but clearly she looked forward to it only because it meant Groucho out there would be gone.

"He's riling up the entire place."

Laughter burst through the tension-coated air. Voices rose and fell. Deline's heart gave a little skip, straightening her spine.

"Sounds like a big group just came in."

This time, Deline wasn't panicked. "Sounds like David and Jolie." Grabbing a glass of ice water, she blew a stray strand of hair from her face as she spun through the half doors. She sailed into the dining hall, ready to see familiar faces. Settling into a table at the back, Jolie waited as David took her jacket and stretched up to hang it on a hook. As he slid back into his chair, he grinned and said something to his fellow ranger, Logan Knox.

Logan's soulful blue eyes hit Deline, and he dropped his gaze.

"There she is!" David announced with a wide smile.

Jolie waved, ever perky, ever perfect. Oh, to be so pristine and poised. Deline wondered what food was stuck to her shirt or face today as she stepped up next to them. "Hey, guys."

"Wow, you look fried," Jolie said, her expression the image of innocence.

"Yeah, thanks a lot." She set the water glasses down, smiling at ranger Logan Knox who had yet to speak.

Her eyes widened. "Oh, I didn't"—she swallowed hard—"I'm sorry, Deline. I didn't mean—it's just you look like. . . I mean—"

David laughed. "Quit before she kills you, Jo."

⁂

The stunning beauty of Denali had nothing on Deline Tsosie. But to Logan, they were both as formidable and forbidding. He lowered his gaze and sipped from the water glass, all too aware she had her hand on the back of his chair.

"It's just so busy in here. I only meant—" Jolie tried.

"I think she looks fine," Logan finally spoke. After all, she worked in a restaurant and he knew how crazy that could be. And Deline always looked more than fine. Which made his heart pound worse than being in that Otter with her.

Standing beside him, Deline laughed and swatted his shoulder. "Very sweet, Logan, but we all know that's a lie."

Indignation stamped across his chest. "I don't lie."

This time, David thumped him. "Easy, chief. She's teasing." David glanced at their host. "Is it crazy here today?"

"One of the worst." Deline flicked that long dark hair out of her face. "But hey, Roger Bender just left, so. . ."

David held up his hand for a high five. "Any day without him is a good one."

Even though she tied it back with one of those elastic bands, her hair always seemed to defy the constriction. Logan wished his heart would. And he hated the way fear smothered her delicate features when Roger Bender came into the picture. He had firsthand knowledge of that man's meanness.

"I've got another hour here, then heading up."

"Tours after this insanity?" David asked, waving around the standing-room-only café. "That's a long day," he said as he snagged a bowl of bread the other waitress delivered. "How many tours you doing?"

"Four that I know of, but Curt said there might be another." Deline took their orders. "How'd you two manage to avoid Base Camp this week?"

Jolie smiled.

"I think I can answer that one without getting in trouble." Logan laughed. Then realized he was the one now in trouble, but David had been smart enough to hide his smile.

"Anyway," Jolie said with a glowering look at Logan, "David got his schedule arranged so he can take a few weeks off for our wedding."

"Oh, wow. That soon?"

"I figured I'd better get him tied down before someone else tries."

"What? David? Why would anyone want him?" Deline winked and headed back to work.

Was she flirting with David? Right in front of Jolie? Confusion tightened Logan's chest. Arms folded on the table, he watched out of the corner of his eye as she moved through the restaurant with grace and speed. She'd been here her whole life. The regulars and locals greeted her by name. Asked about her dad, and she shared he was still in the hospital but much better.

She hadn't been flying much since taking care of her dad and the café became her priority, but she said she was going up today. How had he missed that?

Logan stood and excused himself. He headed for the restrooms and plucked his phone from his pocket. Dialed.

"Talkeetna Flightseeing and Air Taxi."

Chapter 2

The air up there in the clouds is very pure and fine,
bracing and delicious.
And why shouldn't it be? It is the same the angels breathe.
MARK TWAIN

Easing her Jeep up to the rustic cabin structure that served as the office for her flightseeing tours and glacier landing business, Deline eyed the group of five playing basketball off to the side. Comfy in her lightweight thermal jacket, jeans, and boots, Deline stepped into the brisk afternoon. Eyes closed, she inhaled and smiled. Shut out the rowdy guys and just focused on the unpolluted, raw power that was Alaska. Her home. Her heritage.

"Hey, baby!" a guy called from the group.

Moment of silence severed, Deline rolled her eyes and made her way onto the boardwalk. Though tourists paid her way into her business, sometimes she was so over them. Especially the reckless adrenaline junkies.

"Going up to the glaciers? We got room in our tour. Want to j"—he pitched forward with a grunt, then spun around— "Hey! Watch it."

A tall, muscular guy in a bright blue jacket broke through the group. "Sorry." His electric blue eyes hit hers, and Logan shrugged. "Guess I tripped or something."

Hiding her smile, Deline stepped into the building. The

new ranger was all right. Quiet, a bit geeky or nervous or something, but he was nice.

"Hey, boss!" Shawn Graves, her business manager, reached to the side and lifted a clipboard from the cluttered desk, scanned it, then smiled at her. "Got a full complement today."

"Thanks." Deline took the schedule then headed to the office. She rapped against the jamb. "Knock knock."

Salt-and-pepper hair belied Curt's age. He looked up from his computer. "Hey, Deline." Curt eased back in his chair and pointed to the monitor. "Drawing up the final papers. Met with the lawyer via conference call about an hour ago."

Glee streaked through her. "Seriously?" She eased in. "So, you're still good with everything?"

He frowned. "Yeah. Aren't you?"

"Yes!" On her toes, she bounced. "Definitely. I just know that with the way...certain people..."

"Bender isn't going to get this business as long as you and I are alive."

"Right." It was almost too good to be true. "Well, I'll be praying nothing happens to you or me, then. Or that Roger doesn't get any strange ideas." She nodded, wishing she could shake off the disbelief that taking over at TFAT would really happen. "Okay, send me those documents when you have them." Her dream was coming true! "Well, I'd better get up there."

"Yep, take care. And stop worrying about Bender. He's an old coot, but he wouldn't do anything stupid."

Deline smiled. "You've always seen the good in people." *Even when there isn't any.*

"Hey, Dee," Shawn hollered and waved her back over. His eyes twinkled with mischief. "You've got a last-minute add-on. And here he comes."

The door squeaked open. A familiar scent and thud of

boots flooded into the small office. Deline didn't have to turn to know who'd come in. She dropped her gaze to the clipboard but could feel Shawn's knowing smile.

Shawn smiled as he bounced his eyebrows at Deline then looked toward the door. "Well, look here. It's Ranger Knox again."

Why the man kept coming on the tours she didn't know. He told her it was for the view, and she got that, she honestly did, but the cost was too much. "Logan, I am sure there are better ways to spend your money."

"Hey." Shawn swatted her arm. "His money's the best kind—it comes from the mountain. Besides, he practically pays your check with as many trips as he makes. Don't discourage paying customers, boss."

Again, she rolled her eyes. "He does *not* pay my check." But his frequent visits went a ways in keeping things consistent. "You sure you want to do this again, already?"

"Of course I am. It's a perfect day." He grinned that lopsided grin that made him a little geeky and a lot handsome. "You know I couldn't resist. Besides. . ." Logan bobbed his head toward the door. "Seems you got a rowdy one on this trip. I might be able to help."

"By throwing him out as we fly over the Great Gorge?"

Steady and unwavering, his eyes pinched. "It'd be a soft landing. All that snow. . ."

Deline laughed and started for the door. Most certainly would *not* be a soft landing from that height and with the jagged, brutal terrain. "Back in a bit, Shawn."

Out in the sun again, she slid on her sunglasses and stalked toward the first of five flights for the day. First, she carried out her preflight check of the DeHavilland Turbine Otter, verifying her baby was fit for the run. Finally, she waved to the tourists hovering a safe distance away but clearly anxious.

"Morning, everyone." Deline walked toward the Otter and started opening the doors. She set her clipboard on the pilot's seat then turned to her tourists.

"Wait," the guy from earlier squawked. "You're our pilot?"

After the morning she'd had, she *so* did not want to mess with this guy.

"Brent, hush."

Deline stifled a smile. "Okay, once the engine's on, the intercom system will be working." She held up a headset, going over the instructions as she had dozens of times. "Put this one so the thick part of the band sits squarely on your head and"—she pointed two fingers to her mouth—"adjust the microphone so it's directly in front of your mouth."

Brent muttered something and earned another shoulder jar from Logan.

"Hey, dude," the teen said. "You need to learn how to walk."

Logan nodded and pursed his lips as he trudged to the rear of the crowd. He leaned against the plane, hands tucked in his jeans pockets, and set his gaze on hers. As if to say, *Rowdy's under control. Carry on.*

When the passengers were tucked inside and belted, Deline shut the doors, tested them, then climbed into her seat. Engine running, she adjusted her mic, verified they were clear for takeoff, then aimed her Otter down the runway. The lift was smooth, and soon they were sailing over the varied landscape.

She began her spiel. "First, let's be clear." She pointed to the mountain hovering over them. "That is Denali, the High One. If you want to call it Mt. McKinley, I'll drop you at the summit and let you fight it out with the mountain." She winked at the crowd. "I promise Denali will win." She went on to mention that it held the great distinction of being the tallest peak in North America at 20,323 feet. Telling them the

Talkeetna River flowed into the Susitna River. "The railroad came through in 1914, and in 1972 the highway made it out here. Talkeetna was a miners' town and a mecca for tourists. There are sixty miles between Talkeetna and Denali, and in that distance you'll find thick pine forests, rivers draining the mountain, boggy wetlands, lakes, grasslands, foothills, and of course—the mountains."

Though she let her mouth and brain go on autopilot giving the official tour as the half-hour trip ticked down, she let her mind drift to her father and the doctor's concerns. What they said—*he'll be fine*—did not match the worry on their faces. She knew that was because most of the doctors had either grown up in the tribe with her father or knew her father from helping him through her mother's illness and death.

The old, familiar raw ache thudded against her conscience.

She blinked as her body navigated the plane automatically. "That, ladies and gentlemen, is the Great Gorge of the Ruth Glacier. Granite walls around it are five thousand feet tall. That's a vertical mile of relief. The ice on that glacier is 3,400 feet thick."

Gasps and whispers of awe and excitement filled the headsets. Deline smiled. She loved when others saw and experienced what she did. Though wanting to give up the café felt like selling her soul, she loved Talkeetna, loved Denali.

"If you think that's impressive, you should've taken the deluxe tour to see the Wickersham Wall. That's 14,600 feet of vertical relief."

"It's also over five hundred dollars!"

Laughter trickled through her headset, but Deline remained undeterred. "But I promise it's an experience you'll never have anywhere else."

"We heard from friends you were the best because you're native."

"You heard right," Deline said, her modesty gone for the sake of her business. The oil pressure gauge caught her eyes. Her heart tripped. That couldn't be right. She'd checked the plane over. The pressure had been fine.

She double-checked. Tapped the gauge. Her heart thunked against the realization. They wouldn't make it back to Talkeetna airfield.

❧

Gripping the edge of his seat, Logan dug his fingernails into the cushion. Muscles taut, he forced himself to look out the window. When he did, the familiar cold swirled through his gut. Face the formidable with ice clinging to his nose hairs. No problem. Hover over the beast of a mountain in a plane—

Logan jerked back, grateful he wasn't up front with Deline, where he had to pretend to like flying.

Something sifted through the fog of dread. The fear of heights.

Kahiltna Glacier?

"Okay, folks, I've got a surprise for you," Deline's voice crackled in his ear. Her tone sounded sweet. *Too* sweet. "Since it's such a beautiful day and I need to make a stop, you'll get an upgrade on your tour."

Upgrade? Since when? Deline needed the money to seal the merger with Curt.

The woman and her preteen daughter in front of him spun toward each other, gleam lit in their eyes. Rowdy beside them gave a *whoop* of approval.

Something's wrong. Logan felt a nudge to let Deline know he knew something was up. But. . .what if he was wrong? What if she'd been sincere about that generosity?

Logan nearly snorted. It wasn't that Deline wasn't a sweet girl. She was. But she had a lethal will. "Perfect day to see

Base Camp," Logan spoke into his mic.

He noted the slight lift to Deline's chin. "That's right, Ranger Knox. I thought you might be lonely for some of your fellow rangers."

The engine was still running. No sputtering as far as he could tell. But what did he know about planes? Besides the fact he didn't like them.

They circled Kahiltna once more. Logan pushed his spine into the seat. The feeling of descent threw a wave of hot-then-cold chills over him. Man, he hated this part. He could almost tolerate every other aspect, but the descent. . . It didn't help that he'd heard somewhere that the majority of accidents happened on takeoff and landing.

He fixed his gaze on the back of Deline's head, trusting her, not the Otter, to glide them down to safety.

Ha. Safety. She was landing on a glacier. The Otter glided down as Deline made her approach. Smooth and without a hitch, the landing spoke of nothing other than Deline's supposed generosity. Anticipation ran high among the tourists.

Logan took a death grip on his seat again. Prayed harder than he had when he first climbed in here today. *Yea, though I walk through the valley of the shadow of. . .*

Okay, enough with the death references. He wanted to live. Had to live if he ever intended to ask the Aleutian beauty out on a date.

'Course, it might take a few years at that rate of progress. Or lack thereof.

Then again, dying might just solve that.

"Okay, folks. Hop out, snap some pictures, and enjoy this gift."

The steady vibration that rumbled through the hull slowed. . .then stopped. Logan removed his headset as the others disembarked. Outside, he returned the headset to Deline, who received an abundance of excited thanks from the others before they trudged off to check out the camp and the views.

Logan stood over Deline. She seemed frail, as if needing protection. But saying that to her would only get him punched. Or worse. He stuffed his sweaty hands into his jeans pockets. Shouldered in toward her to hide their conversation in case someone happened by. "You okay?"

Surprise winged up her eyebrows. "Me?" She looked at him, the sun hitting her beautiful brown eyes. "I'm fine. My Otter's not. Need to radio back to TFAT and get a replacement plane and some tools."

"What happened?"

She brushed her hair from her face. "Not sure. The oil gauge dropped. Must've had a leak or something. We wouldn't have made it back to TFAT." Then she eyed him a little longer. "You okay, Logan? You look a little pale."

He swallowed. Stepped back. "Yeah." She'd never understand. "Just worried. . ." He let the rest of the sentence die on his lips.

She clapped a hand on his bicep. "Well, fear not. I got us down safely." She looked around then climbed back into the pilot's seat and lifted the radio.

Stooge. He was a complete stooge. How did one express concern and care for a woman who could do everything on her own? She'd never need him.

Chapter 3

*I*t's dangerous up there, Deline. Wouldn't want to see you get hurt."

Roger Bender's words earlier in the café sailed through her mind and pounded against her chest. Surely, he...it couldn't be...

"What do you mean, you're out?"

Snapped back to the phone, Deline let out a breath. Should she tell Curt her suspicion? "If I said what I thought, you'd call me crazy." Deline squinted, watching her passengers taking pictures, changing angles, and taking more. No, better not say anything. What could she prove? Nothing. She'd have to check the oil lines. "I need tools, some oil to get me back, and a plane to pick up my passengers."

"Deline..." The tone in Curt's voice wasn't anger, but it wasn't far from it. "Every plane is booked."

"Curt, I did preflight. Everything was just as it should be." Had the gauge been a little low? Had she just overlooked it? "I know this is a pain and I know this messes things up. I'm sorry. I have no other options save crashing on my way back." She didn't mean to get testy, but for cryin' out loud. It wasn't negligence that caused this, and that was exactly what hung at the back of his mind.

"Easy, Deline. I'm not accusing you. I wouldn't be willing to hand over my baby if you weren't dependable. I just..." He sighed. "Let me figure out—okay, wait."

Swiping a hand over her face, she wanted to scream,

punch something. What else could go wrong today?

She really shouldn't ask that question—this high up, this close to heaven, God just might answer. He'd been pretty much silent over the last two years. Or maybe it was Deline who'd been silent. He'd taken her mom. And now He was trying to snatch her father from her.

"Doing okay?" the soft, firm voice beside Deline pried her eyes open. She tilted her head to the side and looked out at Logan. Stalwart and steady. "Yeah." She lifted the radio. "Waiting on—"

"Deline?"

She smiled. "Speak of the devil." She pressed the lever. "Go ahead, Curt."

"Mason's on his way up to deliver a crew to Base Camp for climbing. He'll have what you need."

Eyes on the High One, she smiled. "Perfect. Thanks, Curt."

"Yeah...and...I guess we need to talk when you get back. TFAT out."

Deline drew back and started at the radio as if it'd spit at her. Talk? What did he want to talk about? And why didn't he leave her time to reply? It seemed too much like he wanted to back out of their agreement. Or maybe something had gone wrong while she'd been up here. She'd better not find out that Roger Bender had visited with Curt. Told lies or defamed her. She wouldn't put it past that coyote.

"You okay?"

Frustration exploded through her chest. "If you ask me that one more time—"

"Okay, okay." Logan held up his hands and stepped away. Shoulders caved, head down, he slunk toward the rangers' tent.

Something in Deline's chest tightened. He looked like

scolded puppy and it was her fault. She wasn't anything sweet like Maggie. Instead she was every bit her Athabascan-Aleutian ancestry, their dogged determination, their hardy work ethic...

"Stubborn bullheadedness." Deline sighed. Which was why at age twenty-five she was still single. She had this innate ability to snap off heads without meaning to. Thank goodness her friends knew she wasn't trying to be mean. She just wanted to get things done. And she had to get her Otter out of the way before Mason showed up. She cranked the engine. It sputtered but sprang to life. She gave it some thrust and guided it to the side. Even as she positioned it so she wouldn't be in the way the engine sputtered. Then croaked. Deline groaned.

Was God punishing her? For what? She hadn't done anything.

Maybe for the silent treatment.

A glint in the sky pulled her gaze upward. A Beaver angled in, headed for the glaciers. Mason. She smiled and relaxed. So perhaps she'd jumped the gun on that whole God-punishing-her thing.

She hopped out of the Otter, closed the door, and headed toward the rangers' tent, determined to make sure Logan knew she meant no harm. Why it was so important to her, she had no idea, but he didn't deserve the way she'd unleashed her frustration. The small ten-by-twelve space felt crowded with the last-minute supplies of granola, waste bags, and two oversized rangers staring back at her.

Zack Taylor nodded. "Having some trouble, eh?"

"Just a leak. I'll be out of your hair in no time."

"Not a problem, though Mason's about to make a drop."

"Yeah, already talked to Curt." She shifted her gaze to the blue-green eyes that looked more like the Mediterranean

Sea than the sky. "Hey." Her courage dumped as she shifted nervously on her feet. Jamming her fists in her TFAT jacket she hunched her shoulders. "Say. Logan." Ugh! Why was it so hard? "Sorry about what I said. It. . . I . . ."

He came toward her and handed her a thermos. "No worries." He smiled at the silver canister. "Hot cocoa. Not David's special recipe, but palatable."

She smiled and the tingling warmth of chocolate wafted up at her. Why was he always so nice to her? "I. . ." She flipped her gaze to him. "I'm sorry, Logan. Really."

The smile almost went full throttle. "Deline." He craned his neck toward her. "Don't worry about it. I didn't mean to hover. Just could tell this really was eating at you."

"How?"

Logan shrugged. "I could see it in your eyes."

Eyes. . .Mediterranean blue. . .bet if he wore blue they were more azure and if he wore green, they were more that color.

Logan angled toward the open flap. "Plane landed." A scowl gouged into his features, his gaze on the open flap.

"What is he doing here?" Zack thrust down his jacket and stomped past them. "He doesn't have clearance."

Confusion twisted her mind as she turned around. "Mason doesn't have—"

"Bender! You can't be here. I've got TFAT doing a drop."

Bender? Roger Bender?

"Relax, Zack. Just wanted to make sure Deline was okay."

Deline shoved into the open. "Make sure I was okay? How'd you even know anything was up?"

"Guess it came over the wave." Bender, a semibalding man, smirked. "Curt must've said something on the open channel. Just wanted to see if there was anything I could do."

"Like what? Run me out of business? Take over the

merger? Or make sure your plan worked?"

"Deline," Logan's soft, stern voice snaked around her outrage. Hauled her back a mental step.

She flung off Logan's touch on her arm.

"Hey, now. No call to get ugly," Bender said.

Deline bit back the retort singeing her tongue as Logan faced her, his shoulder partially blocking her view. She took her cue from him, to relax, turn her back—figuratively—on this coward.

"I don't care what concern you had, I need you and your plane off the glacier," Zack said.

Scruffy and a bit haggard, Roger held her gaze. Challenged her with his eyes and his very presence. Deline made no move to back down. But she also kept her sharp tongue inside her mouth and siphoned from the courage and strength of the man standing less than twelve inches away.

"Now, Bender!" Zack roared, his anger darkening his already tanned face.

"All right, Ranger Taylor. Don't get your hackles up." Bender shifted to conciliatory. "Now that I know a fellow pilot is okay. . ."

Baloney! That guy didn't care about anyone but himself and getting what he wanted. She watched Bender climb into the pilot's seat and start the engine, his passenger still pent up in the plane.

The plane sailed into the sky. A good pilot. She couldn't deny that. But a lousy person.

"There's Mason!" Zack shouted.

Deline turned to see the relief plane, hand shielding her eyes.

"Going to drink that cocoa?" Logan said, next to her.

Deline felt the tension drain from her. Let out a soft sigh as she lifted the thermos and took a sip. She looked at him, expecting censure or disappointment. Instead, she found calm and steadfast strength.

"Hey," Zack said as he slapped Logan on the back. "Trying to steal the only Aleutian beauty in Talkeetna, huh?" He kept moving.

Deline laughed. She hated when guys teased her like that. "He's annoying."

Logan's face flushed red. Neon red. He tucked his chin, swiping a hand down the back of his neck.

"Aw, don't take him seriously. Zack's only teasing. Besides, he's just mad because I wouldn't go out with him."

Nodding, Logan looked around the camp, still red. "I'll see if Mason needs help or something." He darted her a glance before he trudged across the snow.

Chapter 4

Dude, that was your opening."

Two weeks later as Logan sat in the ranger station, he peered up through knotted brows at David. "It wasn't an opening. It was a closing. A sealed-shut closing, at that." He tossed his napkin onto the table and slumped back. "I can tame that mountain, save my friend from a crevasse, but I can't figure out how to talk to Deline, tell her what I feel."

"Gotta admit," David said as he stood and walked to the fridge at the ranger station, "I was wondering about that, too. Never seen you so. . .jittery."

"That's just it. I'm not jittery." Logan cleared his spot and leaned back against the counter, his arms folded. "I just. . ." Shut down. As if someone walked into his brain and turned out the lights. Navigating time around Deline Tsosie was like trying to walk through the piney forest without a flashlight.

But it wasn't just that. She had this way of looking at him that made Logan feel like he had already failed.

"Hey, don't get me wrong," David said as he returned to the table with a bottled water. "Deline's one of the most intimidating women I've ever met."

"Exactly!" Logan slipped into a chair next to David. "She has her own business, runs her father's café, she's an expert pilot, she's completely unshakable."

"Until Roger Bender enters the picture."

"No kidding. He showed up at Base Camp when she went in for that emergency landing."

"I bet he just did. Flying down to check out the competition, see if she'd been wiped out."

"The fury in her face. . . I pray she never aims that at me."

David laughed. "You've got her pretty well pegged." He took another swig, his gaze probing as he stared at Logan.

"What?"

"You really like her."

Denying it would be futile because David would persist until he had Logan on his proverbial knees. Arguing it would only elicit David's certainty. Best bet was straightforward. "Why'd you think I do the tours?"

A shrug. "You like flying like the rest of us."

"Not this country boy," he said with a halfhearted laugh. "If God meant us to fly, He'd have given us wings and self-deploying parachutes."

Another chortle from David. "That's what the wings are."

"I'm glad for the backup in case the wings fail."

"You're seriously afraid of flying?"

Logan felt like a kid again, admitting he hadn't yet learned to swim.

David pitched his bottle at the recycle bin. "Look, I'm not going to lie to you. Going after Deline is like trying to scale Wickersham Wall—without gear and in a whiteout." He snorted and stood. "Trust me, you're safer in her plane than going after her heart, which is protected by more ice than Ruth's Glacier."

Put like that. . . "Not trying to win her heart." Wow, he was a bad liar. "Just want to get to know her."

David paused in the doorway. "To what end?"

To win her over. Logan hung his head.

David laughed.

On his feet, Logan trudged around him. "Don't we have some climbers to rescue?"

More laughter.

Deanna pointed to the reception area. "You're up, Logan." She offered a sad smile that said she'd heard everything.

"Don't say a word," Logan muttered as he entered the room that sported leather chairs and a massive fireplace. Plastering a smile on his face did nothing to mask the ache in his chest. David was right. Getting Deline to notice him, to realize he liked her, to have her like him back—it'd never happen.

"Morning, folks," he said to the waiting climbers. "My name is Ranger Logan Knox." Launching into the familiar routine and spiel of his ranger duties afforded him some time to separate the heartache of knowing Deline Tsosie would never be interested in him from the undeniable draw she held over him. It wasn't just about her looks, though she definitely had that in spades. It was her tough exterior. The one that hid the soft side of her, the one he could tell she didn't want anyone to see. The side that took care of her father and covered at the café, though Logan knew the hours there combined with the flying were taking their toll on her.

Briefing and equipment check done, Logan started for his truck.

"Heading to Tsosie's for dinner?"

The taunt in that question didn't even deserve a response. He climbed in.

David laughed and caught up to him, holding the door open. "C'mon, man."

"Do I need to remind you of how disgustingly lovesick you were over Jolie?"

"No." Waving a hand, David shook his head. "No way. Point taken." He sobered. "Hey, seriously. If you're looking for her, she's not at the café."

Logan frowned. "Dude, it's not like I'm going to stalk her."

David closed the door then tapped the window ledge.

"Her dad's release is today"—he glanced at his watch—"two o'clock."

How on earth did David know something like that?

"Jolie offered to go in and help cover so Deline could run down to Mat-Su."

It was nearly noon. The regional medical center was nearly two hours away. A strange compulsion to be there with her swirled through Logan's gut. The thought of her petite form caring for that large, Athabascan man made him tense. If Mr. Tsosie pitched forward, no way could Deline hold him up. Not that she was weak. "Let's see if she needs help."

David blinked. "Help? You do remember this is Miss Independence herself, right?"

"Which is exactly why we should just show up."

After a slow nod, David gave a firmer nod. "Two for two."

"Huh?"

"Points." He jogged backward toward his truck. "I'll meet you there."

Logan stuffed the irritation. Why hadn't Deline told him? It'd been a week since Zack humiliated him in front of her. All but exposed his attraction to her. She hadn't really talked to him since.

He smoothed a hand over his face, noting the stubble. Probably should've gone home, showered, and shaved. Maybe he should.

He checked the in-dash clock. Not enough time. Might be okay.

He sniffed his armpit. And groaned. Great. Sasquatch probably smelled better.

Why? Why could things not be easy or go right so he could just have a chance. . .

At the hospital, he parked then hustled toward the entrance, searching the area for David. Where had he gone?

After checking with the front desk, Logan headed to the third floor and inquired about the room. The nurse pointed him down the hall and to the right.

Logan slowed his walk. Didn't want to *look* as nasty as he smelled. He smoothed his hand over his short crop.

"You can't do it by yourself, Dee."

"Dad, there is no one else. Who do you want me to call?" Deline sounded a year past frustrated.

"How do I know? But you can't do it all. You're cracking—I can see it. Ask David."

"He's getting married. He's a bit distracted."

Logan eased forward a bit and peered in, staying back just enough to be concealed. Deline knelt in front of her father, who sat on the edge of the bed. From the right, she lifted his other boot and guided his foot into it.

"What about that Logan boy?"

Logan's chest thumped against his ribs, pushing him back, out of sight.

"Dad, please." Deline moved back on her haunches and looked up at her father. "It's just you and me."

"He seems to have taken a likin' to you."

An avalanche couldn't compete with the roar of Logan's heart. Did *everyone* know he liked her?

"No, Dad. Logan's just a nice guy."

"Oh *pffft*."

"Dad, Logan would no sooner want to date me than he would a coyote." She stood and dragged the wheelchair closer. "I'm too mean for someone like him."

"I suppose that's my fault," her father groused as he heaved himself up—with Deline's small arms wrapped around his upper torso—and plunked into the chair with a hefty exhale. "Man, that hurt."

"You need to do it slower."

"You need to get more help."

A firm slap on the back threw Logan forward. In the shock of the moment, he registered David parading past him and into the room with a boisterous, "Help has arrived!"

Logan stepped in, willing away his thoughts of killing David Whiteeagle.

Deline's lips parted as she met his gaze. Hesitation and question hung in her rich, dark eyes. It did something weird to his stomach. She finally blinked and looked at David. "What are you two doing here?"

"Jolie said you were down here. I figured this guy"—he clapped a hand on Mr. Tsosie's shoulder—"might be giving you a hard time."

"Me?" Mr. Tsosie bellowed. "It's her. She's too hardheaded."

"You taught her well." Logan warmed at the guffaw from Deline's father then froze beneath her icy glare.

Stumping downstairs, Deline noticed the telltale exhaustion plucking at every fiber of her being even over the hollering of her father. Daddy said she'd wear herself out. So had everyone else. But nobody seemed to realize there *wasn't* anyone to help. This town might be the mecca for tourists but it was the escape-from mecca of locals. She trudged around the stairs, down the hall and into the kitchen. At the fridge, she reached for the glass pitcher of lemonade, Daddy's favorite. Lydia couldn't come for another month—when it was convenient for her—and her brother, Enli, was out of the country. Mom and Daddy had plenty of friends, but they were just as old as him.

She'd let the rangers help, but the thing of it was. . .

Deline sighed. She didn't know what objection she had. Maybe it was pride. She'd inherited that in buckets from both parents. They'd taken care of themselves all these years. . . .

But she had to admit it was nice—real nice—to have Logan and David here. And Jolie covering for her. It'd worked out this time. But Jolie split her time between here and Anchorage, and with all the wedding planning, Deline knew she couldn't count on her and David long term.

Another ache wormed through her. She longed for what Jolie and David had. Up here with the mountains, the snow, and the wilderness, they'd found something rare.

Thumping boots sounded behind her. "I'd better get moving. Jolie's going to string me up if I'm late," David said.

"Thanks for your help."

He planted a quick kiss on her forehead. "You bet. Don't let him get on your nerves."

"Oh, I know how to handle Daddy."

David grinned as he opened the back door. "I meant Logan." The clatter of the door signaled his departure and drew her attention. She should lock it. Deline took a glass from the shelf, set it on the counter, and lifted the pitcher. A shadow flitted behind the lacy curtain that hung over the door. Had David forgotten something?

"He's asleep."

Startled, she gripped the pitcher tight. Her arm flexed. Lemonade splashed over her hand. She sighed, her mind finally processing Logan's words and presence that pervaded the room

"Sorry," Logan said, lifting a towel and passing it to her. "Didn't mean to scare you."

"No." *"He seems to have taken a likin' to you."* The words rang in her ears as she wiped off her hand. "No, it's okay. I'm just tired."

"There's a surprise. You're carrying the world on your shoulders."

"It's not like I have a choice."

"Hey." A soft touch to her shoulder drew her gaze to his mesmerizing blue eyes. "Give yourself a break."

"Yeah? Exactly how am I supposed to do that?" Why was she being so unreasonable? "I have the café responsibilities, my flying, along with the merger, and now my father to take care of. And what do you know of my life, Logan? Nothing. So just back off!"

The words had tumbled out and barreled into the thick air without her permission. Frightened at the volley of anger she felt, Deline swallowed. Hard. Saw the shock on Logan's face. The disappointment. Hurt.

Unable to bear that expression, she shifted to the counter and whispered through a raw throat, "I'm. . .I'm sorry. You didn't deserve that."

"No worries." His casual pardoning did not have the lightheartedness that normally defined Logan. He stuffed his hands into his pockets and backed up. "I'll get out of your hair."

Stop him. Apologize. Ask him to stay.

But the walls inside her were shifting and colliding. Freezing Deline to her spot. Why couldn't she just let a guy in? Because. She'd seen what letting guys in had done to her sister. She wasn't going to embarrass and shame their family like that. Besides, Daddy needed her. The café needed her. The business needed her. She didn't have time for a man to need her, too.

She looked up at the window, framed by the daisy-embroidered yellow curtains Mama had always loved. Deline saw her own reflection, strangely like her mother's, in the window. But something seemed a bit. . .off.

The eyes. They weren't quite. . .right. Just a little too—

They moved!

She drew back. Had she moved her eyes? She hadn't. The

face seemed to blur into two. Warmth squirted through her belly. A chill scarped down her back.

The images divided.

Only then did it hit her. *Someone's out there!*

She shoved herself backward and screamed.

Chapter 5

D eline!" Logan plowed through the living room. Lunged around the corner and into the kitchen. Glass shards lay amid a yellow puddle of lemonade. The back door sat open. He darted for it. Heady scents of pine and dirt pressed in on him. The darkness suffocated his vision.

Deline came toward him.

"You okay?"

She frowned. "Yeah. I saw someone—something. Just startled me." She pushed past him and stepped back into the kitchen and stopped short.

Logan nearly collided with her.

She cursed. Kicked the kitchen cabinet.

"Hey."

She spun around, her face twisted in rage.

Logan yanked backward. "Whoa. Hey."

"What? Are you going to say I need you now that someone tried to break in? Let me tell you, I've done fine by myself for years. And I'll be fine now."

Heart tromping over her words, Logan tilted his head. "Did someone—someone tried to break in?"

"Yes!" She squeezed her eyes. "No. I don't know. I saw someone staring back at me, but when I went outside. . . nothing." Her eyes glossed. She jerked away and started for the stairs.

Without thinking, Logan lunged after her. Gently caught

her arm. Pulled her back. He braced for a fist in the face. Or the gut. Instead, Deline flung into his arms. Buried her face in his chest. He felt his shirt tightened against his pecs—she must be fisting. Instinct wrapped his arms around her.

But seconds later, she pried out of his hold. Kept her chin tucked. "I'm sorry, Logan. I can't. . .can't do this." She looked at up him, eyes glossy, apologized once more, then hurried up the stairs.

Heart thundering, Logan stood there. Stunned. What had he done wrong? Why wouldn't she let him in? Who'd been outside her window? Maybe he should take a look around, make sure she and her father weren't in any danger. Silly idea, but he couldn't shake it.

He strode back into the kitchen and secured the dead bolt and chain. As he let himself out the front, he made sure it locked behind him. Logan took the flashlight from his truck's glove box and walked the perimeter. Several boot impressions remained around the dirt, but he was no investigator. Could've been David or even Deline, though she had small feet to match her petite frame.

Back in his truck, he tried to shake off the adrenaline dump. He would never forget hearing her scream. But. . .she didn't get paralyzed. She took action. *Proof positive that she doesn't need you. And doesn't want you either.*

"*. . .I can't do this. . .*"

Logan banged the steering wheel. He started the engine, but. . . Breathing hard, he sat there. Stared at the house. Thought of Deline, the fire in her eyes, the single moment of perfection, then the icy facade.

"God," he began, unsure of where he was going or what he should pray for. He huffed and closed his eyes. "If I need to let go of her, help me. Take away what I feel for her. *Please.* Because I can't take much more of her rejection."

❧

Two Weeks Later
Kahiltna Base Camp

"You make me proud."

Logan frowned. "How's that?"

"You just don't give up." David shook his head. "Deline practically shoved you off a cliff, and here you are planning a party for her dad."

Logan tried to fend off the heat flooding his face. Up on Kahiltna, his cheeks should be red from the bitter wind, not from taunting. He hated that he could be embarrassed so easily when it came to Deline. But facts were facts. "This isn't about her. It's about her father."

"Yeah." David walked the camp with Logan, checking to make sure the caches were covered and protected, no litter had been left behind from those who'd cleared out around midnight, and verifying the remaining campers were well. "But it's a sweet way to get in under her radar."

"That is *not* what I'm trying to do. Mr. Tsosie has been cooped up in the house for two weeks. I know it's driving him crazy."

"It's doing that to Deline, too. She nearly threw a frying pan at me when we were in the café."

Logan laughed. "You had that coming. How is it you always bring out the worst in her?"

"It's my special gift." A wide grin flashed. "It's why we gave up dating. She wanted to kill me all the time and it just made me laugh."

A curling in Logan's gut warned him of the green-eyed monster. "You dated?"

"Now, don't get all jealous on me, man. I realized I saw her more like a little sister than a girlfriend. Same with her—she looked up to me. Literally."

"Logan, David!"

They both swung around and hustled back to the rangers' tent, snow crunching beneath their boots and slowing them as Zack ducked back inside.

Logan hurried in. "What do you have?"

"Climber headed up to 7800, passed a guy coming down who has AMS. Guy could use an escort."

"On it," Logan said as he grabbed his gear. Acute mountain sickness could happen to anyone. There were precautions to ward it off, of course, but the mountain had a way of weeding out climbers. But if the climber didn't descend immediately, things could get ugly fast.

It took him an hour to meet up with the climber. Battling a nosebleed, the guy slumped against a rock. "Unbewevabuh," the guy muttered as he tried to stem the flow of blood.

"Hey. What's your name?" Logan asked as he led the guy toward a boulder.

"Barry."

"Well, have a seat, Barry." Shrugging out of his gear, Logan knelt. "Ever had mountain sickness before?"

"No." Shoulders down, head shaking, the guy sighed. "I've climbed a dozen mountains."

"Yeah?" Logan smirked. "Well, the High One takes her climbers seriously. When d'you start feeling sick?"

"Night before last."

"What Base Camp?"

"9500."

"When were you at 7800?"

"Tuesday night."

Doing the math, Logan figured out the guy had ascended too fast. Probably a bit cocky with his "dozen mountains" rating and a little anxious to get to the top. "Any drug allergies?" He dug out a two-milligram tablet of dexamethasone.

"Nope."

"Okay, take this, sip water, and we're going to head down."

The guy grunted but complied. "I'm a pro climber."

"Yeah, well, happens to the best of us."

"Happen to you?"

"You have water?"

"Yeah." The climber unclipped his high altitude water bottle, popped the pill into his mouth, then swallowed.

Logan shouldered his pack then reached for Barry's.

"Hey."

"Relax. I want you to focus on staying upright and alert. Can you do that?"

"I'm not—"

"Or we can do this the hard way, and I strap you to a litter and haul you down. Most important thing is that you *descend*." Logan tempered his frustration. "If you don't, this could turn fatal on you, Barry. With your dozen climbs, that should be something you know."

Defeated, Barry nodded.

"All right, then. Let's get it moving back to Base Camp. No talking. Conserve your energy and focus on moving down this mountain."

Together, they set out as Logan keyed his mic and notified Zack of the climber's situation and that they were on the way back down to Kahiltna. Once they'd reached Base Camp, the guy seemed sturdier, more alert and confident. Logan checked his pulse and breathing. "You made the right decision to turn back. Denali's a beast to conquer. Guess she wasn't ready for you."

"Apparently not," Barry groused as he walked toward his cache.

"You can stay here or head down to Talkeetna with the

next plane." Logan headed to the rangers' tent and slumped back against the supplies. The scent of cinnamon and apples wafted through the tent, pulling him to the large dispenser. "Ah, thank you."

"Knew you could use some when you got back." David sat on the stool at the back, arms folded and hands tucked under his armpits. "Jolie's sin."

Logan shed his gear and stilled. Surely he hadn't heard that right. "Come again?"

"Jolie—she's in. The party. She's in."

Oh. Good. Because he didn't want to know anything about Jolie and her sin. "Dude, you have a wedding, and I have no plans other than a thought percolating in my head."

"Well, now you have a party. And Jolie." David guzzled his cider. "Thank goodness. She's starting to drive me crazy, asking if I like this flower or that flower. They're red. That's all I know. Who cares if one has straight petals or not?" He scratched the side of his head. "But she did say she didn't think Deline would like not knowing beforehand."

"If I tell her about the party before, she'll say it's not necessary or tell me to stay out of her life."

David's eyebrow winged up. "She's already given you the brush-off."

"Why'd you think I agreed to switch with Josh?" He sat down and sipped the cider, glad to have a reason not to talk. But then again. . .

"Want my advice?"

"No."

"Too bad. Just keep doing what you're doing."

Logan gave him a sidelong glance.

"Deline's used to having her way, used to casting off men when she thinks they're getting too close."

"You're saying the harder she fights, the more she likes me?"

"No," David said, dragging it out. "I'm saying ever since Deline's sister, Lydia"—he snapped his mouth shut. "Look, just don't stop."

Logan set down the thermos. "What's this? You're encouraging me now? I thought I was dumb and dimwitted."

David stood. "Hey, you said it, not me." He snickered. "I think you'd be good for her. And I like how you pay attention to her. It's not just you going after her body or something, you know?" He shrugged. "But if you hurt her. . .I'd have to call Enli home."

"Who's that?"

With an evil laugh, David moved toward the flap. "Her brother. And if you thought her dad was big. . .wait till you meet Enli. If he finds out you like Deline, he will rip you up worse than a grizzly."

Grizzly. "That's what everyone calls you."

Brown eyes bore a strong message. "Exactly."

Chapter 6

Rain dumped its relief on Talkeetna. Clouds stomped over the horizon, their anger dissipating as they reached Denali. The wipers groaned and smeared rainwater over the windshield as she aimed her truck down the street.

"Looks clear at the peak," her father said from the passenger seat. "Tell me again why I'm going out in a storm?"

"Jolie asked for you to come, Daddy. And it's about time. You've been in the house for the last six weeks."

"I need my rest."

"You're hiding."

"Getting just like your mama."

"Thank you." She couldn't hide her smile.

Sunlight peeked through the clouds and gave a portent of the pretty day ahead once this storm passed. Funny, that was exactly how she felt, too. Then again, good things hadn't come since Mama died. Two years. Ironically, that was how long it'd been since Logan had shown up. Even to her, the analogy felt unfair. Logan was a good guy. Even if she didn't want to get involved with him.

She aimed the truck up to the front of the café.

"What're we doing here?"

Deline rolled her eyes. "We're meeting Jolie and David here. They invited us for dinner."

He grunted and climbed out.

Heart twisting as she watched her once-strong father

lumber out of the truck and stumble to get himself righted. Shoulders stooped, head down, he trudged forward, but she could see the pain knotting his handsome features.

He gripped the rail and pulled himself up the steps.

As she watched his feet, her gaze careened into a license plate. Washington. Her heart vaulted into her throat. No, it was just a coincidence. Enli had told her he couldn't come back: *"Too many clients, Line-de."* She'd always loved how he inverted the syllables of her name. Whereas Lydia had taunted Deline, calling her "Line Spleen." It was stupid. Sure they rhymed, but *spleen* didn't exactly conjure up any images, good or bad.

They stepped inside. Her mind snagged on the dark environment and she slowed.

"What's wrong?" her father asked as his hand automatically swung toward the light switch.

Lights and shouts erupted. "Surprise! Happy birthday!"

Deline took a step back as the words and smiles and faces registered. Trembling from the momentary fright, she shifted quickly to a smile. A laugh. Especially when she saw her father's weathered, aged features smooth from terse to pure delight.

Arms enveloped her from behind. "Don't hate me," Jolie said then kissed her cheek.

With a laugh, she turned to her friend. "Why didn't you tell me?"

"Sorry, I was a little busy planning a huge birthday bash for my friend's father."

Another laugh. Oh, it felt good to laugh! As Jolie and David led her to a table, she found herself wondering about Logan. Had he come? Surely they'd invited him.

The humiliation over their last encounter, though, made her hope he hadn't come. Never would she forgot how it felt to be cradled in his arms. How the strength of his hold told her how seriously he took the task of protecting her. Of his feelings. She knew that night, right there in his arms, that her father had spoken the truth. And she pushed Logan away.

"So, have you seen him yet?"

Deline's heart kick-started. "Who? Logan?"

David and Jolie shared a look before David went on, "No, I meant—"

"David," a voice boomed. "You bothering my sister again?"

Deline whipped around. "Enli!" Launched into the arms of her big brother. Tears erupted. Fled her hold. His arms were tight and hard, crushing her against him.

His laugh vibrated through his chest and against hers. "Line-de!" He planted a noisy kiss on her cheek and set her down. He tugged one of the curls that dangled over her shoulder. "See you're still trying to trap a guy with that Aleutian beauty."

She tugged her hair out of his hold. "No such thing." She patted his arm. "What are you doing here? You told me you had too much to do!"

"I did. But he said you needed me. That you wouldn't ask."

"Well"—she glared at David, then back at her brother—"nobody seems to want to let me grow up."

"Oh please!" Jolie laughed. "Girl, you're already there. And there are gawking men to prove it." She bobbed her head in the direction behind Deline.

Glancing over her shoulder, she only saw her father.

Then a dark blue shirt caught her eye. And the blue eyes that matched. Logan stood talking with her father.

"*Who* is that?" Enli demanded. "Do I need to know something?"

"Just that you haven't been home in two years." The jest

fell flat, since he'd left after their mother's death—two years ago—he misconstrued her meaning. "Enli, I only meant Logan showed up after you left."

"Logan, huh?" He deflected the hurt well, just like her. "Do Logan and I need to have a talk?"

"Leave him. He's a nice guy. Dad likes him."

"Even more reason for this guy and I to have a little one-on-one."

❧

"That must have been hard on you."

The compassion of Mr. Tsosie floored Logan. He hadn't met a man like this in. . .well, since he'd lost his father. "Yes, sir. It was. His death was the reason I came out here."

"Searching." Understanding pinched wizened brown eyes. "Denali is a good place to wrestle those demons."

"Yes, sir. Tried it out in the military, but I found it enabled and encouraged the anger rather than sated it." Oh good. *Smart move, champ. Just tell the guy you're sadistic.* "I came out here to find peace."

"Did you find it?"

"Well. . ." That was a tricky answer. "I stopped blaming God."

"But the peace isn't there, not like it used to be?"

Raised in a good Christian home, Logan felt sinful. "No, sir. It's not." He saw Deline standing across the café, gorgeous in jeans and an orange shirt. Not a T-shirt. This was a blouse. A slight ruffle around the collar mimicked her curls—

A hand reached over and touched that curl.

Demons had nothing on what he felt right now. *Let it go. She told you how she felt.*

Realizing Mr. Tsosie watched him still, Logan took a sip of his punch. "However, I am learning to surrender my dreams to the supreme High One."

Again, a smile wrinkled the man's eyes. "You mean the Lord."

"Yes, sir. I do."

"Please, call me Kuzih."

Honored that the man made the request, Logan couldn't help but battle nerves. Now if only Deline would be as easy to find favor with. "If you insist, sir."

Mr. Tsosie laughed and slapped Logan's shoulder. "Knew I liked you. Now if I can just—" His gaze slammed into something. His jaw went slack. "No. It can't be." His hand went to his heart.

Logan reached for Mr. Tsosie as he felt a dark shadow drop over them.

"Dad." A man the size of an elephant embraced Mr. Tsosie.

Logan automatically took a step back. With that guy around, there was no such thing as personal space because he ate it up.

"Son! You came." Tears streamed down Mr. Tsosie's face. "You came."

"Easy, Dad." Tsosie Junior—okay, that was just downright wrong—eased his father back. "They said you needed someone to keep you in line."

Dad?

Mr. Tsosie thumbed away his tears. "Did they?" he snorted. "When did you ever listen to them?"

"This time." For a guy the size of Foraker, the younger Tsosie had an incredible gentleness about him. An ache twisted inside Logan for the family he didn't have. The family that rounded out Thanksgivings and Christmases. Family that came to the rescue when things went south.

Smiling, Logan turned to the big guy again.

Fierce, narrowing eyes nailed him.

Logan shrank back.

A meaty hand thrust toward him.

Half expecting to feel an impact against his gut, Logan tensed.

"Enli Tsosie."

Deline's brother. As if to confirm the thought, she snaked around in front of the guy. "Logan, this is my brother. Enli, this is Logan Knox, a friend. And a mountaineering ranger."

A friend. The knife of that word severed his hope that she'd see him as anything but a ranger and a *friend*.

"If he finds out you like Deline, he will tear you apart faster than a grizzly."

So maybe *friend* had been a safe word and Deline saved Logan's life. Because the guy's grip felt like a vise. Logan prayed Enli wouldn't break anything. Thanked the Lord the grip wasn't around his neck. He was heading up to 9500 for the next month to relieve Mario. He'd need everything— including the limb—for that stint.

"Mr. Tsosie," Logan finally managed, wading through his morbid thoughts.

Enli didn't release him. "Saw you watching my sister. You like her?"

Visions of him laid out in the snow—bleeding, eyesight fading, dying—danced through his mind. Where was the gentle giant who'd just addressed his father?

Deline spun toward him. "Enli, stop it!"

The grip tightened. Logan felt the flicker of a frown. Surely he wouldn't...

Maybe he would. "Yes, I like her." Logan swallowed the adrenaline spurting into his throat. "Liked everyone I've met since arriving in Talkeetna...till now." He flicked his gaze to the death grip.

"You don't like me?"

"Depends on what condition you leave my hand in. Breaking it sort of ruins things for me." Logan raised his eyebrows when nothing shifted, not the grip, not the tension, not the posture. "I'd have to take that personally, since it'd put my job at risk."

Enli released his hand with a loud laugh then slapped Logan on the shoulder. "Welcome to Talkeetna." He turned back to Mr. Tsosie then went to retrieve glasses of punch.

Welcome? He'd been here two years!

"I'm sorry," Deline said. "He's a little overprotective."

He shrugged. "He's doing what big brothers do best."

David waded over to them. "Wow. I thought I was going to need to put some field medic training to use."

"You and me both." Logan laughed.

Deline gave him a look.

"What?"

She shook her head. "Nothing." But she kept watching him as the evening wore on. Though he didn't hover—not technically—and didn't try to constantly engage her, Logan had a finger on her location for the next two hours. He couldn't help it. Something about her served as a beacon in the midst of a storm.

He hoped for some time to talk with her, break down another protective layer. "Hey, so you think—"

"I'll be right back." She hurried off.

And did another three times. Every time he tried to engage her, in fact. Frustration pinched his shoulder muscles as the party wound down.

"I'd better get him home," she said to David and Jolie, then her gorgeous eyes skittered over to his. "Sorry. I just think he overdid it."

"Want help?" Logan offered, tossing his plastic cup into the trash.

"No. No, it's okay." She smiled at him. "Enli will help us."

"We're heading over to Jolie's for a movie in a bit. Logan, why don't you come over." David lifted a crate of drinks from the table and started for the back.

Logan watched as Deline hooked her hand beneath her father's elbow and walked with him out the door. Out of his life. His relationship with her felt like one step forward, two steps back.

A solid thump against his chest startled Logan. He jerked. "What. . . ?"

"It's not polite to stare." David grinned as he bent down and caught a table, nodding to Logan. "Grab the other end?"

Logan sighed and moved into the tedious process of cleaning up. Anything to get his mind off the hopelessness of his attraction to Deline. He was better than this. Bigger than this. He was a mountaineering ranger, for cryin' out loud!

Hollow but distant, a noise rocked through the air.

What was that? Maybe. . .Jolie and David. No, they were in the kitchen, laughing and talking. The sound repeated, and only then did he realize it was a scream.

Logan started toward the front.

Light flickered and danced along the curtains. Not bright enough for someone to have pulled up in front of Tsosie's. He pushed open the door. It looked a lot like—

"Fire!" a woman who stood in the street screamed. "Their house is on fire! Kuzih and Deline's—the Tsosies'!"

Chapter 7

Adrenaline surged. Logan sprinted across the road. Flames roared into the dark night. His heart cramped as he rounded the corner and saw the Tsosie home. Cracking and popping beneath the consuming fire, the two-story structure groaned.

"Deline!" Logan shouted as he palmed her Jeep. Hoping against hope they were inside that and not in the house. Front—empty. Back—same. Logan pounded on the hood. "Deline!"

A growl came from somewhere.

He rushed toward the steps that led up to the front porch. Flames erupted, as if attracted to his presence.

He threw himself backward. His boots slipped on the gravel walk. "Deline!" Shielding his face and eyes from the glare of the fire, he searched for a sign of her. "Deline!" The veins in his temples competed with the fire for oxygen. *"Deline!"*

Small and entirely too weak, a voice came from. . . somewhere.

Bright and angry, the fire roared. Licked the walls. Ate the wood.

"Help!"

The voice jolted him out of the stupor. From the right. He lunged toward the side deck. There, legs still inside the house, lay Mr. Tsosie. Collapsed, his large frame blocked Deline, who was bent, trying to wrangle her father. Hair framing her ash-coated face, Deline looked up at him. "Logan!"

He propelled himself up the steps. Flew the four feet to them. "Go, go! I got him."

❧

Scrambling a safe distance away, Deline struggled to make herself stay, to stop coughing. Logan scooped her father up and started forward.

A fiery beam slammed down in front of him.

Hands over her mouth, Deline froze.

David darted in front of her and raced to help Logan. He lifted her father's feet, and the two shuffled his unconscious form to the side. Helpless. He looked helpless. She felt helpless. Nothing she could do. . .

Have to do something. She'd always been able to take care of them. Fix things. Make things better. Stay in control when others couldn't.

With her dad on the ground Craig and Jared, two volunteer EMTs, raced into the fray. They knelt on each side of her father, taking his pulse, strapping on an oxygen mask. Jared threw a question over his shoulder to the man behind him.

Logan.

Holding his knees, he muttered something as an IV slid into her father's arm. Yes, Logan. He'd been there. Saved her father.

He saved my father. The thought rang like a dinner bell in her ears. Over and over.

He'd put his life in jeopardy to save her father. To save her.

Of all the men she'd met, of all the mountaineering rangers she'd known. . .Logan was the only one who unnerved her. She didn't know what to do with him, with his kindness, his quiet strength. The other guys were loud, boisterous, full of themselves. Like David.

Logan was. . .Logan. Confident. Quiet. Strong.

Like Daddy.

She hauled in a breath—smoke and ash caught at the back of her throat. She coughed.

Logan's gaze snapped to hers. "Where's Enli?"

Around another coughing fit, she said, "Hotel. . .back at the hotel."

He frowned as he straightened, his brow knitted.

Though she tried to stop the coughing, the taste in her mouth felt like sandpaper scrubbing her tonsils. More coughing. She turned away. Eyes burning. Limbs aching. Heart tearing.

"Here," came Logan's deep, strong voice as he produced a water bottle. "Drink slowly."

Fist over her mouth, she nodded as the urge to cough continued. She lifted it to her mouth but instead of swallowing, she swished and spit. Then took another gulp and let it slide down.

Lights swirled and a siren squawked. The crowd broke up and moved away as two more EMTs hopped out of another vehicle.

"Need a board," Jared shouted.

Attention back on her father as they transferred him to a board, Deline panicked. She couldn't lose him. Not now. "He's a fighter. He's going to be okay."

Logan said nothing, just watched.

"Mom used to always say he was strongest man she knew, inside and out. Thickheaded, too."

Rocks crunched as Logan shifted toward her.

"She said I was just like him, thickheaded and all. He'll be fine. I know he will. He has to. . ."

"Deline." Logan's voice was softer this time.

She snapped her gaze to him. "He will. I know he will." She smiled, but it warbled like the heat plumes that had erupted from the kitchen when they'd entered. "Right? He will, won't he?"

"Yes. He will. Just overcome with smoke. You got him out in time."

She didn't know whether to nod or shake her head. She did both.

"Deline, we're going to take him up to Mat-Su to make sure he's clear, since he just had the stroke. Do you want to come?" Jared asked.

"Yes!" She surprised herself with how loud that was. They led her to the ambulance. But it felt like a draft, a chilling, death-enshrouded emptiness cocooned her. What. . . ? She turned.

Logan. He hadn't moved. He swallowed. "He'll be okay. You'll be okay. You're tough, Deline."

"Will. . ." If she did this, things would change between them. At least, for her. "Will you follow us up there?"

His hands came out of his pockets. No smile. But there was a distinct realignment of. . .something. "I'll meet you there," he said with a nod. "And I'll get hold of Enli."

Her heart thumped. "Yes. Please." How could she have forgotten her brother? Staying at the hotel, he was probably already asleep. "Thank you, Logan."

When she thought of a handsome mountaineering ranger before her own flesh and blood. . . Definitely changing.

❧

Logan trekked into the ER, having seen the ambulance parked outside that had taken Deline and her father away from Talkeetna. Inside, he made his way to the waiting room. That's where she'd be, right?

As he strode the long, sterile halls, Logan whispered a prayer. That God would keep Deline's father safe. That He'd keep Deline safe. And that He'd help Logan be whatever Deline needed right now, though he hoped it was more than just the "friend" she'd introduced him as to her brother.

He turned the corner and entered a small waiting area. A family huddled close, arms around a woman who sobbed uncontrollably. Heart in a knot, Logan swallowed and diverted his gaze—right into Deline's.

Her expression went from exhausted and weighted. . .

Oh, he so didn't want to go there. To think that she had hope in her eyes, and relief—it meant too much to him to hope and find out he'd misread it.

"Hey." His heart felt a thousand pounds lighter as he joined her.

Lips apart, she started to rise.

"No, don't get up." Glancing down, he stilled. Spotted the butterfly stitch on her forehead. He eased into the chairs. "Any word?"

Tucking a strand of hair behind her ear, Deline let out a shaky breath. "Yeah, well—no." She bobbled her head back and forth, as if trying to sort her thoughts.

"Hey," Logan said, touching her knee—then realizing his mistake. He pulled back and gave her a reassuring nod. "It's okay."

"Sorry. I'm just tired." She let out a long sigh and eased back into the chair. "Daddy came to on the way over. Jared said things looked fine, but they wanted to check him out, possibly keep him for observation."

Glancing at the butterfly bandage again, Logan felt a knot in his gut. If she'd died. . .if she'd gotten hurt. . . And the last thing she needed after all the things happening—her plane losing oil, the house fire, her mom's death—losing her dad would be too much. "How's your head?"

Long, delicate fingers went to her temple automatically.

She winced. "Only hurts when I touch it."

Logan chuckled. "Maybe you shouldn't touch it, then."

A small smile teased the edges of her lips as she tucked her chin. She sat there for several long minutes, staring at her hands. Finally, she lifted her gaze to his. "I'm really glad you came."

Ping-Pong had nothing on the competition in his chest. "I wouldn't want to be anywhere else."

She tilted her head a fraction. "I meant—that you showed up at the house."

Heat stomped into his face. "Oh."

Deline touched his hand. "You saved our lives, Logan." Her chin trembled. "I can't thank you enough."

"When I heard it was your house. . ." Logan pushed his attention around the room. He huffed. "The thought of. . ."

"You really meant that, didn't you?"

He jerked back to her. "What?"

"What you said, about not wanting to be anywhere else."

Logan sat forward, his elbows on his knees. He could tell her. Tell her right now what he felt for her. He considered her. Those beautiful eyes that were layers of different shades of brown, like a rich wood. Her long, wavy hair that so perfectly framed her oval face and accented her pink lips. How his heart danced a jig every time she looked at him.

And. . .*she's looking back at me.*

Did she feel the same way? She'd asked him to come up here. Hadn't asked anyone else.

"I mean it, Deline. I'd do—"

"Miss Tsosie?"

Deline flinched, breaking their visual lock, and looked up at the man standing over them.

Where had Sheriff Wellesley come from?

Logan stood and shook hands with the man. "Sheriff."

He motioned Deline back into her seat. "Mind if I ask you some questions?"

"No, of course not," Deline said, glancing to Logan again. As if for support. Backup.

Parked on the edge of the seat, Logan folded his hand around Deline's. Her delicate fingers curled around his as she squeezed her appreciation.

"Can you tell me what happened, in your own words?"

"Sure." Deline wet her lips. "After Daddy's party at the café, we drove back home. It's just a short stint, but with Daddy's surgery, we thought it'd be best not to push it by walking. When we got to the house, Enli and I helped him out of the truck. Then Enli had an emergency call and left. I helped through the side door."

"Into the kitchen."

"Right. You've been there, had coffee with Daddy."

Wellesley nodded.

"We were about halfway to the hall when we could smell something strange. About the same time, I saw the smoke and fire thick as night pouring down the stairs." Deline's grip tightened. "That's when Daddy collapsed. I don't know if it was the smoke or the fear, but he just went down. I got him back through the kitchen but. . .his feet. . .they got stuck."

Logan eased forward, taking a firmer, more protective hold of her hand to bring her back to the present. To the fact that things were fine.

She blinked and turned those wide eyes on him. "That's when Logan came around the side."

Wellesley frowned. "You were there?"

"I was at the café. Heard something and went to check it out. Someone shouted that the Tsosie home was on fire, so I sprinted down to the house. Found Deline trying to get her father to safety and interdicted."

"Did either of you see anything or anyone unusual?"

"No," they both replied.

Deline shrugged. "I just don't know why it started. I hadn't cooked. We didn't have the heat on."

"We don't believe it was a heater," the sheriff said. "The investigators believe an accelerant was used."

Logan tensed, drawing Deline's attention. "Arson?"

Hesitating as he looked at both of them, Wellesley finally nodded. "One thing we are pretty sure of, it wasn't an accident."

Chapter 8

Leveling off as they circled Ruth's Glacier, Deline spoke through the microphone. "Do you want the whole tour?"

Logan's laugh, filtered through the crackling of the coms, carried through her headset and shot straight into her heart. "Not necessary."

"You've only heard it—what?—a dozen times."

"About that."

The flight was smooth, seamless. It felt good, right, to be up here, in the clouds. Thank goodness Enli had gone home—he'd hovered and smothered until they got her father settled into Jolie's loft apartment, loaned to them while the heiress was in New York on a bridal shopping trip. More power to her. Deline would go simple and quickly down the altar.

Squirts of warmth darted through her stomach. Wedding? Since when? She'd vowed not to get married while Daddy was still alive. And she'd nearly lost Daddy with that fire. Who. . . ?

"Did you hear anything else about the fire?" she asked Logan as she stared down at the five thousand feet of relief surrounding the glacier. So gorgeous. So amazing. God's country. How about they go a little higher? Check out Wickersham? He'd bought out this tour, so why not?

"No."

His voice sounded funny, off. Deline glanced to the side,

noting his hands gripping the seat. Face pale. "You okay, Logan?"

Gaze darting to hers, he nodded.

He almost looked afraid. Scared.

"Hey," she said, catching sight of the sleds that marked the high Base Camp. "Look at 9600. Good crowd down there."

"Clear weather. No surprise." His hands smoothed along his jeans, then returned to the seat. "I'm heading there tomorrow."

Deline glanced at him and frowned. "Isn't that like a monthlong rotation?"

He nodded. "It's my turn to go up."

Disappointment lurked beneath the comfort of their togetherness. That meant no flying with him. No sharing the most beautiful vistas and views in America. That meant no more Logan smiles.

"Hey, did I say something wrong?"

"No." She flashed a smile at him. Why did she feel so nervous? Keep him talking—that way she didn't have to think about her squiggly stomach. "Spending weeks at a time on the High One—you must really like mountaineering."

"Love it."

"Why?"

Logan sighed. "Long story."

"You paid for an hour."

He laughed. And it warmed her, despite the frigid elevation. "You know my dad died in 9/11."

"Right."

"Well, after his death, I went into the Army—"

" 'Be all you can be.' "

"Hooah." He seemed more relaxed now. "But I was keyed up on adrenaline 24-7. I realized about three years in that I was in it for revenge. Somehow, knowing that I was killing people of the same heritage as those who killed my dad—well, it fed my fury. I was angry. And I wasn't getting any better. So,

I didn't re-up when the time came. I got out. Headed here. As your dad said, I wrestled my demons summiting."

She eyed him. "You made it? You actually summitted?"

He nodded. "About froze to death, but yeah. Then, I realized it was a good, safe outlet for the anger. I found more peace at the summit than I did anywhere else. I felt like I was meeting God there."

"Were you?"

"Yeah." He met her gaze. "And angels."

Me? He's talking about me! Deline watched him for a moment, unsure what to say at first, then just let loose with a good belly-busting laugh. "You smooth talker."

Logan chuckled. "Clearly not."

"So you came up here to get rid of your anger?"

"That's about the size of it."

"Army guy, huh?"

"As were my father and grandfather before him. Don't get me wrong—I'm all for the military but I had things in me I had to take care of, and with the ongoing wars, I couldn't get what I needed."

"Smart man to recognize that."

"What about you?"

Deline frowned as she kept the plane level, eyeing the High One and trying to stay relaxed as he probed her soul. "What about me?"

"Why do you stay here?"

"Hello? It's Alaska!" She motioned to the windshield. "Look at that. Tell me that doesn't inspire you, stir a realization that there is something much bigger out there than us. God really shines here. It's hard to deny Him when you see this kind of beauty, you know?"

"Yeah."

"When d'you start flying?"

"I went up with Curt as soon as he'd allow me—fifteen. He wouldn't let me have the controls, but he showed me what to do, taught me. Helped me get my license."

"So, that's why he's willing to let you take over TFAT."

She shrugged. "Not sure why he's willing to do that, but it's a dream come true for me. I won't argue."

"So. . .you think Bender might be behind the fire?"

Deline's heart pounced on the idea. "I've thought about it, but I don't want to go there. If I get it in my head he did that. . . I'd go mental."

"You and me both. Doesn't it drive you crazy wondering?"

"Night and day." She had to stay alert all the time. She had to double- and triple-check the locks. Deline started the descent back to the airstrip. "Do you think he's behind it?"

"That's not my territory, but I find it peculiar that he suddenly hasn't been seen around much."

"Hadn't thought of that."

Logan shrugged. "Eh, probably not a big thing that he's not here, but considering how much he liked to annoy you. . . it looks suspicious."

"Good point."

He gripped the seat again. "Let's not ruin our last twenty minutes talking about him. After all, I paid for this." He laughed again.

"Why do you keep hiring me, my plane?" Oh, why did she ask?

"For the view."

There was a strange inflection to the way he answered. She checked and found him watching her. Not Denali.

Back on terra firma.

Logan let out a breath as he climbed from the Otter

and waited for his land legs to solidify. The things he did for. . .love? Seriously? That was a leap. Yeah, a twenty-four-thousand-foot leap. They'd gone that high and he really didn't want to do it again. But he would.

"Hey, what'd you think?" Deline walked with him toward the offices. "That was your first solo with me."

"Loved it." He'd go through a lot worse to be alone with her.

Jaw out, she narrowed her eyes at him. "Well, I enjoyed the tour." She leaned against the rail, a few feet from the door, and folded her arms. "After all Daddy and I have been through, it was really nice to just get up there and fly." Her gaze rose to the sky and though she put her aviator sunglasses on, he didn't mind. She was still the most beautiful woman he'd met.

Now or never, chicken.

"So, do me a favor?"

She pulled straight. "Sure. What?"

"Go out with me."

Deline froze.

Silence gaped.

Two tourists tromped up the stairs and wedged between him and Deline, but he refused to break their visual connection. After the tourists passed, Logan stepped closer. He reached down and hooked her fingers with his. "Nothing serious. Just dinner at the café—"

"No." Deline snapped out of her frozen stupor. "Not the café. Anywhere else, but not there."

So that wasn't a no. "Sounds good. Pick you up around six?"

"Tonight?" Panic etched into her face.

"I head up into Denali tomorrow."

"Right." Deline wet her lips and swallowed. "Okay. . ."

Logan grinned. He'd rattled her. The unrattleable girl. "See you then."

He turned and forced himself to walk away. Before he gave her an out. He hated seeing her look nervous and scared. She didn't wear it well. But he loved the blush that colored her cheeks in the midst of that. And she hadn't said no.

He hopped into his truck, started the engine, and peered through the windshield. Nah, it'd be too much to hope she was still standing there watching. She probably realized her mistake. Would call and come up with a reason why she couldn't go.

His phone belted out a country song.

Logan smirked. Turned on his radio. Cranked the volume and headed back to his house. No way would he give her an out.

❧

He hadn't meant to burn their house down. It wasn't supposed to go up like that. But he needed to make a point. Needed Deline to shift her priorities to her father. She had family left. She had other things that should matter more than an air taxi business. And if he could just get her to realize that, get her to step out of the way, he could save his entire life savings.

Couldn't she see that? Why did she think she had the right to so many good things at such a young age? Sure, her mama had died, but that happened to a lot of people. To him, in fact. But he moved on. Life went on.

Till the creditors came. The tour company was his only lifeline, his only way to save everything he had worked so hard for.

After nearly dying in that fire, she should've seen what was important. But no. She didn't. She went up in the plane, took that fool young ranger who had the hots for her. Now the two of them sat at the table, eating, laughing, talking. As if they had not a care in the world. And they probably didn't.

Well, he'd fix that. He'd make sure she didn't steal this from him. He'd have nothing to live for if the business went down. If she continued with this merger talk.

He fisted his hands. Didn't want to do this. Didn't want to cross any *real* ethical lines. But she had to wake up.

Unless. . .unless she didn't wake up.

Ever.

Chapter 9

Tranquility embraced Deline as she stepped from between a cluster of pines and stood overlooking the pristine Christiansen Lake. Moonlight spread its light along the glasslike surface, illuminating the area. Rocks and gravel crunched behind her as Logan came alongside.

Clean, crisp air swirled at his approach and brought with it a scent of something Old Spice-ish, yet not. Lighter scented, but all masculine.

Can't believe I'm out here. Alone. With Logan Knox.

It'd been a long time since she felt like she was sixteen and had a crush again.

Logan took a hand out of his pocket, bent, and retrieved a rock. He bounced it in his hand then took a step and flung it along the moon's reflection. The rock skipped off the water, leaving ringlets. Hit again. More rings. And one more time before dropping out of sight.

Standing a couple of feet in front of her, Logan watched for a moment then slid his hands back into his pockets. Broad shoulders hung beneath his navy and bright blue jacket. Dark hair. Borderline electric blue eyes. A strong jawline and profile. Strong character. But quiet.

Unnervingly quiet.

She and Enli had been loud and antagonistic all their lives. But their love for each other went to the ends of the earth. But Enli was her brother.

I don't want a brother. She wanted. . .

Well, what did she want? She had it up to the summit and back with tourists who wanted to score with her because she was a native.

She knew what she wanted—to break the ice between them. To somehow shift from friends to. . .something else. Was that what he wanted? Was that why they'd trekked from the restaurant through the forest, alert for bears, moose, and droppings, to come out here and be alone?

How exactly did one break that ice?

"It's beautiful out here," Logan said, his gaze still on the water, on the trees, rising to the High One, in the distance, that held the moonlight captive.

"You come out here a lot?"

"Most nights I'm not up there"—he nodded toward Denali again—"I'm out here, jogging, thinking, praying."

A perfect in. "What do you pray for?"

He lowered his head, lifted another rock, and sent it hopping across the water like a frog over lily pads. "The future. Safety." He shrugged. "The usual."

Logan angled his shoulder down and toward her. "What about you? What do you pray for?"

She smiled at him out of the corner of her eye. "The usual."

With a breathy snort he shook his head and stood beside her, just watching the surroundings. Deline retrieved a rock and sent it sailing over the water. It skipped six times.

"Show-off," Logan muttered.

Laughing, she took another. "Contest?"

Amusement sparkled in his eyes, the light of the moon bright on those eyes. She liked when they were on her, the way they warmed her. Because his gaze wasn't just a gaze. It was probing, searching, considering, thoughtful.

"All right." He squatted and ran a hand over the rocks.

"What is this? Jedi mind tricks?"

Logan straightened, running his thumb over a rock as he looked down at her over his shoulder. "What's the prize?"

"Another date." Her insides felt like jelly. Would he think her too forward or too flirty?

"Okay, and what's your prize if you win?"

She blinked. "A date—that was *my* prize."

Logan shifted, pulling straight as he stared down at her. "You want another date. With me?"

"No, with the moose who left that pile on the trail."

"How do you know it wasn't a bear?"

"Oh, just throw the rock."

"I haven't told you what prize I get if I win." His lopsided smirk and lazy gaze swirled her stomach with giddy excitement.

"So you think you'll win?"

His left eyebrow winged up.

Deline giggled. Oh man. Maybe she was letting up a little too much. "Okay, Ranger Knox, name your prize."

Logan's smile slid away. His expression went serious. Heady serious that left swarms of nervous and buzzing fireflies in her belly. The way he looked at her, considered her, sent waves of heat crashing through her. What was he thinking?

He twitched and turned away. "Another solo flight with you." He flung the rock with expert precision.

One, two, three, four, five. . .six. . .

"Ah—"

He held up his hand as a final *plop* sounded through the still lake.

"Now who's the show-off?"

Logan stepped aside and motioned her forward to launch.

"Okay," she said, choosing her weapon. "I want to come

out here again and do a boat tour for our next date."

"Planning to win?"

She cast a flirtatious smile over her shoulder. "Always." Facing the water, she lifted her rock, blew on it, and then lowered her shoulder and whipped it over Christiansen Lake.

Plop!

"One."

Plop!

"Two."

Plop. . .plop!

"Three, four."

Plop.

"Five."

She waited.

And waited.

"I think I won."

Huffing, she spun to him. "Fine." She raised her hands. "You won. When do you want to go up next?"

Logan's eyes pinched beneath a hidden smile. "As soon as I get back."

"Speaking of getting back. . ." She tried to angle to see her watch. "Probably need to get back."

"Probably." Logan headed up the bank, hands in his jeans pockets.

Deline slid up next to him and looped her arm through his. The move splashed a bit of excitement through her, but she didn't know how else to shift their relationship beyond friendship.

He gave her a sidelong glance but no resistance to her clinging. And for once in her life, she didn't mind being a clinging female.

They chatted about his mountaineering and the climbers as they made their way through the forest back to his truck.

It'd been one of the best nights of her life. Again she asked herself why she hadn't loosened up long ago.

Because Logan wasn't here.

He was the reason she'd been willing to brave getting hurt. To brave enduring what Lydia went through. Of course, that was her sister's own fault, being an endless flirt and clingy. . .

Oh man. Was she doing it? Had Lydia felt like this with her boyfriend? Was that what made her so willing to cast off propriety? To end up pregnant and dumped? Twice.

And now I'm doing it.

Deline straightened and slowly slid her arm free.

Logan noticed. "Something wrong?"

She took a step back.

Holding her by the shoulders, Logan crouched to see her eye to eye. "Deline. . .what're you thinking? You went stone-cold on me. Why?"

"How. . .?" Was it wrong to talk to him about it? "My sister. . .Lydia."

"Yeah?"

Breaking off a small branch as they walked, she told herself to talk this through. Not shut down. She wanted to explore this with Logan. She'd never been willing to go here with a guy before. So it had to be different, didn't it?

"She was this insatiable flirt. Always dating a new guy. Going out with just about any climber who came through." Deline lowered her head, already seeing the differences between herself and her sister. "She got pregnant—twice. Lost the first baby. Gave the second one up and finally left Talkeetna."

"Is that why you don't date?"

Surprise leapt through her as she considered Logan. Then slowly, she nodded. "Yeah. I didn't want to be like her. I wanted the town to know that our parents raised good kids."

Logan paused and turned to her. "Deline, they know that." His gaze traced her face. "They know you're not like that."

"Do you?"

Chilled but strong, his hand cupped her cheek. "Yeah. I know it."

How a guy's hand could be cold yet zap her belly with fire, she didn't know. She blinked, startled by the intimacy of his touch, and glanced down the trail. Away from him. Away from the awareness that flared through her.

Too much. She couldn't think. Couldn't function.

She lifted a hand to her forehead. "What. . . ?" She grabbed that thought. "Back there at the lake, that prize you wanted—it wasn't flightseeing, was it?"

Logan smirked.

"So, what was it?"

He chuckled, his deep resonating laugh, and started walking. "You don't want to know."

Deline rushed in front of him and pushed against his abdomen. "Yeah, I do actually."

They'd stepped out of the forest. The gentle waxing of the moon caressed his face, making his skin look darker yet softer.

For a moment, he studied her. Then shook his head and looked toward the not-so-thriving town. "I think we should just call it a night."

"Chicken." She nudged his gut again and drew his attention back. Hands on her hips, she lifted her chin and stared defiantly back. "What was it, Ranger Knox? I'm not moving out of the way till you tell me what you were going to choose. *That* should be your prize. Not some second-preference pick."

He scratched the back of his head, yet again looking around. "Deline. . ."

Laughing, she leaned into him. "Oh, come on. What is it? What did you really want?"

His face went all serious again. He watched her eyes—*eyes are good. They lead to the soul.* He could look into hers—she felt the clearest and most open she'd felt in a very long time. Her nose. Okay, so it was a little stubby at the end, but otherwise straight. Then his gaze dipped to her—

Mouth. Lips.

Oh.

His breath skated along her cheek as he lowered his face to hers. Her stomach—*yes!*—and brain—*no!*—went to war, paralyzing her.

Chapter 10

The world funneled down into a laser-sharp focus until only Deline remained on his radar. Like some gravitational pull, he honed in on her lips. Doing this, going in for the kill, was one huge risk. He wanted it to shift their relationship. He wanted things to be different. This moment would tell him if that would ever happen.

In the microseconds before his lips met hers, Logan noticed she'd frozen.

But she didn't resist, either. That was a good thing, right?

He pressed in. Kissed her. Oh, soft lips. She smelled of something flowery.

Logan lifted his head, noticed her eyes closed, and kissed her again. This time, lingering. He slid a hand to the back of her neck and savored the moment.

She eased off, her breathing shaky as she lowered her head, gaze down.

Unwilling to move, to sever this connection that had formed. Afraid to move and have her tell him—

"I. . .I think. . ." Deline stepped back, the wind tousling her wavy hair across her face.

In that split second, he saw it.

She glanced toward the city, as if looking for an escape. The light of the moon reflected off her eyes—and in them, he saw tears. *Tears?* "I need to get back."

Logan took hold of her hand. "Deline—"

"I had a great evening, Logan." Tugging free, she sacrificed a smile for the sake of his feelings. At least, that was what it looked like. "Thanks."

And she started walking.

"Deline, please." His brain caught up with her movement. Several large strides carried him to her side. "Talk to me, Deline. Don't just walk off."

"I'm not walking off." Her words were stiff, yet trembling. Just as her breathing. "Really, I'm fine. Just. . .give me room. . ."

"Let me drive you back."

"No." Her voice firmed. "I want to walk. Need it."

Someone wielded a baseball bat against his heart because the wind was knocked out of Logan. Should've known better. He took a leap in kissing her, a risk the equivalent of jumping off a skyscraper. Now his guts and heart had splattered all over the ground floor of her rejection.

Logan clamped down on his words and slowed. She gained a lead, a long lead. And he watched her go. Down the road. Into the darkness. Right. Out. Of. His. Life.

Molars grinding, he shoved his focus to the rocks and dirt. He couldn't believe his idiocy. Their first quasi date and he made a move like that. Ruined everything. Logan shoved both hands against his face and huffed, then scrubbed his cheeks as if trying to rub away the stupidity.

Hands in the pockets of his jeans, he trudged back to his truck. Climbed inside the cab and started the engine. Shouldn't have kissed her. Should've just let the good time they'd had hold. Given her time to realize he wouldn't hurt her. That was what this was about, right? She was afraid he'd hurt her? That was the last thing he would want. He'd been crazy for her since coming to Talkeetna. She was like a fresh breeze in the storm of his life. All this time flying with her. Spending hundreds of dollars, hoping to get to know her, to win her.

Fail. A complete fail. All because he let his heart get ahead of his brain.

Well, at least now he knew how she really felt.

He stomped into his house, flipped on the light, and spotted his gear. He let out a long sigh. A month on the High One would give him plenty of time to cool off. Get over her.

He shed his boots and jacket then dropped onto the bed. "Yeah, keep telling yourself that."

Chapter 11

It'd been three weeks since she'd taken the long road home. Walking anywhere in Talkeetna didn't take long, but that road away from Logan felt like hours. That kiss, Logan's tenderness, awakened what had died in her.

Startling. Terrifying. Beautiful.

Deline suppressed a smile as she stepped from the TFAT office, hands in her lightweight jacket. Though she knew he thought she was walking away for good, she'd just needed time to sort through it, figure out what she felt.

No, not true. She really had to stop lying to herself.

"I know exactly what I feel when it comes to Logan Knox." Warmth. Happiness. Joy. . .

"You gotta be kidding me."

Deline's hiking boot hit the dirt just as the man's voice registered. Roger Bender. Hauling in a breath, she took a step back, up onto the porch. Steeled herself as he came around the corner, his attention on his cell phone conversation.

"What do you mean? I thought you said those rangers had backup." He grunted. "Yeah, well, suits him right." He snorted. "Fine, I'll tell her, but I'm not doing your dirty work anymore, Curt."

Deline felt fury color her red. She looked over her shoulder. Curt wasn't in the office.

Roger Bender met her gaze. "Gotta go." He ended the call. "Deline! Thank God, I found you!"

She recoiled at his touch. "Get away from me."

"Now be nice. Curt asked me to find you, and I'm sorry to be the one to tell you this, but that ranger fella you took a shine to is in trouble."

"Logan."

A smile, a greedy, slimy smile, filled his face. "That's the one. He got in trouble up there. I don't know what. Curt was too frantic. Said to get you up in there, help them search. If they don't get him off the mountain he's going to die."

Trembling, she dared not believe this man. But. . .what if it was true? She turned and rushed into the office.

"Where's Curt?"

One of the new hires shrugged. "Search and rescue, I think."

Breath backed into her throat, Deline threw herself out the door. Sprinted over the tarmac to her Otter, trailed by a terrible, terrible feeling.

❦

Thoughts of Deline and her soft kiss haunted his dreams that night and for the next week, chased him up onto the mountain. Up to High Camp. Through his patrols with the volunteers. Through a rescue. Through his duties—nothing like making sure people were using their CMCs, leaving the Alaska Range clean for those who came behind.

Why didn't she like him? What was it about him that kept her from letting things happen? He saw the way she looked at him. As if it pained her to like him. At High Camp for a week and still moping around over Deline. Fourteen thousand, two hundred feet, and he couldn't get away from her or the memories of that night at Christiansen Lake. That kiss. *Am I that pathetic?*

To himself, he muttered, "Yeah, you are."

"What's that?" Dr. Reginald Malcolm asked as he stirred

a pot early that morning. Malcolm had come from Colombia to volunteer—it was as much adrenaline as it was experience that compelled the burly man. Despite his age, the doctor was in peak physical shape.

"Nothing." Logan snapped out of the mental fog and focused on patrolling. *Shake it off. Get your head in the game. Or you'll end up in a crevasse the way you found David.*

He could really use his friend right now. To talk to. To bounce this insanity off of.

Logan trudged to the kitchen tent and nodded at the other ranger working with him—Josh. The normally brilliant sun shielded itself with a thick storm cloud.

"Looks ominous," Josh said as he handed a bowl to Logan.

Cradling the soup that wafted the warm, delicious scent of chicken and broth, Logan sat on the ice bench. "Yeah, Deanna told me a nasty one was coming in." It was his curse, he guessed, for pushing things too far too fast with Deline. Why was it he could save lives and be a hero on the mountain but down there, where the air and people were normal, he couldn't even save face? "I'd hoped the storm would change its mind."

Josh laughed.

Logan peered out the tent, amazed at God's creation. Smooth glittering tufts stretched over the pristine landscape. Jagged peaks thrust up out of the sunset-softened snow. Clouds enshrouded Mt. Foraker. Serene and stunning. Brutal and beautiful. Fierce and forbidding.

Just like Deline.

After cleaning up to erase as much carbon imprint as possible, Logan trekked out of the tent.

Laughter carried from one of the tents, and he spotted a team who'd spent yesterday ferrying their equipment back and forth to seventeen hundred. One of the men had taken a tumble and wrenched his ankle. Logan and his patrol had come upon him and the other three with him shortly after. The guy vowed, however, he wasn't turning back. Said he'd take a day to give his ankle time to rest, but he wasn't descending without summiting first. *I'm too close to give up now.*

Hands in his ranger jacket, Logan stood staring up at the last three thousand feet of Denali. A perfect parallel to his relationship with Deline. The climb behind him had been the last two years. Summiting Denali was as much a feat as it would be to summit a relationship with Deline Tsosie.

And like the mountaineer, Logan wasn't going to give up. Months ago, he realized she was the girl of his dreams. A bit out of his league, if anyone asked him, but she was the one he wanted. He'd consider it the ultimate prize to win her heart. He sent up a prayer, asking God for one chance, one opportunity to find out if Deline would accept him.

Exhausted after another patrol of checking the CMCs and monitoring hikers and helping in any fashion necessary, Logan dropped into his bedroll. Closed his eyes and let the numbing silence and cold embrace him.

Somewhere in the howling wind, a noise squawked.

Logan eased up, confused. His mind blurred.

The noise again.

Sat phone!

Logan grabbed it from the ice shelf and answered, "Ranger Knox."

"Logan!" Deanna's shaky, frantic voice drew him up. Sitting, he waited for her to continue. "Logan, it's Deanna."

"What's wrong?"

"Have you seen Deline?"

His gaze darted back and forth. "Deanna, did you forget? I'm at fourteen hundred."

"I know! I know—she was doing a tour, radioed in and said something was wrong."

On his knees, heart pounding, Logan yanked the tent's zipper.

Snow and ice barreled in. He ripped it closed.

"What're you saying?" he asked, her panic now tangible in his own body.

"Radar shows nothing, Logan. She went down. We lost her."

Chapter 12

It'd been too easy. So easy, he felt guilty.

But she'd taken the bait like a starving rat. Gobbled it right up. Hopped in her plane and lifted into the skies. . . never to be seen again.

He wasn't proud of what he'd done. Not really. She'd been a nice girl. Pretty, even. But she wouldn't give up that fool notion of taking over TFAT. *He* needed that business. She didn't. She wanted it, but she didn't need it. Not the way he did.

She pushed me to do this.

Hadn't even noticed the tampering he'd done. She'd get up there, think she was on some rescue mission, then. . .

"Breaking news at six!" he exclaimed with a chuckle.

"Roger Bender."

Over his shoulder, Roger saw the sheriff stalking toward him, one hand hovering over his holstered weapon.

❧

Weightlessness coupled with deadly silence engulfed her. She attempted to restart the engines. Eyes glued to the rapidly slowing propeller that went from looking like a heat plume in front of the Otter to a slowing ceiling fan blade.

"Mayday! Mayday! This is November 5-6-2 Tango Foxtrot. Having trouble—"

A wind gust caught her. Threw her Otter sideways. With no engines she had no control. Panic thrummed against the silent scream.

"Mayday! Mayday! This is November 5-6-2 Tango Foxtrot—"

"November 5-6-2, this is Control. What is the problem?"

"I—" Deline bit off the sentence as she saw the sheer granite relief of Ruth's Gorge storming toward her. "Oh, God, help!"

"November 5-6-2! Deline—talk to us."

Hearing her voice name snapped Deline back to the present. "I. . .engines. . .something's wrong. Losing altitude."

And fast. The plane glided down. . .down. . .no control. . .right toward a ten-thousand-foot wall of granite. "Great Gorge. . .not—"

A loud moaning vibrated through the hull. Deline looked over her shoulder. The left wing sheared off. The plane canted.

Glacier and granite rushed up at her.

Pop!

Deline jolted upward.

Pain howled. She threw herself back with a scream, clamping a hand over her left leg. Her stomach threatened to heave against the agony and smell of fuel mixed with blood. Something pressed into her face—the headset. She pushed it off with a grunt. Feeling suffocated, trapped, upside down. . .

Her mind whiplashed as her awareness surged to the forefront. The plane. . .it sat tilted. The right wing propped against something. The weight of sitting at an odd angle—for however long she'd been here unconscious—proved painful. Her shoulder and leg pulsed a fresh wave of pain with each heartbeat.

Have to get out of here. Through the fiery shards and nausea, she groped for the headset that clattered against fiberglass and steel. "November. . ." It hurt to talk. What was she saying? Her code—ID—whatever. "This is. . .November 5-6-2 Tango Foxtrot. . . ." She panted against the exertion.

Nothing. Not static. Not anything. . .why wasn't it working?

She slumped back. . .sideways, bracing herself as she remembered what happened. The conversation with Roger

Bender. His warnings that Logan had been badly injured, that Curt wanted her to fly up to retrieve him. That she had to get him off the mountain or he'd die. Of what happened.

Wet and hot, her thigh felt...weird. *What...?* She peered down and grimaced. Her breakfast came hurtling back up. She hurled to the right, all over the passenger seat that now lay crumpled and littered with glass.

Must move. Get out. She released her harness and tried to extract herself without falling. Gravity exerted its force. Her leg slipped. Fire lit through her muscles. And shoulder. She couldn't give in to it. Had to get out. Carefully, she lowered herself.

Fire lit down her leg. And shoulder.

Her other arm collapsed.

She dropped. Pitched forward. Slid toward the back of the Otter.

She hit her head. So hard her teeth clamped. Cold pain shocked her body. Sent her reeling back into blackness.

Chapter 13

Wind ripped at Logan. The driving snow taunted him. Dared him to continue the rescue mission. Hoodie up, mouth and nose covered, he used the poles to probe for crevasses and keep moving forward. The weather hadn't devolved into a storm, but the snow had proven relentless, as if Denali were as angry as Logan that Deline had crashed. TFAT couldn't do flyovers because a lenticular cloud had formed around the peak, making it impossible to see. The only option was to climb it. Find her.

Roped up with Josh and the patrol volunteers, he skied in the direction her plane would have most likely gone, judging from the known facts. Karon said climbers on Ruth's Glacier saw an Otter's wing get sheared off as it glided northeast until it vanished over the amphitheater and into a cloud. That meant, if his guess was right—and he hoped it wasn't—the normal flight path would take her right around to the Wickersham Wall.

Which apparently matched the last communication the control tower had with Deline, who'd mentioned the Great Gorge. Freezing tundra. Granite walls. The mental image of her plane collapsing accordion-style against those sheer reliefs propelled him onward. A mile or so north of Camp 3, they were at the Edge of the World. His breath caught every time he saw it, but right now—Deline was all he cared about.

They made it past Washburn's Thumb, watching the

terrain, watching the distance. *God, help me find her. Let her be alive. Please.*

Another forty minutes, they crested and started along a ridge. Something glinted to his right. Logan squinted. Heart in his throat, he spotted a hint of—

"There!" Josh shouted. "Down on the glacier!"

Red. The tail of the plane peeked out from behind a jagged upshot of granite. The front end tucked behind it, as if to shield Logan from the awful truth. Was the plane compacted or was there room back there for it to rest? What a miracle. If she'd hit a few feet to the left, it'd be like picking up LEGO pieces from a white carpet. As they traversed the incline, roped up and picketing as they went, Logan radioed to the ranger station that they'd located her plane.

"It's upside down. Missing a wing. Can't tell anything else. Partially hidden." Breathing hurt. The thought of finding her injured sucked the life from him. "Approaching it now."

"Zack just got clearance to lift off. He's en route to your coordinates."

"Good. Knox out." Logan stowed the phone. Within five hundred feet, his gut churned as the snow crunched beneath his crampons. Pieces of the plane littered the flat surface of the glacier. What he thought merely the glittering snow was, in fact, glass from the Otter.

Locked on the plane, Logan had to force himself to act with caution and wisdom. Probing for crevasses—*especially* on a glacier—with each tromp forward. Though it only took minutes, it felt like hours. He hurried along. As he closed in, he realized the plane had cartwheeled into its present position. How it hadn't broken up was beyond him. But he was grateful. Because it gave Deline a shot at surviving.

Once clear of the frozen glacier, he unhooked from Josh and Dr. Malcolm and climbed the jagged rock and peered over it. The right wing had hooked on rock. "Deline!" He peeked into the cabin.

Pilot's seat sat empty.

"She's not there."

"Look around," Dr. Malcolm shouted. "She might've been thrown."

Then Logan noticed the blood. On the seat. On the hull. Gulping panic, he pulled himself up on rock, leaned against the hull, and looked at the—"Here! She's here. Help me."

On his knees, he pried the door open and had to crawl into the tail of the Otter. Glass and debris littered the space. "Deline," he said, his voice firm but quieter.

Blood streaked across her forehead, nose, and lip. Her head sat an awkward angle. Was she even breathing? "Deline!" Logan pressed two fingers against her carotid. Barely beating. "Give me a neck brace," he shouted.

On one knee and with the other stretched awkwardly over her because of the lack of room and the position of her body, Logan checked for breathing. "Deline, c'mon. Deline. Talk to me."

Her eyebrows rippled in a half frown. A small moan. As if trying to wake from a bad dream.

A noise behind him alerted him to Dr. Malcolm's insertion into the plane. An inflatable brace appeared over his shoulder. "Breathing?" Dr. Malcolm asked.

"Shallow." Logan slid the neck brace on and inflated it. Touched her face as he scooted aside so the medical professional could do his work. "Deline. Deline, I need you to wake up." He held the sides of Deline's face to make sure her neck didn't shift as the doc began assessing her.

"Her leg's broken. Possibly her arm." Experienced hands searched her abdomen.

Deline moaned. Then whimpered.

"Deline, you there? Deline!" Logan angled, half-bent over another seat, so he could see her face. "Deline, let me see those beautiful eyes."

Her eyelashes fluttered.

"That's right. Fight your way out."

Malcolm probed her side.

Deline arched her back with a yelp. Then slumped down.

"Deline. Deline, you okay?"

A tear slipped free from her closed eyelid.

⁊

"Hey," came a warm, calming voice. Logan's. She could feel his hand wrapped around hers as he lifted it.

A pinch plucked the top of her hand.

She hissed, but that pinprick—an IV?—was the baby of the pains ravaging her body. "Hurts," she gritted out. "Hurts." Hot tears streaked across her cheeks.

"I know, but you're alive. That's all that matters."

Deline forced her way past the black wall of pain that competed against Wickersham Wall. She'd struggled with the plane to avoid that monster.

Monster.

Bender.

Her eyes shot open. She stared into eyes the color of the sky. "Bender."

Logan frowned. "Shh, relax."

"He told me you were up here," she managed, ignoring the fire licking through her side. "Told me you were dying." A flood of tears washed her face.

"I'm here. I'm fine—now that I know you're alive." The worry gouged into his face told her the story. He'd never been in danger. Bender wanted her out here.

No. Not out here.

Out of the way.

"He tried to kill me." She wrinkled up her nose and fought the sobs that were pulling against whatever agony took over her abdomen.

Logan squatted closer, touching her face. "Deline, take it easy. It's okay. You're okay. I'm here. I won't let anything happen."

Brave words. So sweet.

A bolt of fire and then ice stabbed through her. She howled.

"Sorry," an older man with dark skin—Dr. Malcolm— eased into view. "I had to stabilize your leg."

She looked down and saw the makeshift splint.

"We need to get you out of here," the doctor said with an expression of sorrow. "But there's not enough room to bring a board in here."

She understood and gave a nod. She'd have to get herself out before they could secure her.

"I'll help you," Logan said. "We need to turn you, so I can support your weight as you exit."

Together, they made the position switch. Sweat beaded on her brow and nausea cinched her stomach at the pain. The incredible pain. As they worked their way out of the plane, down, and into the snow, her hearing hollowed.

Logan hooked his arms under hers and drew her out. White-hot fire erupted through her torso. *I'm going to pass out.* Her vision grayed as she vaguely became aware of Logan lifting her into his arms.

Her head lobbed.

Seconds later, the suffocating constriction in her abdomen and pounding in her head eased. Cold—terrible cold— snapped through her body. "I'm dying."

A laugh massaged her worry. "Not if I can help it."

Opening her eyes, a blinding sheet of white stabbed her

corneas. She flinched. Then felt something slide along her temples. When she looked again, the world was. . .less bright.

And Logan didn't have sunglasses anymore. He knelt beside her, gently adjusted a belt that held her neck and head in place. Ah, that explained the cold—lying on the ground, being strapped to a board.

"Chopper!"

"I'm a pilot," she mumbled.

"Not this time," Logan said with a smile.

She caught his hand with her uninjured arm.

Wind gusted and whipped the loose snow into a powdered frenzy.

Logan's gaze flickered to hers.

She wanted the gap bridged. She wanted to apologize for panicking when he'd kissed her. "The thought. . .of life without you. . ."

The left side of his mouth quirked. "Don't say something you'll regret later."

"Let's go!" the doctor shouted.

The litter lifted into the air and within a few minutes, she was secured to the chopper and flying thousands of miles over the mountain that nearly claimed her soul.

Chapter 14

I have a broken rib, not a broken head."

"One might think you had both," her father groused. "What were you thinking, flying up there without a flight plan, without—"

"Mr. Tsosie, she followed protocol. The tower communicated with her and gave her clearance. There was a lot of miscommunication that went into this—"

"You going to sit there and tell me Bender *miscommunicated* his attempt to kill my daughter?"

Sheriff Wellesley tipped his head down. "No, sir. Bender is under arrest and charges are pending. We've got evidence that places him at the scene of the fire that burned down your home, and"—his gaze cut to Deline, who sat on the sofa, her leg elevated with pillows—"we've learned from the mechanic that the oil line on your Otter had been tampered with from the first time you had to make that emergency landing. There's video footage that shows Bender out there."

"What about this time?"

"The Chinook is scheduled to retrieve your plane tomorrow. We'll do a full investigation on the plane once it's back on level ground."

"I just don't understand why he'd do this. It's insane."

"Well, he had a mountain of bills and debts he had to pay off. When he lost his last job and opened up his air taxi business, every last dime went into the air taxi. He was losing thousands every month and couldn't keep up. With you out of the picture, I reckon he thought he could save his financial future."

The sheriff stood and waved the papers. "Thanks for your time, Deline. If I need or hear anything, I'll let you know."

"Thank you." Pushing off the cushions, she grimaced.

"Don't get up. I'll see myself out."

Deline watched out the door, strained to see up and down the street.

"He's not coming," her father muttered. "Told you he has to finish out his month at High Camp. There's no rescue for a ranger."

"There's always a rescue." Just not for a broken heart. She slumped back into the cushions.

"Why you so worried about this boy now anyway? You didn't seem to care none when he was hovering over you and paying you all that mind."

"I'm not worried about Logan." *I miss him.* She wanted to talk to him.

Antsy from a week on the couch, she pushed herself up. Wobbled, then righted herself.

"What're you doing?"

"Going to cook myself some sourdough pancakes."

"That's what you always make when you're worried."

Deline groaned as she moved into Jolie's kitchen. With the wedding this weekend, Jolie had opted to stay with her family in Anchorage. David was out there, too, doing last-minute preps. Which gave Deline and her dad time to find a new home. "Oh, hey. I heard the McClellans are selling their home."

"Too close to the highway."

Highway—in a town this small, to call it a highway was crazy.

Deline grunted. He'd found something wrong with just

about every place she'd suggested. "We have to find someplace, Daddy." She drew the fry pan from beneath the cabinet, set it on the Viking stove, then dug through the drawer for a spatula and fork. Once she had those, she opened the pantry door and rifled through to find the ingredients, careful not to aggravate her injuries.

"I like Logan's place," her daddy announced. "Think he'd sell it to us?"

"Logan likes his house just fine. I'm sure he isn't interested in selling it to us." Armed with a box and some spices, she closed the door with her toe. "Besides, I think he's forgotten about me." She turned.

And found herself staring into blue eyes. "Logan," she breathed.

"Is this part of your 'life without me' plan?"

Afraid she'd drop the contents in her arms, she set them down. Her insides quivered as she felt his gaze on her. Intense gaze. This wasn't just a social call. She braved a glance.

Hand on the granite island, Logan leaned in. "I need to know, Deline."

She brushed the curls from her face and folded her arms, hiding a cringe at the pain.

Logan tugged her closer. "Do you want life without me?"

Whistling, her dad sauntered out of the living room and into the hall. She couldn't resist the smile at his "told you so" posture as he vanished into the back room.

Logan's hand traced her cheek. "Finding you on that mountain, unconscious—" He bit off his sentence.

She let the bravado drain out and looked up at him. "I've never needed anyone, Logan." With a bob of her head she indicated her father in the other room. "I've taken care of him and Enli since I can remember, even though I was the youngest and Mama was around—until, well, you know."

Defeat deflated Logan.

"But when Roger told me you were dying, that they needed someone to fly you out—" She gulped the memory back. "I realized I needed you more than I ever realized."

His expression shifted to one of surprise, then joy.

"When I woke up in the Otter with you there, seeing you. . .when I thought I'd never see you again. . ." Tears threatened. "Stupid tears." She stomped her foot, cringing as tingles ran up her casted leg. "I think. . .I think hope is taking flight." She placed her hands on his abdomen. "I'm not good at this stuff, so just—as I tried and failed to say that night at the lake—give me room *to adjust*."

"I'll give you the rest of my life."

"Easy there, cowboy. That's a little fast, don't you think?" She smiled at him. "Maybe a few more flights up with me?"

He flinched. "If I have to."

"What. . .don't you like flying with me?"

"I *love* doing anything with you."

"But?"

He looked like a sheepish schoolboy. "I *hate* flying."

Stunned, she stared at him. Wanted to laugh. But. . . couldn't. "Then, why. . .?"

Logan eased in closer, his hand around the back of her neck as he guided her into his arms. "Deline, this whole thing with you—for me, it's *love* taking flight."

Ronie Kendig grew up an Army brat, married a veteran, and they now have four children and a golden retriever. She has a BS in psychology, speaks to various groups, volunteers with the American Christian Fiction Writers (ACFW), and mentors new writers.

DENALI
GUARDIANS

by Kimberley Woodhouse

Dedication

To the Talkeetna Rangers. For everything you do, everyone you rescue, and all the crazy authors you put up with on a day-to-day basis (well, okay, so at least *this* crazy author). You're all amazing.

Missy—this one's for you.

A Note from the Author

What a joy it has been to share this journey with you all. I'd like to give a big shout-out to my friend Ronie Kendig. She's brilliant, and I love her dearly. We've had a blast with these stories and characters, and we hope you've enjoyed a taste of Alaska, mountaineering, and the incredible rangers.

More than anything, I hope you can walk away with a sense that God is with you at all times and His joy is *always* there for the taking.

Never let go.

In His Abundant JOY,
Kimberley Woodhouse
http://kimberleywoodhouse.com

Chapter 1

Mountaineering ranger Josh Richards grabbed his gear off the helicopter and headed back to the station. This last thirty-day stint on upper mountain rotation had kicked him in the rear. Twenty-seven rescues, two plane crashes, and three acute cases of HACE. Must've been a record. With over twelve hundred people climbing Denali during the short summer season this year, it shouldn't surprise him. But his body protested, clearly saying it would have liked some warning.

A whiff of unsavory odor rose up to meet him. Ugh. He stank. Needed a long, hot shower, a haircut, and a good shave. And then sleep. Real sleep in a real bed.

Kyle greeted him at the door. "Good to have you back, bud."

Josh nodded. "Feels good to be back. I'm glad I don't have to look at the side of that mountain again for a while. I'm worn out. Shredded."

Zack joined them. "Yeah, this season's been a mess. Just goes to show that even the most experienced climbers aren't prepared for everything."

"I'm glad the official climbing season is *over*." Josh shook his head. "Can I just say how much I'm looking forward to winter?"

Kyle smacked him on the shoulder. "You and me both."

The rangers laughed together.

A smile crinkled Zack's eyes. "You definitely earned your position, Josh. Good to have you with us." He started to walk away, then turned. "Hey, Karon will kill me if I don't ask if you brought her book back."

Josh dropped his duffel. Pulled out a gallon Ziploc with two books inside. "Tell her thanks, here's the one from David as well. She's a lifesaver."

"That's my girl. She's becoming the mobile library for the camps." Zack grinned from ear to ear and left the station.

"You know every time I see him now, he can't seem to wipe the smile off his face." Josh laughed.

"Yep." Kyle walked with him to the conference room.

"And when I first met him, I thought he was the most arrogant grouch I'd ever encountered."

Kyle nodded. "That's because he let go of the rope, before Karon entered the picture."

"Let go of the rope?"

Kyle smacked his shoulder. "That's a story Zack will have to tell you sometime. It's a good one. . . ."

Josh's attention diverted. Deanna Smith walked by talking on the radio. Fellow ranger and heartbeat of the station. She kept everything and everyone moving. He couldn't take his eyes off her. Wait. Kyle was still talking. Was he supposed to respond? He couldn't remember. "Uh-huh."

"Josh?"

"Uh-huh."

"Josh!"

Oops. "What?" His gaze remained on Deanna as she rounded the corner.

Laughter answered him. "You didn't hear a word I said, did you?"

Huh? Oh right. He panned back to Kyle. "Uh, no. Sorry."

"And another one bites the dust." The other ranger—his senior—mumbled and patted him on the back again. "Turn in your paperwork, then do us all a favor and get some sleep."

Josh watched him walk away. He'd better focus. He had a job to do.

After he found all his paperwork and took care of his equipment, Josh ran a hand through his scruffy hair and headed toward Deanna's desk.

The highlight of any day, she'd smile at him and talk to him as though they were best friends. But that was her way. She made everyone feel special, every day. But just once, he wanted it to be different. He wanted to be the one. Would she ever turn that smile his way? For him alone?

He shook his head. *Focus, man!*

When he found her, Deanna had her head bent over her desk. Long, auburn hair pulled back with a simple elastic band. She never wore any makeup—didn't need any, in his opinion—and he'd never seen her in anything other than the green ranger uniform. But she was beautiful.

The same question had plagued him for months: Why did she keep everyone at a distance? Everyone loved her. But it was like she didn't want any attention drawn to herself. Ever. But she certainly drew *his* attention.

Get a grip, Richards. He shook his head. He was acting like a hormonal teenager. If he didn't watch it, he'd start drooling all over her desk. Not a good look for a twenty-six-year-old.

Deanna's head popped up, those green eyes landing square on him. She put a hand to her chest. "Oh! Sorry, Josh. I didn't know you were standing there."

"Didn't want to interrupt your train of thought."

"You're never interrupting." She smiled. "What do you have for me?"

"Paperwork." He grimaced. "Your favorite." Hopefully his sarcasm wasn't over the top.

Deanna's light laughter washed over him as she took the file folder. "Oh joy. Well, someone's gotta do it." She flipped through the papers. "Bet you're glad to be done with your first full season."

Small talk. He could do that. "Yeah, I am. Looking forward to the work around here this winter."

She nodded. "Just wait until we need your help with a winter rescue. Those are always fun."

"And...cold...I bet." Couldn't he come up with anything more clever to say? He needed to quit now before he made a bigger fool of himself. Walk away. Out the door, into his Jeep. He could do that. Get some sleep and maybe smack his head against the wall a few times.

But Deanna had the courtesy to laugh. "Yeah, just a little." Then she pointed a finger in his direction. "But don't get your hopes up that things will be easy over the winter—there's always a million things to be done."

"Okay." Escape. Run away. Before he stuck his foot in his mouth and couldn't remove it. "Well...I better get cleaned up." He took a few steps backward and waved. "Thanks...for taking my paperwork." *Good one, Richards.* He wanted to roll his eyes at himself. What an idiot.

Those green eyes looked up at him. "You're welcome. See you soon."

"Yeah, see ya." The door couldn't swallow him up fast enough. Did he really just thank her for taking his paperwork? He needed more than sleep. Maybe he could get a brain transplant before he saw her again.

❧

Deanna watched Josh walk away. For the first time in fifteen years, she found herself interested in a guy. At the age of twelve, Deanna made a vow to never allow herself to be attracted to or fall in love with a man. Her sister's stalker and murderer could take the credit for that.

Now at the ripe old age of twenty-seven, she couldn't keep that vow. At least the attraction part. She wasn't in love. Yet. But her heart had other ideas. Josh Richards pulled her in like a magnet.

She'd watched him with the other rangers. Eager to learn, not overly cocky, though he knew his stuff. Whenever he came around her, he stumbled over his words. She'd never say it aloud, but his nervousness endeared him to her heart. Josh never had trouble speaking to anyone else. Which told her one thing—he liked her. And for some strange and wonderful reason, she wanted him to.

But it could never be. She'd hold the attraction deep in her heart and treasure all the memories she could make with the handsome ranger. And that would be the end of it. No attachments. She nodded to emphasize her point.

For seven years, she'd worked at the Talkeetna Ranger Station. Everyone knew who she was. And yet no one knew who she *really* was.

Depression clawed its way up and threatened to take over. How she longed for a real life. A loving relationship. Friends she could confide in.

But that was just a dream. One that could never be.

John, the head ranger, dropped by her desk. "Hey, Deanna, thanks for all your work on that last project. Your spreadsheet was incredibly helpful. The guys were able to see everything plain as day. I know that took a lot of extra work."

"You're welcome." She gave John her classic I'm-always-happy-to-do-whatever-needs-to-be-done smile.

"You're a trouper. I don't know why you enjoy paperwork so much, but the other rangers appreciate it." John tapped her desk and walked away.

Most of the others would be gone soon. She'd lock up the building and head to her small two-bedroom house, shut the blinds, bolt the door, and eat her dinner. Alone.

When Missy waved good-bye, Deanna sat down at her desk, her thoughts returning to Josh. Memories of her past tumbled in. What would he think if he knew the truth?

She'd arrived in the small Alaska town a fresh graduate from college. Young and eager to learn, she knew how to avoid people prying too much into her history. From their perspective, she was just getting started in her life anyway, right? Everyone thought she was an orphan, loved Alaska and mountaineering. They were correct, in that much at least.

The truth—the real truth, buried under layers of lies and years—was horrific. After her sister's murder, her parents were stalked by the murderer. During her junior high years, the most insecure time in her life, they changed her last name and sent Deanna away to boarding school in an attempt to hide her from the madman. For a year her parents stayed on the run. The FBI told her it was for her safety. But that wasn't how it felt to a young girl about to become a teen.

In reality, her parents had been prey. They'd been hunted. Until one day, her father couldn't take the hiding or running anymore. He drove their car off the highway into a ravine. With himself and her mother inside.

Deanna had been taken into protective custody and placed with an unfeeling police couple to hide her true identity. Her teen years were filled with schooling, but love and laughter weren't part of the equation. The officers kept their emotional distance.

The killer had never been caught. But every once in a while, the FBI received a note or tip.

And so she'd hidden all these years. From everyone, even God. Never allowing anyone to penetrate her walls.

Every few months her mind took this path and wounded her heart anew. The memories were so vivid, the pain still resh. The childhood she could never get back.

She slumped over her workspace as the grief tore through her yet again. A few tears escaped her own prescribed barrier and dropped onto the file folder on her desk.

Josh's file.

Loneliness ripped her protective walls to shreds. In the silence of the moment, her heart ached for what could never be.

Chapter 2

Snow was coming. Deanna could feel it in the air.

A slow smile stretched across her face as sh
finished her five-mile walk around town and the flake
began to fly. The guys would hate her for sure.

It took a good three-hour pity party to put herself t
rights last night, but her confidence and shield were back i
place. She'd done this a long time. Her will was strong.

By the time she reached her house, a half inch stuck t
the ground. Oh, she was good.

An hour later, Deanna walked into the ranger station'
conference room and poured herself a cup of coffee. "Morning
guys!"

"Morning, Dee." Zack handed her a fax. "Looks like th
reports are correct, termination dust in Anchorage for thre
days. And an inch on the ground here already. You know wha
that means."

"It *means* I win the pool again, doesn't it?" She teased an
held out her palm to the other rangers at the table. "Pay up.'

Dollar bills were smacked into the middle of the table
and her palm. "How do you do that?" Logan gave her hi
dollar.

She grinned. "I smell it."

"Well, your uncanny ability has won the past four years.
David shook his head. "I'm beginning to think I've lost m
touch."

David Whiteeagle had been the long-standing winner o

the rangers' pool before Deanna arrived. The massive guy was intimidating, but once you got to know him, he was more of a ginormous teddy bear.

Deanna gave him a gentle pat on the arm. "It's okay, David. I'm sure Jolie still loves you."

The guys guffawed around the table.

Missy giggled. "Seriously, girl, I don't know how you do it. You name a date. The guys in Anchorage confirm the termination dust, and then it snows here. Every time."

"Yeah, and we all thought we had a chance this year, since you picked an early date." Kyle stuck out his bottom lip. "It's not fair."

"You just don't like being beat." Deanna laughed along. "But I'm sorry—it's time to pay up. And I don't just mean your dollar bills. You know what you have to do, boys."

Josh jogged into the room, out of breath. "Sorry, guys. I, uh, forgot to set my alarm."

John welcomed him. "No problem, you didn't have to be here today anyway. But you just missed Deanna winning the pool."

"Stinking termination dust." Zack held up the fax. "Had to go and prove her right. Again."

"Wait a sec," Josh piped up. "What's termination dust?"

Laughter rounded the table again. Deanna smiled, enjoying the camaraderie of the station.

"Hey, take pity on the guy, would ya?" Zack wrapped an arm around Josh's shoulders. "He's from the lower forty-eight."

More laughter. Deanna watched Josh from across the room. She took a slow sip of her coffee. He took the banter all in stride.

Logan pulled a tattered book off one of the shelves. "We save this book for all the non-Alaskans who come up here." He showed the spine to Josh. "*The Dictionary of Alaskan English* by Russell Tabbert." Logan cleared his voice and turned pages. " 'Termination dust—an Anchorage area term for the end-of-summer snows that fall on the surrounding mountains and hills, signaling that the traditional construction season is about over and that workers will be terminated soon.'

"And Deanna here bases her guess for our first real—meaning it sticks to the ground—snowfall on their termination dust."

Josh met her eyes. "Ah, so the lady has won." With people around, he always seemed to have more confidence to talk to her. She found it charming. Like everything else about him.

She loved the admiration shining in his eyes. If only she could do something about it. Deanna cleared her throat.

"Again." The cheer came from Missy. "And she deserves it because she puts up with all of us." Her friend winked at her.

Logan tossed the book in front of Josh. "Here ya go. This might help you out."

More laughter.

Josh nodded and flipped through the pages, receiving all the slaps on the back with a smile.

Deanna couldn't help it, her eyes went back to Josh's only to find his steady gaze. "Well"—she attempted to break the connection—"it just goes to show that none of you should mess with me. I mean business." She pointed a finger at each one of them but couldn't keep a straight face.

Balls of paper, napkins, and coffee straws flew across the table.

John stood at the head of the table. "All right, you guys have had your fun. You can bow to her and kiss her feet later. And anything else you might owe her for winning—I'm sure chocolate is involved somehow." He winked at her. "But right now, it's back to business. There's a lot of debriefing that needs to be done. We've had a doozy of a season."

❧

Josh leaned back in his chair and threw the Nerf basketball at the hoop on the door. It missed and bounced onto David's desk. "Sorry, man."

"I *would* say, just go talk to her. But this is Deanna we're talking about." His fellow ranger turned pages in the new mountaineering guide they were proofreading.

"What do you mean?" Josh tossed the Nerf again. Missed. "Deanna's like the sweetest person around."

"Nobody's saying she's not, dude. But she's been here a long time, and there's little to nothing any of us know about her." Another page turned.

That seemed odd. Deanna's bubbly personality made everyone feel welcome. She was the encourager, the go-getter, the glue that held them all together. And her people skills far exceeded his. "I don't get it."

"And you probably never will. It's like an unwritten rule around here. Nobody can get too close." David shrugged. "I'm not trying to discourage you, but lots of guys have tried and failed. And those of us around here who know her, or just want to know her better as a friend, have tried and failed as well. Don't get me wrong. We all love Deanna. But there's a wall—no, make that a force field—around that woman that I don't think anyone can penetrate."

Josh shot the ball again. This time it went in. What if he was the one to make it past her defenses? Or maybe David was right and he was just trying to save him some heartache. One thing he'd learned working with everyone here these past six months—they stuck together. They encouraged each other. Even when they were teasing, they were looking out for the best interests of their fellow rangers.

This was the first time he'd heard one of the guys

discourage another about a relationship. Had he not been here long enough to earn their trust? What was it about Deanna? Or was it him?

The auburn-haired ranger made him feel things he'd never felt before. Could she be the one for him?

If only he could convince Deanna.

Chapter 3

Snow boots laced up, Deanna headed out the door to brave the wind and snow. A simple walk to the post office would calm her crazy thoughts, but maybe it wasn't the brightest idea. Ever since the snow had started two days ago, it hadn't stopped.

All the rangers razzed her. It was *obviously* her fault the snow came so early. At the moment, she wasn't too happy with her prediction, but snow was always good. At least in her point of view. It meant the end of tourist season. Less people.

And less people meant less chance of a stranger entering the area without her knowing.

The habits she'd developed over the years had protected her. They'd been her constant companion.

Stomping her feet outside the door, she turned the knob and entered. Deanna waved at Mrs. Malcolm behind the counter and headed for her P.O. box. She pulled off her gloves and inserted the key.

The stack was larger than she'd expected. Bill, bill, bill, bill, advertisement, and at the bottom, a handwritten letter. She turned it over. Hmm. Postmarked from Fairbanks. Who did she know in Fairbanks that would have her box number? A moment of fear passed over her. She shook it off.

Her curiosity won out and she opened the letter on her way out the door. Nothing could have prepared her for what she read.

The words struck at the secret places inside. Tears burned

her eyes. Her heart caught in her throat. No. No! This couldn't be happening.

Fear crept in. She pulled her sunglasses down from the perch atop her head and forced her eyes to search every door, every nook, every alley around her.

The first instinct was to flee. Her feet started running before she even realized she needed to get home. Run as fast and far as she could.

The house came into view. She ran around the structure and checked all the windows and doors from the outside. Checked the garage. She intentionally never left anything outside that could hide someone. No trash cans. No shrubs. No storage containers.

When she thought it was safe, she unlocked the front door and put a cautious step forward. Nothing seemed amiss. Everything was just as she'd left it. Dropping the mail onto the coffee table, she scanned the room. She picked up the baseball bat she kept by the door with her umbrella. Raised it with both hands. *Calm down*. If she gave herself a heart attack, he'd win. And she couldn't allow that to happen.

The safe was upstairs. Deanna closed her eyes and counted slowly to catch her breath and climbed the stairs. Checked each of the rooms. She unlocked the closet and approached the safe. After entering the combination, the door popped open and she pulled out the satellite phone. Turning it on, she prayed for God's peace. For safety. Then she punched in the number and codes she had memorized.

"Hello."

"He found me," she croaked, her emotions spilling out. "I've been compromised."

"Understood. Stay calm. Wait for instructions. I'll call back in less than fifteen."

The phone slipped out of her hand and she crumpled to the floor.

When every tear was spent, Deanna uncurled her limbs and wiped at her face.

A new realization hit her in the gut. This wasn't her. This fear. This frail human being. She'd allowed him to take control, and that wasn't acceptable.

On wobbly legs, she rose to her feet, picked up the phone, and headed back downstairs.

The letter lay on the table where she'd thrown the mail after locking the door. With a steadying breath, she straightened her shoulders and walked over to it.

Her fingers shook as she reached for it.

Little Girl,
You thought you could run.
But I've found you.
There's nowhere to hide.
Surprise.

The note sickened her. She jutted her chin out, refusing to give him any power over her. She could do this. Closing her eyes, she prayed again. *Lord, You're the only One who really knows what's going on. I need help. I need protection. Please, God. Don't let him get to me.*

Minutes felt like hours as Deanna waited. Busyness didn't help. Nothing helped but prayer. In the dark, she drank her third hot chocolate, trying to ward off the chill invading her body. She watched every shadow and light as cars and people passed her window. She prayed some more. As much as she'd made herself not call this place *home*, she'd been lying to herself. It was home. She was comfortable here. Had felt safe up until now.

She clutched the phone to her chest. Waiting stunk. What would she do? Where could she go? How would she say good-bye? Again.

Josh's face flooded her mind. Tears streamed down her cheeks for the second time that evening. The sobs overtook her. She'd always be alone. For the rest of her life.

The beep jolted her. A call came in. She sucked in a breath and clicked TALK. "Hello?"

"We've got an agent on the way to you now. Stay put. We've got a plan."

"Should I pack?"

"That remains to be seen."

"How long?"

"Three hours at most. Use the passwords. Don't let anyone in without them."

The beep on the line confirmed the call had ended.

Three hours. Seemed like an eternity.

❧

Watching her windows from across the street made him antsy. After all these years, she was still alive. The thought excited him.

She was smarter than he'd anticipated. Her job kept her surrounded by people. Stayed hidden for a long time. But here, in this small town, he'd found her. Finally.

The FBI thought they had him, but it had been far too easy setting someone else up to take the fall.

A chuckle rippled through him as he took a long drag on the cigar. Revenge would be sweet.

Even after fifteen years.

❧

Josh didn't know what kept him up so late. He was bone tired. But the thought nagged him that something wasn't right. His mom would tell him to pray when he felt these proddings. Maybe he should. Faith was strong in him, but he had a hard time showing any outward evidence of it. Maybe it had been his time in the Army, or just the simple fact that his dad disliked his mom and her "religion."

He folded his hands behind his head and looked to the ceiling. *God, I know You're listening and I haven't been the best talker, but I feel this urgency in my heart. You're the only One who can help in a time like this. You know what's going on. I don't even know who I'm praying for, but You do.*

A simple peace flowed through him then, but the urgency stayed. With sleep miles away, he decided to go for a late run. Maybe the brisk air would clear his head and help him sleep.

The road disappeared beneath his sturdy shoes. Long strides worked out the stress and worry in his muscles. He probably just needed to decompress. The upper mountain rotation was a tough one, and add to that David's words about Deanna. No wonder he was feeling uneasy.

Josh turned a corner toward the station. Deanna only lived a few blocks away. Maybe he would see if there were any lights on.

Who was he kidding? That wasn't even remotely appropriate. His brain must be malfunctioning. But as he passed the station, he turned toward her home. She lived on the corner. There. He could see the house. But there weren't any lights on. Bummer.

Maybe he'd better just head home. This was a bad idea.

As Josh turned to head back, a black car raced up the street. No lights. Dark windows.

Who would drive at night with their lights off? And that fast in this little bitty town?

Josh ducked behind a tree one house over. The black car stopped in front of Deanna's! The engine died, door opened, and a man climbed out. He shut the door without a noise, glanced around him, and walked to Deanna's house.

Who was that guy? And what did he want with her?

On the other side of the street, Josh heard rustling. Someone else was moving in the opposite direction. The man had been watching Deanna's house? He started running toward the woods.

What was going on?

Josh felt as if he was in a spy movie. Except he wasn't supposed to be here. He had no idea what to do next. He crept toward Deanna's front door, keeping a close eye on the guy who stood on her stoop. The man barely tapped on the wood.

Snow muffled Josh's steps until one shoe slipped and he grabbed hold of a tree branch.

Before he could right himself, Josh heard Deanna scream and he was staring into the unmistakable barrel of a Glock .45 pistol.

Chapter 4

Her heart wouldn't stop racing. Thank God it was Josh out there. But what *was* Josh doing out there? Deanna looked to the agent for help.

"Get inside. Bolt the door."

"But I know him. I work with him. He's not the stalker."

"You sure?" His gun still trained on Josh.

"Yeah. I'm sure."

"Get inside. Let me talk to him." The guy was serious. Didn't flinch.

"Um, Agent..." Deanna said. "I'm sorry. I don't even know who you are, but you should probably bring him inside before the neighbors start talking."

He lowered the gun. "Make it fast." The guy looked to Josh. Signaled for him to come to the door.

Josh approached with his hands in the air.

"Put your hands out in front of you so I can see them," Agent-man whispered. "Okay, now put them behind your back."

Josh's eyes widened as he was frisked at Deanna's front door. With a shove from behind, he stood in Deanna's living room. He looked to her. His usual awkwardness replaced by a steely look in his eyes. "Wanna explain what's going on here?"

"I'll ask the questions." The man in black stood tall.

Deanna held up her hands. "Please, stop." Every part of her shook. "Josh, what are you doing here?"

His eyes softened just a little. "I was jogging, when I saw

this black car drive up with no lights. And then it stopped at your house and the guy went to your door." He stepped closer. "I got concerned."

For a brief second, she wished she could spill her guts. Tell him everything. But the agent spoke instead.

"She's all right." The agent held out his badge. "I'm with the FBI. Everything's fine. You can go—"

"So the other guy across the street was with you, too?" Josh looked from the agent to Deanna.

Deanna's heart sank. The trembling started in her feet and worked its way up. No. It couldn't be.

"What other guy?" The agent went to the window and peered through the blinds.

"A man. Watching the house. He walked a few steps then ran away when you went to the door." Josh scratched his forehead and took off his cap. He turned to Deanna. "What's going on? Are you okay?" He stepped closer.

Deanna fell into the chair behind her. Her legs would no longer hold her up. Tears sprang to her eyes. She could've sworn she'd spent them all earlier. How could this be happening?

The agent turned to them and holstered his weapon. "I'm Agent Williams. I need to know everything you saw. Can you describe the other man?"

Josh shook his head. "I'm sorry. Too dark, and he was covered with dark clothing and a hat. But if I saw him again, I could recognize him by the way he walked. Is Deanna in danger?"

"I can't answer that at the moment." Williams shot her a look.

If she could just stop this trembling, she might be able to think. How could she explain this? If she disappeared now, what would Josh do? Would he search for her? What would everyone at the station think?

She placed her head in her hands. This *couldn't* be happening.

But it was.

Josh's sneakers appeared by her feet. He squatted down in front of her and lifted her chin. "Deanna, talk to me. How can I help?"

She shook her head. No one could help. This nightmare would never end. Not until the murderer was gone or he got to her first.

Agent Williams approached. "I didn't catch your friend's name."

Josh stuck out a hand. "Josh Richards. Ranger Josh Richards."

"Ranger Richards, could you go outside for a few minutes? Keep an eye on things? I need to make sure that guy doesn't return, and Miss Smith and I need to chat."

Josh looked to her, stared into her eyes. Then he nodded and walked to the door. "I'll be just outside if you need me, Deanna." Doubt clouded his eyes as he left.

What had she done? Where had she slipped up? There was no way out, was there?

Agent Williams sat on the couch opposite her. "Deanna, we need to talk. I knew your father and have worked in the background on this case for a long time. I asked specifically to be given your detail. But let me be blunt. This guy has taunted us far too long. He's a professional assassin. The only reason he's after you is because it would be a failure on his card, and the profiler says that's completely unacceptable to him. The director thinks the best plan of action is to move you to a safe location and bring in a decoy. If we can bait this guy, we think we can catch him."

Her eyebrows shot up. "There's no way you can bring in a decoy in this little town. I've lived here seven years. Even if I have kept them all at arm's length, they would know Especially everyone at the station."

"You're in serious danger—you need to reconsider."

She shook her head. "No. Someone would tip him off unintentionally. Even though *he* hasn't seen me in a long time—these people here know me. Have lived around me."

Williams sighed. "Can I see the note?"

Deanna handed him the letter.

It only took a few seconds to read. He shook his head "And now he's here. At least, I'm assuming that's whoever your ranger friend spotted."

"I can't go on like this. I thought I could. But this hurts too much. I love this town. I love these people." The tremors returned. "I don't think I can take it."

The agent stood and moved closer to her. "It's understandable you feel that way, you've dealt with this for a long time. But your father was a good man and you've got the same tenacity as him. It's time to bring justice to so many senseless deaths." He walked back to the window. "Maybe there's another way."

"What?" She was afraid of his answer.

"I'd have to make a call. But maybe we can get the help of some of your ranger friends. Are they trustworthy?"

She nodded. "Of course they are, they're the best people I've ever known. They risk their lives every day. . .but I wouldn't want to put any of them in danger."

Williams pulled a phone out of his pocket. "I'll be just a minute. Can I go into the kitchen?"

Another nod. With all the tremors and shaking and nodding, she felt like a bobble head. Her eyes caught a glimpse of the letter.

Rage started a slow burn in her belly. All these years, she'd hidden because of him. He'd stolen her sister, and in effect her mom and her dad. Now he threatened everything and everyone else she'd ever held dear. The shaking stopped as heat seeped through every pore of her body. A new understanding hit her.

She would stop him.

No matter what it took.

It ended here.

Chapter 5

Josh awoke from the most miserable night of his life. Agent Williams ordered him home without a word of explanation or a good-bye from Deanna. He said it would all be explained today. Yeah, like that would help him sleep.

He ran a hand down his face and then rubbed his eyes. A glance at the clock told him it was only 6:00 a.m. Williams said he and Deanna would be at the station at 8:00 sharp.

Enough time for him to take a shower and rally the troops.

At 6:45, Josh met with David, Logan, Kyle, Zack, and John at Tsosie's Café. He realized he was the new guy, but he trusted these men with his life. None of them had flinched at meeting immediately when he said one of their own was in danger.

It took him all of two minutes to lay out for the other rangers what he'd seen and heard the night before.

Logan whistled low. "Sounds like there's way more to this than we know. But I don't care if we're in over our heads, this is Deanna we're talking about."

"FBI, you say?" John rubbed his jaw. "And you saw the badge?"

Josh nodded. "I've never seen Deanna so shaken. She trembled from head to toe."

David leaned in closer, his huge frame filling up the table. "I don't know about the FBI or anything else. I'm inclined to agree with Logan. Deanna's one of us. We're her family.

And we best be out there knocking any heads together that threaten her safety."

The guys nodded in agreement.

Kyle looked at Josh. "There's something else you aren't telling us, isn't there?"

Josh breathed deep. "I've only known her for six months—you've known her much longer so feel free to correct me if I'm wrong—but I've never seen her afraid of anything. She's always been in control. Always a smile on her face."

Josh watched each face around the table. David's eyes narrowed. "And?"

"Well, that's just it. The woman I saw last night. . .let me rephrase. . .it was her eyes. They spooked me."

"Why?" Kyle took a sip of coffee.

"They were pure fear."

❧

By 10:00 a.m. Deanna's exhaustion was complete. Every ranger she worked with, except for a few still at Base Camp, sat in the conference room with her and Agent Williams. Their faces all displayed different emotions—anger, fear, pity, shock. The gamut was covered today.

Mark Williams was a good man. Many years he'd been a shadow for her father, and now, he asked for this position to honor the man he respected. She couldn't have asked for a better agent to be by her side, but she wished the need for one would disappear.

Her head pounded.

Williams stood. "Ladies and gentlemen, thank you for taking the time to be here. I'm Agent Williams with the FBI. Ms. Smith has been in our protection for over fifteen years. This case involves a highly dangerous assassin. Her sister was killed by this guy. Since the town is so small, Deanna has requested that a decoy *not* be brought in, which means we are going to need your help. Your eyes and ears."

After briefing everyone in the room on his plan, the questions began. Ideas were thrown out. Testosterone oozed from every corner as the guys all wanted to protect her.

Missy leaned over and grabbed her hand. She whispered, "It's gonna be okay. I promise. We're family, remember?"

Deanna managed a slight nod but kept her jaw clenched so the tears threatening wouldn't spill. She closed her eyes and her mind to the conversation around her. What did all her friends think of her now? Would they hate her for lying to them and putting them in danger all these years?

What about Josh? No. Stop it. She should've never allowed herself to get attracted to him. Never allowed those feelings to grow. Now her heart just hurt. For everyone she'd failed. For the life she'd never get to live.

Maybe she needed to run now. The emergency cache was still there. The locker in Canada. The cabin in Montana. All she had to do was walk out the door, hop into her truck, and disappear.

But the thought of starting over after all these years horrified her. He'd follow her or find her. No matter where she went, no matter how long she hid.

"Deanna?"

Someone called her name. She opened her eyes and blinked. "I'm sorry. What?"

John was talking to her. "Everyone here wants you to know that you're a part of us. We're one family. And we don't take that lightly. You don't have to do this alone anymore." He smiled and nodded at each person around the table. "In fact, we won't be leaving you alone at all. Ever. Until this is over."

What had she missed? "I'm sorry, John, I'm confused. What are you saying?"

One by one the guys all stood, then the few women stood as well. Arms crossed, shoulders set. She looked up to the wall of rangers around her.

John thrust a hand out to Agent Williams. "We're saying that at least two of us will be with her at all times. Whether you like it not." He leaned toward Deanna, his face a mask of stone and determination. "Prepare to have your space invaded, Ranger Smith. Because your guardians are here to stay."

So she thought she could hide with the rangers? Might make it more difficult at first, but they didn't know who they were up against.

He leaned against the tree, puffing on his cigar. The bitter cold of the air stood in contrast to the warmth of the smoke as he inhaled.

She was surrounded as she left the station. Her gaze darting all around.

Excellent. He'd gotten under her skin.

He could almost smell her fear.

First, the agent would have to go. Then he'd deal with the rangers. One by one. He'd find their weaknesses. Besides, the addition of extra players made the game more fun.

All he needed was a little time. Then the little speck on the map called Talkeetna wouldn't know what hit it.

Chapter 6

Three long days had passed since the meeting in the station. John had suggested—no, ordered—that she stay home a few days and rest. Deanna wasn't quite sure what to do with herself. Oh, she had plenty to do. She always did. Living alone all these years had taught her to keep busy with projects, crafts, books, anything and everything she could learn how to do herself. She'd built her own craft cabinet, taught herself how to sew, quilt, tat, knit, crochet, and weave. Her latest craze had been scrapbooking—that project alone could keep her busy for the next decade since she had no lack of beautiful pictures. She lived in Alaska for heaven's sake.

But what she had trouble dealing with? People. Now. In her home. All the time.

For the first time in fifteen years, she was constantly surrounded by people. Granted, these were people she knew. But people she'd spent the last seven years keeping at a distance. And it was just plain weird.

At the station, every day, she dealt with people. Worked with people. Answered people's questions. But she always went home alone. Shut herself up in her little house and did her solitary confinement. There was never a girls' night out, or movie get-together, no Tupperware party or book club. So when John warned her that her space was about to be invaded—he wasn't kidding—she really had no idea what to expect.

Her skin had crawled the first day just because it was different. Day two brought on claustrophobic feelings. Today, the thought of running away sounded good. Would she ever get used to this?

David, Logan, Kyle, Zack, and Josh were the worst. They hovered. Like mother hens. And when David was around, he seemed to suck all the air out of the room just because he was so stinkin' huge. Kyle challenged her to keep praying and reading the Word. Zack tried to get her laughing, while Logan filled her in on everything at the station and the café since Deline fed him new information every day.

Their hearts were in the right place. But adapting to this new life proved hard.

Then there was Josh. His hovering...well, *it* was different. She longed for it and didn't know how to deal with it all at the same time.

For years, she'd wondered what it would be like to give her heart to someone. Shoot, she'd wanted to know what it was like just to hold someone's hand, to be wrapped in the arms of a man who loved her. But those ideas and dreams seemed so far-fetched.

Then last night, she'd had a dream. A beautiful dream.

Several nights she'd endured nightmares created by the letter, but this dream erased them all. Deep in her heart, she wanted it to come true.

The only way that could happen?

If the predator took the bait and they caught him.

Williams had spilled the truth to the rangers. But not the whole truth.

Everyone knew what happened to her sister, and as a result her parents.

But no one knew why.

That secret would have to remain buried.

❧

Another minute. Another hour. Another day.

Passing by with the slow tick of the clock on her mantel.

Deanna wanted to scream. Acclimating to people in her home was worse than acute mountain sickness. But she had to admit the only thing keeping her sane was the other rangers. Every moment they stayed with her, helping her survive the mundane life as a fugitive in her own home. This had to change. Could she leave? Or was it her own fear holding her back? She allowed that thought to take root. The first day, they'd encouraged her to think about getting out, acting "normal." But the thought of that scared her. More than she wanted to admit. Her abrupt refusals had ensured they wouldn't ask anymore. She could see that now. No wonder no one had offered to take her anywhere the past couple of days.

Resolve to stop the stalker bubbled up again.

Agent Williams entered the living room where she'd tucked herself into the couch. "How are you doing, Deanna?"

"Okay, I guess. Under the circumstances." She wasn't ready to admit her struggle with fear.

"We need to discuss a plan. Our man hasn't shown himself."

"I think I need to get out. What do you think?" There. She'd said it.

His eyebrows raised. "I was actually going to suggest it."

She threw off the blanket and sat on the edge of the couch. "This roller coaster of emotions will eat me alive if I don't get out. I'm scared to death, I'll admit that, but then I get angry and want to stop him. I feel like a mouse sometimes and a lion at others."

"That's understandable. Your life has revolved around hiding from him."

"Yeah, but the swing of the pendulum is getting to me. One minute I want to hide, the next I want to strangle him with my bare hands."

He nodded.

"I don't want to put others in danger," she said.

"You forget that everyone volunteered for this."

She nodded. Time to suck it up.

A knock at the front door made her jump. Williams peered through the side window. "It's Josh."

Relief poured through her as the agent allowed her favorite ranger entry. "Hi, Josh."

"Hi." He glanced around the room, a worried expression on his face. "Am I the only one here?"

Williams patted his shoulder. "The others are outside getting some fresh air. We're done for now, Deanna. I'll check in with everyone else and come back later."

"Okay, thanks."

Josh paced in front of her. "So, how are you doing?"

"Good."

"Getting enough rest?"

"Uh-huh." She watched him go back and forth. "Josh, you're going to wear a hole in the carpet. Why don't you sit down?"

His feet stopped, and he sighed. "Sorry."

"It's okay. I know this is stressful for everyone."

"Yeah, it is." He looked up and captured her gaze. "Especially since it's you."

That got her attention.

"You're special, Deanna."

Heat crept up her neck, into her cheeks. He thought she was special?

"More than just a fellow ranger, and more than just a friend." He looked down.

The front door opened before Deanna could respond.

John stood there, glancing back and forth between Josh and her. "Am I interrupting something?"

"No," Josh said, face flaming as he glanced at Deanna. "I just wanted to check on Deanna." He smiled.

"Me, too." John moved forward. "I brought some paperwork I was hoping you could help us with."

Deanna stole a glance at Josh as he backed toward the door. He winked and slipped out.

Maybe next time.

Chapter 7

Today was the day. After prodding, ribbing, and teasing from all the guys, Josh was going to make his move.

The bouquet of flowers behind his back would hopefully make Deanna smile.

David sat on the porch of her little house as Josh walked up. The smirk on the big guy's face couldn't be missed. "About time."

"Don't think it's insensitive? Bad timing?"

"Nope. Go for it, dude. She needs you."

He nodded. "Let's hope so." The door stared him down. Deep breath. Shoulders back.

"But if you hurt her, you realize how many big brothers will kill you, right?"

Right. Nothing like a bunch of brawny, scared-of-nothing, mountaineering rangers after your tail. He gave a mock salute to David. "Understood."

He opened the door. "Hey, Deanna."

"Josh." She smiled from her perch on the couch. "How are you?" Feet tucked underneath her, she looked at total ease, except for the haunted look in her eyes.

"I'm great." He handed her the flowers. "Especially now that I'm off."

"What are these for?"

"You." Realization hit him square in the jaw. He'd just referred to her as a "what." Well, kind of. "I mean, who. . . well, you said, 'what' and I said 'you,' but I meant that they're for you. And you're a who, not a what. . . ." The hole he dug

305

couldn't swallow him up fast enough. "Just because."

Laughter surrounded him. Deline stood in the door from the kitchen. "You're adorable when you get nervous, Josh. didn't know you were such a chatterbox." She handed a cu of steaming liquid to Deanna. "You better snatch this one u I think he's a keeper."

Adorable. Just what a guy aimed for. Wasn't *adorab* reserved for puppies and babies?

A slight blush rose in Deanna's cheeks. She lowered he head to sip from the cup.

It made Deline laugh harder. She turned to Josh, gav him a smack on the arm. "So, have you seen Logan today?"

"Yep, just a little bit ago."

"Is he behaving himself?" She pulled on a jacket.

At least she had the courtesy to change the subject. Jos swallowed his embarrassment. "Yes, ma'am. In fact, he's o his way over here for a little while. He said something abou a hot date with a beautiful woman."

"Did he, now?" She winked at Deanna. "I'll come back b tomorrow, but I need to go check on my dad."

"Thanks, Deline. It's been fun." Deanna tossed her lon auburn braid behind her shoulder.

"You're welcome. Promise me it won't take another seve years to do it again." And in a blur, she was gone.

Josh stood in the living room feeling awkward. Were the actually alone? Oh boy. What was it about Deanna that threw him off like this? Every single time.

"You can sit down, you know." The cup in her hands hi the lower portion of her face. Her cheeks were still pink.

"Okay." The spot next to her on the couch invited him.

"Thank you for the flowers."

"You're welcome." Good grief, he was an idiot. Couldn' he come up with something better than that? "Look, I know things are really tough right now. But I want you to know I'm here for you." Here for you. Uh-huh. What did that mean exactly? Open mouth. Insert foot.

Warmth seeped through his jacket as she touched his shoulder. Her smile was small, but it reached her eyes. She didn't seem to care that he turned into a bumbling fool around her. "I don't know what to do with my feelings, Josh. I'm scared. Really scared. And for the first time as an adult, I'm not alone. But I don't want to risk anyone else's life. Especially yours." A soft sigh escaped as she uncurled and sat forward. Her bare feet rubbed the carpet. "I haven't been able to trust a soul. No friendships, no dating, no one allowed in my life." She turned her head toward him.

A lock of hair escaped her braid, and he longed to brush it back.

"All these years, I've wanted to live a normal life—be around people, hang out with friends—you know the drill. But now that people *know*, I don't know what to do with myself." She bit her bottom lip. Then breathed deep. "And I don't know what I would do if anyone got hurt because of me."

"No one's going to get hurt. We're going to protect you."

"You don't know that, Josh."

"But I believe it."

She huffed. "Look, I know we share the same faith, but you haven't seen what I've seen. Haven't been through the horror this man has put me through. Yes, I know God is there, and I believe, but I've also got to keep a clear head and protect those around me."

"So you don't think God is big enough to do that?"

"That's not what I'm saying." Deanna stood and paced the living room in front of him. "I know He's big enough, but I also know He allows bad things to happen. So if *I* can keep them from—"

"Whoa there, Deanna. That's not how God works and you know it. This is a sin-filled world, so yes, bad things are going to happen. But you can't supersede His position and say that even if He allows something to happen, you can stop it because you don't *want* it to happen."

Her back to him, she stopped her pacing. Her shoulders slumped and began to shake. Was she crying? He prayed David wouldn't decide to come in the door at that moment. The big guy would probably lay Josh flat for making her cry.

He stood and moved closer to her. "I'm sorry, Deanna." He reached out and touched her elbow. "I didn't mean to upset you, but I would be a lousy friend if I didn't tell you the truth."

Deanna turned to him. Sobs shook her whole frame. "No, I'm sorry. I need you to be honest with me. And I need to be reminded that I'm not in control." She stepped closer and smiled. Patted his chest with her hand. Her voice broke as she walked back to the couch. She sat on her knees in the far corner and pulled a blanket up around her. "I'm sorry. I'm an emotional mess right now."

"It's okay, you have the right. And maybe someone should remind you that the killer isn't in control, either." He handed her a tissue.

"Thanks." She sighed. "And you're right again. But don't let it go to your head."

"I won't. And you're welcome. Anytime." He meant it. He would love nothing more than to pull her into his arms and hold her for the rest of his life. As the connection between them grew, Josh couldn't pull his gaze away. Change the subject. Do something. He was in way over his head. "So, I have an idea. Maybe it will cheer you up."

"Sure, what is it?"

"I was hoping we could go out to the café. David and Jolie

said they'd go and sit at another table. Kyle, Zack, and John will be in there as well."

The haunted look left her eyes for a brief moment. "You mean, a date?"

"Well, I. . .was hoping for one. . .eventually that is. . .but this doesn't have to be one, if you'd—" If only he could stop rambling around her.

"I would love to go on a date with you. . .but. . ."

David burst through the door. "No buts. You can't let this killer rule your life. Besides, Agent Williams thinks he's gone for now. Talkeetna's too small and everyone is on alert for anyone new or suspicious."

Josh crossed his arms and raised an eyebrow at his fellow ranger. How long had he been listening?

Deanna smirked. She yanked the blanket off and stood. "You know what?" Deanna pulled on his hand. "I am dying to get out of this house! And you know what else? I would love to go on a date with you."

"So you're just using me to get some fresh air?" He winked.

David smacked him on the shoulder.

A pillow flew through the air from the couch. It hit David just as another one sailed toward Josh.

"I take that as a yes?"

Chapter 8

The laughter was a balm to her soul. The food was amazing.

And Josh? Well, he was everything. Everything she'd ever wanted in a man. Who cared if this was her first date *ever* at twenty-seven years old? Contentment poured through her. This truly was how life was supposed to be, wasn't it?

Zack had the whole place laughing about a climb. But Deanna couldn't take her eyes off Josh. For almost three hours, she hadn't even thought about the stalker. Or her family. Guilt washed over her. Shouldn't she be hiding somewhere? Her family hadn't given their lives so she could live it up in a café while the stalker was still loose. She shook her head. Thinking like that wasn't healthy.

A hand reached across the table. Took hers. She jolted. He let go but left his hand close. "I'm sorry, Deanna. I didn't mean to startle you."

Tears pooled in her eyes as she tentatively reached for him. "You didn't." She sniffed. Wiped at her eyes. Josh held her hand. The simple gesture meant more than he'd ever know.

She motioned him closer with a finger and whispered into his ear. "I'm almost ashamed to admit it, but it's the first time I've held a man's hand."

He squeezed tighter and sat back in his chair.

After hours of conversation and fun, gone was the man

ho rambled around her. She knew Josh was a great guy, but
t had been fun to watch him be nervous around her. This
ew Josh, the real guy underneath, was amazing. She hoped
hey'd have a chance. A real chance.

"Why don't we get you home?" Josh caught the attention
f the other rangers. "I don't want it to get too late."

She nodded, trying to remember all the wonderful things
bout the evening. They would be stowed in her memory
orever. Maybe they could even replace the ugly memories
ver time. Maybe. If they ever caught *him*.

Josh, David, Logan, and Zack all escorted her out. Josh
pened her door for her, as David climbed into the backseat.
Zack and Logan got into the Jeep behind them.

The distance to the café was so short, they could've
valked, but the guys wouldn't allow it. As they drove up to
er house, she noticed Agent Williams standing on the front
orch.

Once again ensconced between all her bodyguards,
Deanna walked toward the house. Williams escorted her
nside with Josh. John, her boss, sat in the living room.

He stood. "Not a sound while you were gone. But I'll
heck all the rooms, just to be safe."

Her heart raced, this was the part she hated. With a
assion. The stalker had taken her trust away. She never
elt safe. She checked and rechecked everything. All the
ime. The stove, the oven. Windows and doors. Closets and
abinets. Even phone calls and e-mail made her a nervous
vreck. Would the nightmare ever end?

John and Williams returned. The agent holstered his
veapon. "David is on the porch, but he needs a break. I'll stay
utside tonight. John said he would stay inside, and Missy is
oming as well, correct?"

All she managed was a nod. So much for her date. The

fun evening was over. A short reprieve from reality. Cynicism raced through her blood again. Anger burned. The man had to be stopped. He'd stolen everything.

❧

Josh's bubble burst when they returned to Deanna's home. had been such a great night. He'd had hope they could forge But that monster destroyed even the remote possibility. Th look on Deanna's face told the story. Fear, anger, hatre They'd never have a chance until the stalker was caught an put away for the rest of his life.

Good-byes were brief as Josh left Deanna with the FF agent and Missy.

Josh walked to his car and decided to head home. *Lor what do I do?* Hopelessness filled him. He wanted to *a* something. He understood now the prompting of the Hol Spirit the other night. Why he'd felt the need to pray. If Go cared enough to have him pray for Deanna, when he didn even know who he was praying for, then couldn't He car enough to take care of the situation at hand?

For the first time in his life, he'd found someone he care about. The thought of losing Deanna before they even had chance to really begin gave him pause.

He pulled into his driveway and went inside. The re question was bigger. Did he believe God was in control c not? Could he leave everything in the Lord's hands? Eve Deanna and her safety?

❧

"Come on in, Karon." Deanna sipped another cup of ho chocolate. If only the brew could calm her nerves. Two mor long days had passed. No sign of the stalker. No rest for he weary mind.

312

Karon carried an armload of books. She plopped them onto the coffee table and sat cross-legged on the couch next to Deanna. "Okay, boys"—she shooed Zack and Logan—"go sit on the porch for a while. We need to chat."

The guys nodded. Zack turned back around. "You sure you're okay, Dee?"

"Yeah, go ahead. I'm sure she won't tell me anything that will make me think *any* worse of you."

The guys laughed.

The door closed with a soft click. Deanna sipped. What did Karon have up her sleeve?

"All right, friend. We need to talk." She ran both hands through her short black curls. "It comes so naturally to you now, doesn't it?"

"What?"

"The facade. You can joke with the best of them, keep them all thinking you are fine and dandy, while you're really just hiding behind a wall of fear."

Wow. Deanna felt stabbed by the words. The wound bled inside.

Karon patted Deanna's knee and smiled. "Sorry, I've just come to realize that life is too short to mince words. I haven't been here as long as the others, I don't know you like they do. But I'm pretty observant and I've been watching you all summer. You're amazing. So strong. So together."

"I wish that's who I really was." A long sigh escaped. "But it's not. You're right, the facade is my cloak—my protection." She'd never voiced thoughts like this out loud to anyone. "It's safe. Easy. Comfortable."

"Mind if I share something with you?"

Deanna shrugged. "Sure. Go ahead." What could it hurt? Wasn't that what real friends did?

"I know you've heard all about Zack and me. So you know

I'm a cancer survivor."

Deanna nodded. When Karon had braved Denali earlier in the summer, she'd been shocked and amazed at her gumption.

"Well, what you probably don't know is that I just about let cancer win."

"What do you mean?" She set her cup down.

"The battle was long and hard. Everyone coddled me. I was so sick for so long that it simply became easier to let everyone else help and do everything. I didn't make any decisions anymore. I didn't go anywhere. *Exhausted* was my middle name."

"That's totally understandable. I can't begin to imagine what you've been through." Karon had become a big sister to everyone at the station under thirty-five. The woman had more spunk than the proverbial barrel of monkeys. She'd moved from Louisiana to Alaska and opened a coffee shop/bookstore. Just like that. No long, drawn-out decisions. She just did it. Deanna couldn't fathom this bright, lively woman in front of her giving up.

"Now, I have a point. This isn't a pity party about me, Dee. I wanted to share with you what God did during that time. In my exhaustion, I thought about how much easier it would be for everyone else if they didn't have to take care of me, if they didn't have to worry about me. And it was during one of those martyr times that I was lying in bed crying. I realized it was my *fear* of living that held me back."

"I don't get it."

"Fear isn't of God, Dee. He is the Creator of all and our days are listed in His book. But whether the Lord took me home through the cancer, or He let me live—I was still afraid. Of living or dying."

Deanna leaned forward and fidgeted with the fringe of

the blanket. "So what did you do? To get past the fear?"

"I admitted to God that *I* wanted to be in control, and when that control was taken away from me, I let go and allowed fear in. It wasn't about dying. It wasn't even about the cancer. It was about me saying, 'Lord, Your will be done' no matter what. I prayed and asked Him to give me the will to live for Him whether I had one more day, or a million days."

Something about her words struck Deanna deep. A little too close to home. She liked to be in control, too. In fact, she'd controlled every aspect of her life for a long time. She loved the Lord and yet didn't feel the growth and closeness to Him that she'd longed for all these years. "What happened?"

"God used every second in the hospitals. Every person I met. Every second of treatment. Every person I prayed with. Every second of my exhaustion. Every person I saw leave this world and enter into the arms of our Father. I let go and when He allowed me to live a little longer for Him, I vowed to live every moment to the fullest." Karon pulled her knees up to her chest. "No matter how many I had left. I wanted to live. And I'm not saying that my will to live was what saved me or cured me of cancer. I'm saying I wanted to live because He could still use me, use my story, use my *cancer* for His glory." Karon looked down and took a deep breath. "Because the cancer could always come back. But God is bigger than cancer, and there are so many people who need to know Him. *He's* what living is all about. This body, this world, is only temporary. What's important is letting other people know. I can't let fear keep me from sharing the greatest story ever told."

Deanna jumped to her feet as tears pooled in her eyes. *Fear.* The word alone caused her to tremble. She'd allowed fear to reign supreme. Fear was what brought her here. Fear kept her locked up in her house. Fear kept her from relationships and people.

Fear kept her from church and from sharing her faith with others.

Fear. Kept her hidden.

But it hadn't done much good, had it? He'd found her anyway. All this time, alone. Because of fear.

Yet, here Karon sat in front of her, willing to share what God had done in her life even through all her trials. While Deanna had hidden. In fifteen years, she hadn't shared her faith with anyone. Not one soul had she won for Christ. She'd wasted so much time. She'd wasted her life.

Silent tears traced down Deanna's cheeks.

Karon stood up beside her and wrapped loving arms around her.

For the second time in less than a week, Deanna sobbed. She returned the hug of a friend. A *real* friend, and poured her heart out to the Lord.

Chapter 9

Josh jogged with Kyle back up the Parks Highway toward the Talkeetna Spur. He hated being away from Deanna but kept reminding himself that God cared about her more than *he* ever could.

Once a week he and Kyle put in a long run to help keep in shape. As mountaineering rangers in Denali National Park, they never knew what kind of battle they would face next. The beginning of the run had started with a real heart-to-heart. Now that Josh felt he had a better grip on his emotions, he decided to leave the results up to God. No matter what. He just needed to remind himself of that. Every second.

The last few miles into Talkeetna he spotted two moose and a bear. Things he never saw growing up unless he went to the zoo. Here, there seemed to be more of them than there were people. The first time he saw moose poop, he thought he'd fall over laughing—the fact that such a large, goofy-looking creature could create such perfect little pellets in perfect little piles. He shook his head. All the gift shops sold tea made out of it, shellacked earrings and jewelry made out of it. Now, a pile of bear scat was a totally different story. Glad they hadn't tried to sell a mess of that. Although the tourists would probably buy it.

Alaska was definitely the last frontier. He loved it.

They slowed as they neared Josh's house. Kyle gave a small wave and headed toward his own home.

BOOM!

The explosion knocked Josh back a good ten feet. Shocked and stunned, his ears were still ringing when Kyle was at his side helping him up. Flames engulfed his car. People poured out of buildings and homes all over the small town.

Glass cut into his hands, and he felt a trickle down his left temple. He swiped at it. Blood. Josh walked around the wreckage to the front of his house. A note was duct-taped to the front door.

In large red letters it read:

> *You can't stop me.*
> *You can't protect her.*
> *I will win.*

❧

The explosion was fun. People didn't appreciate the beauty of these things anymore. But the simple car bomb was just to get people's attention. Scare them a little. Small-town folks had such a hard time believing that the world actually turned outside of their one-mile radius.

They'd have to get over that.

He'd have a little fun and teach them about reality.

The dark, scary world they lived in.

And the terrifying monsters they lived with. But the ultimate goal? He wanted to scare *her*. Taunt her. She deserved it for hiding from him all these years. Little Girl didn't want to frighten people around here. She liked helping people.

So he'd give her lots of ways to *help* people.

But then he'd kill them all.

❧

No. This couldn't be happening. Josh could've been killed. And all because of her.

Two state troopers stood outside her door. Her ranger family hovered. Josh had finally gone to Mat-Su but only because his superiors ordered it. Stubborn man. Bleeding from his head and hands, he'd run straight to her house to check on *her* while the paramedics chased him down after the explosion.

Karon's words from yesterday skittered through her mind. But the age-old fear fought back. Reared its ugly head and spread its strong tentacles throughout her body. She wasn't strong enough for this. She wanted to scream.

Lord, how am I supposed to deal with this?

Agent Williams entered the living room. "We need to go. Briefing at the station."

Deanna managed a nod.

As the entourage led her to the car and drove to the station, her thoughts ran rampant. Like wheels spinning in mud. No traction. No sense could be made.

What had happened to the confidence she'd felt yesterday? Why couldn't she grab on to God the same way Karon had?

All the doubt, worry, and fears she'd carried through the years haunted her now. One after another they taunted. She was so weak.

They led her into the station. Her home away from home. Every nook and cranny was familiar to her.

Karon sat in a chair in the great room. She stood when she spotted Deanna. "Hey, guys, can I have a minute?"

Williams stood by Deanna's side while the others headed to the conference room.

Bloodshot eyes met hers. "Zack was taken to the hospital a few minutes ago."

Zack, too? All of a sudden all the air had been sucked out of the room. It was because of her. She knew it. The stalker would stop at nothing. "Oh, Karon. . . I'm so sorry." The two embraced.

"I didn't tell you for you to blame yourself, Zack wanted you to know why he's not in there. I'm on my way to be with him right now. The paramedics thought it was food poisoning at first until we found a note." Karon kept her arms around Deanna. "Don't you give in to him, Dee. And don't you dare give in to your fear. This world is not our home, remember? God did not give us a spirit of fear."

She nodded against her friend's shoulder. Sucked in a sob. Karon was right. "Tell Zack I'm all right and I'm praying for him, okay?"

"You got it." Karon rushed out the door.

Bile rose in her throat. Deanna pushed it down and fought the fear climbing her body. No! *Lord, You've got to give me the strength to fight. No more fear. No more hiding. Lord, help me do what's right.*

With purpose in her stride, she walked down the hall to the conference room.

It was full once again. Rangers, FBI, state troopers. They were all here. Deanna fidgeted in her chair. Except, where was David? She did a mental check of everyone in the room. David should be here.

One of the local officers ran into the office and spoke in Williams's ear.

The seasoned agent placed his hands on the table in front of him and spoke to the group. "Looks like our guy's gone after another ranger. David Whiteeagle found an old-fashioned bear trap on his front steps early this morning. David's fine, a few puncture wounds to his leg, but he went after the guy and has more of a description for us. Since he lost quite a bit of blood in the chase, they've taken him in to Mat-Su as well."

Deanna gasped. The others around the table darted looks to one another. Were they blaming her? The old insecurities burned inside.

Logan and John shared a glance, then John looked straight at Deanna. "David's gonna be fine. That big lug's only at the hospital because Jolie demanded it, and you know it. And no one is blaming you, so wipe that expression off your face. We're all in this together, Dee. We've"—he motioned to all the rangers in the room—"had quite a bit of time to talk and we understand why you kept us at a distance, and we totally understand. But even though you don't think we do, we know you. You're one of us. And we take care of our own. No matter what." He chuckled and shook his head. "Can you imagine David chasing a guy down the street with a bear trap on his leg?"

The others laughed with their boss. John nodded to Agent Williams.

"Sanders will be back in a moment with a sketch," the agent went on, "and as soon as we have news on Taylor or Whiteeagle, we'll let you all know." Williams walked around the table. "You all need to be on your guard. Right now, it seems he's trying to get Deanna's attention, trying to scare her. But I can't reiterate enough that this guy is dangerous. He's taken out twenty-seven targets that we know of, probably many more."

He paused and took a sip of coffee. "There's something we weren't cleared to share before, but I think now's a good time." He looked around the room. Tuned in to each face. Dead quiet covered them all like a blanket. "This case is personal. Deanna's the only one who's eluded him, so this is about winning. Our guy has never lost."

Chapter 10

The fog around his mind lifted as Josh worked to open his eyes.

Deanna! Where was she?

His head pounded. What a nightmare. He couldn't protect the woman he loved.

And she didn't even know how much he cared.

A shrill beep pierced his quiet room. Again and again.

A nurse walked in and shut off the annoying sound. "Telemetry called and said your blood pressure and heart rate were elevated." She slapped a manual blood pressure cuff around his arm. "Are you feeling all right?"

"I'm fine. Just want to get out of here." He tugged at his arm and ripped the cuff off, handing it to the nurse. "I'd like to leave now."

She frowned at him. "I'll have to speak to the doctor—"

"I'm fine. I take full responsibility for myself. I'll sign whatever. Lives are at stake and I need to get back to Talkeetna."

The nurse's lips thinned. "I'll get the paperwork and your antibiotics." She dragged the rolling apparatus behind her and closed the door with force.

Josh touched the stitches on his head as he waited. He hated waiting. Hadn't he waited all these months for Deanna? He needed to be back there. Now.

Might as well face facts. He loved her. She might never be ready to hear it, but it was the truth. His heart belonged to the green-eyed, auburn-haired ranger.

Anger boiled in his gut. Whoever this guy was, Josh wanted to personally wring his neck. He didn't care about his jeep. Didn't care about any of his possessions. But if that man got anywhere near his Deanna again, he'd rip him to shreds.

"Mr. Richards." The nurse handed him some instructions, a tube of cream, and a bottle of antibiotics. "Make sure you keep the wounds clean, put the cream on it twice a day, and finish the entire round of antibiotics, okay?"

"Yes, ma'am." He jumped off the bed. Pain pulsed through his legs. "I can leave now?" He pasted on his best smile.

She nodded. "Just make sure you have the stitches taken out properly in ten days."

"Got it." The paper stuffed between his teeth, he jammed the prescriptions into the pocket of his jacket as he threw it on. His cell phone rang. "Richards."

"Hey, Josh, this is Missy. Are you okay?"

"Yeah." He winced. "They released me. Just a few stitches and bruises."

"Oh good. We were afraid you would have to stay up here awhile."

Not if he had anything to do with it.

"Could you check on Zack and David while you're there? Everyone's asking about them and I don't think Karon has her cell turned on."

Josh's heart sank. Zack and David? "What happened?"

"They think Zack was poisoned, and David had an incident with a bear trap."

A bear trap? "Let me guess, our stalker's responsible?"

Fear punctuated her sigh. "Yes. Everyone is on high alert."

Anger filled him. This guy would stop at nothing. If only Josh had known who he was when he'd spotted the guy watching Deanna's house. He could have stopped him.

Missy's voice filled his ear. ". . .meeting later. Just make sure you call me as soon as you know something. Once you know how the guys are."

"Sure thing." He closed his phone. The guys. A bunch of mother hens was what they were. But he wouldn't have it any other way.

Josh retraced his steps back into the hospital to the front desk and inquired about his fellow rangers. At least they were both out of danger.

He found Zack's room first. Karon sat on the edge of his bed, reading aloud from a novel.

"How's the patient?" Josh leaned against the doorframe.

"Ornery." Karon smiled up at him.

Zack's pasty face turned toward him. "I don't *ever* want to be sick like that again." He pointed to the IV tubes. "But whatever they've got flowing through these tubes neutralized it. I won't be able to get to the station for a few days, though."

Karon shook her head. "He won't be able to *move* for a few days. The stubborn man thinks he's going back to work, ha!" She pinched Zack's arm. "He's so weak, he can't even hold the cup."

Zack lifted his head a little. "Dude, you look like you got run over. Are you sure you shouldn't be in here with me?"

"Nah, I'm fine. They released me." Time to change the subject. "So, Karon, what's happening at the coffee shop while you're gone?"

"Lisa's got it under control. And it won't kill anyone if it had to close for a few days."

"Well, I don't know about that. Your coffee is to die for. . . ."

"Your puns get worse and worse." Zack's laugh was weak. "But thanks for stopping by, man. I heard David was in here too. Have you seen him?"

"Not yet. I'm on my way there next. I've been sent on a mission by Missy to make sure the guys know how you all are doing."

Zack cleared his throat. "You make sure they catch this guy, okay? I don't want anything happening to Deanna."

"That makes two of us."

Zack nodded. "Go check on the grizzly bear. I'm sure he's giving the staff a run for their money."

"You got it." Josh hugged Karon and left.

David's room was easy to find. Josh heard the shouts all the way down the hallway. He peeked around the corner. Jolie stood, hands on her hips, fire shooting out of her eyes. "You are the most pigheaded—"

"Ahem." Josh entered. "I see Ranger Whiteeagle is giving the lady a hard time."

Jolie pointed a finger at the red-faced David and headed toward the door. "You have no idea. If I didn't love that man so much, I'd be looking for a way to strangle him." She nudged Josh with her shoulder. "See if you can get him to cooperate before the little nurse comes back with her big needle."

"I am not letting that—" David began.

"I'm not listening, David. Either you get the shot or you're not coming home. End of story. Got it? I don't make idle threats, you big baby." And with that she walked out the door. "Men—"

Josh attempted not to laugh. "That good, huh?"

David banged his fist on the dinner tray. Then he crossed his arms. "That woman gets me so riled up."

"I take it you need a shot?"

"Multiple. It appears our nice little stalker used an old, *dirty*, and recently used bear trap. They're not only worried about tetanus but rabies as well."

Josh stayed out of reach. Just in case David decided to unleash his fury on the closest victim. Him. "Sounds like fun."

"Don't start, rookie."

He held up his hands in surrender. "Hey, I'm just here to

check on the troops for the station. Everyone's worried. So what would you like me to tell them? The truth?"

"The truth? If we're telling them the truth, what about the fact that you look worse than I do? Shouldn't you still be in here?"

"It's just a few stitches. You, on the other hand? You need some serious shots before they'll release you."

"Few stitches? You're all banged up and bruised and look a little like Frankenstein they've sewn you up so much!"

"Hey, don't take your frustration out on me. You don't want me to go back to the station and tell 'em you're afraid of needles—"

"Don't you dare." The grizzly bear of a ranger hissed at him.

Josh knew his time was up. "Just suck it up and get the shots."

David pressed the CALL button. "Nurse, I'm being harassed."

The nasally voice over the speaker oozed sarcasm. "Good. Shall I send in the SWAT team?"

Josh laughed.

"Grrrrrrr. No, just send in the stupid needles." David threw the box down. "Not a word of this to the guys at the station."

"Oh, I wouldn't dare." Josh covered his mouth with a hand and coughed to cover his mirth. At least he could leave now and get back to Deanna. "So when will the ornery one be back to grace us with his presence?"

He ducked out the door before the flying tray could hit his head.

❧

The water in the sink had long gone cold, but Deanna continued to scrub the glass casserole dish. She swirled the scrubby around and around.

How long before he struck again? What would he do next?

At least Josh, David, and Zack were all right. But what if someone died next time? Would she be able to live with herself?

Maybe she should leave. If she stayed, the rangers would stick to her like glue, and that was a serious problem. That meant all the people she cared about most were in danger.

"You've been scrubbing that same dish for an hour." Missy's voice invaded her space.

"Yeah, I guess I have."

"Tell me the truth. Are you in here hiding?"

"Maybe." She pulled her wrinkled and pruned hands from the water.

"Plotting how to leave without any of us knowing?"

Deanna spun on her heel. "Now, why would you think a thing like that?"

"Because you want to protect everyone else around you, but don't want anyone to get hurt protecting you."

Not fair.

"Don't even try to convince me you weren't thinking it. Every person in this town knows to keep you from running."

"But, Missy, don't you see? My being here has put all of you in danger. If I leave, then the danger leaves with me."

"And then there's no one to keep *you* out of danger." Missy placed a hand on Deanna's shoulder. "Get it through your thick skull right now, the idea of leaving is not an option."

A billion thoughts swirled through her brain. She turned back to the sink. Pulled the drain plug and watched the murky water vanish down the pipes.

If only she could pull the plug on the stalker that easily.

Chapter 11

These people were imbeciles. Like a cluster of ants that scattered after a boot kicked their hill.

Did they really think they could protect themselve[s] from him?

FBI. State troopers. Rangers. Local VPSOs. Ridiculous[.] He watched their every move. Knew their every weakness.

Amateurs. All of them.

He was in charge.

He called the shots.

And never lost.

Never.

He placed another pipe bomb in the woods. Let them believe they could stop him. Now it was just a matter of time[.] The plan was in motion.

He couldn't wait to see Deanna's face.

❧

"Another note was found." John and Missy stood in front o[f] Deanna's desk. She'd refused to stay home any longer. At th[e] station she felt needed. Wanted. Useful.

She watched her friend Missy. Waited for the news[.] *Please, God, don't let anyone else be hurt because of me.*

Missy gripped Deanna's shoulder. "Don't freak out. W[e] wanted you to hear it first from us."

"What did it say?"

A glance between the two didn't help settle her stomach[.]

"What?"

"This time it was in a paramedic's locker. Mike called in the state troopers and they found open syringes in the bottom of his gear bag that he'd already loaded into the ambulance." John played with the paperweight on her desk. "They've got them down at the lab now examining what was in them."

"But no one was hurt?"

"No. The troopers are working with the FBI to figure out where this guy might hit next." The paperweight thunked the desk with a soft thud. "But he's unpredictable. And weird."

What was it they weren't telling her? "What did the note *say*?"

Missy looked at John then sat down. "It was a bunch of jumbled letters all over the page and then at the bottom, it said, 'I win.'"

"They've got experts trying to figure that one out, too, in case it's a clue." John walked around her desk and sat on the edge, in front of Deanna. "We're here, Dee. This guy can't scare us off. He'll be stopped. Okay?"

The floor called her attention. No tears. She forbade it. But the stinging at the back of her eyes betrayed her command. She managed a stiff nod. No words would come. She couldn't even move.

In the silence, she heard Missy whisper to John, "Give her a few minutes," then shuffle away. John's solid footsteps followed a moment later.

As she studied the carpet, thoughts swirled around in her mind. This station had been her refuge. Not just a job. Deanna felt like she was contributing to something bigger than herself here. It made her feel worthwhile. Gave her a purpose.

But now the weight of everything on her shoulders—the years of hiding, the danger to her friends, the people hurt because of her—was almost too much to bear.

Why had God allowed this to happen?

Why did He allow *anything* bad to happen?

Why did Karon have to go through cancer? What about Deline and the Bender guy who tried to destroy her and her business? What about David's sister, Mariah? Jolie's brother, Gael? And all the people who died up on the great mountain Denali?

Would the suffering never stop?

Lord, help me see what You're doing here. Please show me how to handle this. I can't bear watching more people suffer.

Her weakness depressed her. This wasn't what her parents had fought for. This wasn't *her*.

A new train of thought pierced through the fog. She lived in a sin-filled world. There would be suffering and disease. Heartache and pain. But she could do something about it. Even if it was just one thing.

She would do everything in her power to stop this madman from hurting one more soul.

❧

Josh didn't like the sound of it. Not one bit. A hiker found what looked to be an explosive device in the woods. Several of the rangers had gone out in teams searching the surrounding areas. He and Kyle had to go with the bomb squad from Anchorage to the actual location.

Something wasn't right. He couldn't place his finger on it, but every nerve in his body felt the uneasiness.

Deanna was working at the station surrounded by dozens of people. She would be fine.

Unless the stalker had planted a bomb there, too.

Josh's thoughts went round and round. Not good.

Traipsing through the woods through a foot of snow was

not an ideal situation to him. He wanted to be where Deanna was. That was the only way *he* could protect her.

A still, small voice told him to leave her in God's hands, but Josh kept bucking it.

Sorry, Lord. I know she's Yours.

Their radios crackled to life. "Kyle, get over here. We've got another live one."

Kyle nodded at Josh and took off in the direction of the coordinates.

Josh stayed on course for the first call. Between the snow and the thick forest, it was slow going. But it shouldn't be far now—

A crack to his skull caught him by surprise. He tried to fight whatever was in front of him, but the darkness took over.

Deanna...

❧

Deanna's dark green ranger jacket now had spit-up on it. The mother apologized, but what a time to have a homeschool group from Wasilla show up. They needed her here at the station, and she wanted to be here, but nothing felt right. She'd been holding the pudgy little baby while she showed the rest of the children the bear paw casts. Each one of them wanted to see how big their own feet compared to the different-sized bear prints. Brown, black, grizzly, polar bear. Most of the kids could fit both their feet *and* their hands inside the paw prints. She really should just be thankful that she had a lot to keep her busy. It kept her mind off the junk going on in her life. If only they could catch the guy...

Missy was showing the kids the huge portraits on the walls taken of the mountains from the air.

Deanna really had no desire to smell like sour milk all day, so she headed to the bathroom to clean up her jacket. As she worked on the stain at the sink, she thought about how sweet the six-month-old had been and how warm and cuddly he'd felt in her arms.

She shook her head. Maybe one day she'd have kids of her own.

A flutter at the window caught her attention. What was it doing open? It must be fifteen degrees outside.

She reached over to close the window but a large cloth covered her nose and mouth. It smelled odd. Before she could struggle, the world around her went black.

❧

Josh woke up with his hands and feet bound. His head spun. The smell of airplane fuel filled his nose. He yelled. The echo of his own voice bounced back to him. Sounded like he was in an empty hangar. But where?

And where was Deanna?

Darkness surrounded him. No lights. No sounds. No voices. Nothing.

He worked at the bonds on his hands but felt his flesh burning and tearing under the stress. No use. He was totally incapacitated.

Josh let his head fall back to the concrete floor with a thud. *Lord, only You can get me out of this. But before You worry about me, please save Deanna. Please.*

❧

The scent of cinnamon rolls woke Deanna up.

"Well, good morning, Little Girl. How are you feeling?" The gravelly voice sent shivers up her spine. She hated the term "little girl" because of him. Now she'd always hate the wonderful smell of cinnamon.

"Where am I?" She needed to stay strong, even though her greatest fear had just come to life. This man. This horrible man. He was the epitome of all her fears. For fifteen years, he'd haunted her. Now there was a voice attached to the nightmare.

"Safe. But not for long. I needed your little guardians to worry a bit longer."

Her mouth was dry. Like cotton. "Who are you?" She forced her eyes to open wider. But there was nothing to see. Only the back side of the blindfold covering her eyes.

"My name is Graham. And I'm an assassin."

"Are you the man who killed my sister?" Maybe if she let rage take over, her fear and shaking would subside.

"Indeed."

Anger surged through her. She balled her fists but couldn't feel anything. The burning helped her feel stronger. More in control. "Why?"

"Because I was hired to do so."

The man had no conscience? No emotion? "I killed your parents, too. Although the accident/possible suicide angle was so much fun to read about in the papers." His crusty laugh lasted only a second. "But they were still my kill. Added to my number. And everyone who mattered knew it."

Deanna's thoughts swam. So her father hadn't driven off the cliff? This man, Graham, had killed them? "Why? Why were you hired to kill them?"

"I was hired to kill your whole family. And many others." The voice moved away. Was he leaving?

"Why?" She needed to keep him talking. So she could formulate a plan.

"Because your father worked for the CIA."

What was he talking about? "No, he didn't. He worked for the United Nations."

More laughter.

The drugs on that cloth must've done a number on her brain cells, because this wasn't making any sense. Her dad had been a noble man. Always talked about world peace. Wanted to be an ambassador of the United States to other countries. At least, that's what she remembered.

"Your father traveled a lot, did he not?" The voice came closer.

"Yes." Where was this going?

"The UN job was a cover. Plain and simple, your father was a spy."

The information washed over her. It didn't matter. Her parents were gone. This madman just wanted to rile her up. "Who hired you?"

"A country who hates American spies." He laughed.

"But I'm not a spy. My sister wasn't a spy. Why did you kill her?"

"Because I wanted to." She felt his sneer all the way to her toes. "She was a warning to your parents." He paused, seeming to enjoy the moment. "I like to torture my subjects before I kill them. Besides, leaving family members only creates a mess. Look at what you've done. You've been a mess for me all these years."

"But—"

"Shut up, Little Girl. I don't ever lose. That's why you have to die. And all the wonderful people of Talkeetna have to suffer as well."

This man was a lunatic. Why hadn't the FBI ever told her the truth? Assuming Graham told her the real story.

Her best bet was to cooperate. Maybe she'd have a chance to escape at some point.

"I'll be back. I've left a few surprises for your friends. I like to go out with a bang."

Chapter 12

A sharp stabbing to his ribs jolted Josh awake. Ropes dug into his flesh at his wrists and ankles. He was lifted by a wiry man to a chair. The man wasn't much to look at, but he was obviously trained and strong.

"Hello there, Mr. Ranger. My name is Graham, and I want you to know that I will be killing your precious Deanna today." He snickered.

How long had he been out? "Where is she?"

"And what will you do?" The man approached. "You can't touch me."

Josh lunged for him and fell onto the floor on his face.

"*Tsk, tsk.* You need to pay better attention to your surroundings, young man."

Who was this guy? He was obviously whacked.

"Now, we're going to go for a little ride, but I wanted to introduce myself. I'd like to think that I at least have the decency to show good manners to my victims."

What? What loony bin did this guy escape from?

Another blow to the head made stars appear. As much as he tried to stay awake, Josh surrendered to the blackness.

❧

Rough hands tore the blindfold off her face. For the first time in fifteen years, Deanna stared into the dark eyes of her family's killer. A chill ran down her spine. His hard face was weathered, worn. Without any life in his eyes, the man looked totally evil. He paced the floor in front of her. Waiting. Watching. What made a man like him turn into a monster?

The only idea she had was to keep him talking. Stall him. For as long as she could. Even if *she* died today, she needed to try to save as many lives as she could. There had to be a way to stop him. Somehow. "What made you choose this line of work?"

"That isn't important. Besides, it found me. And I take it very seriously; it's an art form."

Her gut churned. Nausea swelled and rose. *Get a grip.* God was in control here. Not Graham. No matter what the madman did. "So I take it you are the best in your trade?"

That awful chuckle was back. "Of course."

Change the subject. This was getting her nowhere and only fed his ego. "Have you ever been in love, Graham?"

He spit on the floor. "Love is for fools."

"Have you ever been to church?"

"Religion is for fools as well." He glared at her. "And weaklings."

She tried another tactic. "Have you ever been happy?"

"Happiness is what you make. So yes, I've been very happy."

"But how can you be? You're alone, you chase people down and spill their blood, for what? Money?"

"I don't expect a simpleminded fool like yourself to understand my genius."

In that moment, the clear reminder of sin and its consequences overwhelmed her. The enemy loved it. This was what sin had done to the world. Sin perverted the truth for its own ends. Sin. In all its selfishness and pride.

"Stand up, Little Girl. It's time."

As Graham untied her bonds and led her through the darkness, she prayed. God knew. He'd conquered sin. Once

nd for all. He understood the pain and agony better than
anyone. He understood her worry for her friends, for the
people of Talkeetna. A new thought took root: He knew the
guilt she'd lived with all these years. The blame she'd taken
from Graham for the deaths of her family. God understood.
And she wouldn't shoulder the guilt anymore. Blood rushed
to her limbs and she flexed her hands. There had to be some
way to escape.

Chapter 13

Deanna climbed into the backseat of Deline's Otter as Graham shoved the gun in her friend's back. Josh lay slumped in the seat next to her. His arms and legs tied, the knot on his forehead an ugly purple. She looked to the cockpit. Tears streamed down Deline's cheeks. Somehow Graham had gotten to her, too. Deline was as tough as they came. And he'd made her cry.

Anger burned inside Deanna. She had to stop him. No matter what happened. She had to stop him. This world wasn't her home. Her home awaited in heaven. Her heavenly Father awaited. She'd endured a life of pain and fear because of this madman. No more.

Graham turned back to her. "Not a move, or I'll kill your friends here."

She nodded. Looked around. There was nothing to use as a weapon.

As the plane left the ground, Graham held his gun pointed at Deline. Deanna didn't know his plan, but the outcome would not be good. Several minutes passed in silence.

Deline sniffed. Sobbed, actually. "Please don't kill me. I. . . I don't want to die. . . . Who will take care of my father?"

"Oh, I may have a use for you, beautiful." He reached to touch her hair with his left hand.

Deline shrank into the pilot's seat and whimpered.

He grinned, a gleam in his eyes that disgusted Deanna. She looked at her friend cowering in the front of the

338

plane. Then it hit her. Deline was putting in an Oscar-winning performance. Did she have a plan?

"Leave her alone, Graham. You came for me and you've got me. Why don't you let them go?" Deanna played along.

"That'd be entirely too easy, now, wouldn't it?" He sneered. "You're just getting what you deserve after all this time. I never lose. Never."

A moan next to her brought her attention to Josh. Blood dripped from his nose. He needed medical attention. What could she do to let Deline know she could help?

Graham shifted and pointed the gun at her. "Don't even think about touching him, Little Girl."

A shiver raced up her spine whenever he used that name. For over a decade, he'd tortured her with it. She shrank into her seat, following Deline's lead. If her friend had a plan, she needed to be ready. She braced her feet against the bottom of Deline's seat in the floor and tightened her seat belt.

She looked out the window. Nothing but the National Park below them. Minutes passed too slowly.

Graham reached for Deline again. She whimpered, then jerked and turned the yoke. The plane dropped into a sharp roll to the left. Then she slugged Graham so hard with her right fist that his head slammed into the windshield and he slumped to the floor. She righted the plane and sat up straight. "Grab the gun, Dee." Then she lifted her right leg and shoved the unconscious Graham toward the other side. "You touch me one more time, and I'll drop you without a parachute and then land this plane on top of your broken body."

Deanna laughed, her head spinning from the roll. "That was awesome." The gun felt awkward in her hands. "What do you want me to do with this?"

Deline wiped her face. "Just hold on to it in case he comes to." She lifted her leg and shoved at Graham's limp body again. "I'd like to punch him again, but I think I might've broken some bones the first time." She flexed her fingers.

"You okay?"

"I think so. It was harder to produce tears than I thought, but I'm thankful for PMS."

Deanna smiled with her friend. "For the tears or the slug?" She found a luggage strap on the floor and tied it around Graham's hands.

"Both. I'm gonna land on the Kahiltna. There's backup waiting to take our little friend into custody."

"So this was the plan all along?"

"We didn't know, but we were prepared just in case." Deline shrugged. "This little weasel showed up wanting to rent a plane and a pilot. Something about him didn't sit right. He just *seemed* suspicious, so I got his fingerprints on a piece of paper and sent them over to Williams. Don't you dare tell Logan I volunteered for this, okay?"

"Okay." She smiled. The depth of what just happened hit Deanna square in the face. So many people had risked their lives. For her.

Josh groaned next to her again. "She won't tell, but I will."

"Josh!" Deanna threw her arms around him. "Don't move. You look pretty bad."

Deline laughed. "Don't you dare tattle on me, Josh Richards. I've got too much on you, too, and you know it."

Graham's hands shot out and grabbed Deline's arm. She yanked the yoke again, but he held tight. She bit him, and he slapped her hard. The plane dropped.

Josh whispered to Deanna. "Give me the gun."

She handed it over.

He held it between his bound hands and slammed the butt into Graham's head. The wiry man crumpled. Anger welled up. She wanted to strangle him with her bare hands.

But God had taken it out of her control. Deanna squelched the anger. God provided a way of escape. He'd given her strong friends, people who cared about the *real* her. As they rounded back to the north, Deanna spotted Denali ahead. She definitely had lots of guardian angels, didn't she? The mountain was one of them.

Deline landed on the glacier with deft movements and brought the plane to a halt. She picked up an FRS radio and called, "Come and get 'im."

The ground around them moved as white-clothed mounds turned into men with guns.

Deanna wanted to cheer. The cavalry had arrived.

❦

Graham shot daggers with his eyes to everyone around him. Blood dripped from where Deline's ring had sliced his cheek when she decked him. Two officers hauled him to his feet.

Handcuffs weren't enough to hold this guy. Deanna's stomach roiled. What were they missing? She scanned the glacier and the area around them. Two medics worked on Josh, while Deline and Logan talked with Agent Williams. The glacier swarmed with people.

Could he have set a trap? If so, those restraints weren't enough. She knew it. Deep down. And as their eyes met, Deanna shrank back. What was he up to?

An explosion ripped through the air. Deline's plane blew twenty feet into the air and landed with a sickening thud. In a split second, Graham head-butted a state trooper and yanked the gun from him.

Three shots rang out around her.

The stalker fell, blood pooling in the pure white snow. The gun in his grip still trained on Deanna.

Two more troopers and one of the FBI guys kept their

weapons raised. But it was over. They'd taken him down.

People scurried everywhere.

Deanna sank to her knees.

Josh's arms came around her from behind. "It's over."

"Are you okay?" She turned in his arms and looked at his bandaged and bruised face.

"I'm fine."

"Is it really over?" she whispered. The trembling began in her legs and moved up her body. Emotions from the past fifteen years flooded her body.

"Yeah, it's really over." He gripped tighter around her waist.

Comfort. Pure comfort.

She closed her eyes and wept.

Chapter 14

The porch was slick with snow and ice. Her breath puffed in front of her.

Sunrise. Her favorite time of day.

But today held new meaning. It was the first day without *im*. Fifteen years she'd run and hidden. Lived in fear. Fifteen ears she'd attempted to control what she couldn't. Fifteen ears, she'd kept God at arm's length like everyone else in her fe.

Well, today would be different. Trials and heartache would e in this world no matter what. But she could definitely andle it better. *Lord, I'm sorry. I professed to have faith in You nd yet I kept yanking back control. I didn't trust You enough. I'm sorry. Thank You for saving me, for taking care of me.*

Footsteps approached from the south.

Josh.

Thank You for Josh, Lord.

He reached out a hand to her. She'd never tire of hold-ng it.

"I'm glad you're up. Would you like to go for a walk?" he scent of him surrounded her like a cloak as his arm went round her shoulder.

"I'd love to."

They settled into a slow, steady pace, watching the sun on he eastern horizon. Josh reached into his coat pocket. "I have omething for you."

Deanna's heart raced. "Really? For me?" When was the

last time anyone had given her anything? They stopped and she turned to him. "I used to love presents as a kid, and everyone at the station knows how much I love our secret Santa every year." She bounced on her toes.

"So, you haven't gotten anything just for you other than secret Santa gifts?"

She shook her head. "Not since I was twelve."

"Go ahead and get excited, Deanna. I can't wait to see you open it." His blue eyes shone bright in the early morning light.

The package was small, the paper delicate. She ripped off the covering and gasped as she opened the tiny box. "It's beautiful." The gold ring was embedded with tiny diamonds around the band. Engraved in black script was her name, Deanna. "I love it. Thank you."

"Let me explain my intentions." He cupped her face with his right hand. "I'm probably a little old-fashioned, but I'm looking at this like courtship. You're the only one for me." He breathed deep. "I love you, Deanna. I want to spend the rest of my life getting to know you. I don't want you to feel rushed, so feel free to tell me to back off if you need—"

"I love you, too, Josh."

"You do?"

"I do." She leaned forward and breathed in the man she loved and kissed his cheek. With a hand on his chest, she pulled back. "And there's something you need to know."

"Okay." His eyebrows lowered. "Is it serious?"

"My name is pronounced Dee-na. Not Dee-ann-a."

"I think I can handle that." He sighed and moved closer. "But why didn't you tell any of us sooner?"

"Because it was part of my cover. And it was easier to allow people to pronounce it that way—my dad named me

Just wanted to be different." Tears pricked her eyes as she gazed at the ring.

"It's beautiful. Just like you."

As his lips covered hers, she wrapped her arms around his neck. This was definitely home.

Chapter 15

The café was packed. Voices floated up and down, dishes and glasses clanked. The engagement party for Logan and Deline was a celebration for the entire town.

Josh glanced at Deanna. Her face glowed in the light. Pure happiness etched there.

He looked down the table at David and Jolie—newlyweds. They stole the show wherever they went.

The tables were filled with smiling faces. Faces of family. These rugged and loving people who risked their lives in a little piece of Alaska. The Talkeetna Ranger Station changed his life, and he would be forever grateful. These people had touched his soul, and he would lay down his life for any one of them.

Especially the lady at his side. A glance at Deanna made his heart swell. He leaned in and kissed her cheek. Soon they'd have their own party—because tonight they would make an announcement. He nodded at Zack across the table.

Zack took a knife and banged on his glass. "I've got another announcement to make, but first I'd like to give the rookie the floor."

Josh stood. "I'll be brief." He glanced at Deanna then went on, "I've asked Deanna to marry me and she said yes."

Cheers erupted throughout the room.

Deanna added, "And I've had six volunteers to walk me down the aisle." She winked at him.

"Oh boy."

Karon stood next to Zack and shouted, "And we're having a double wedding with Deanna and Josh, so we hope you all will reserve December 28th on your calendars!"

Applause poured through the room. Everyone passed around hugs, congratulations, and kisses on the cheeks to the brides-to-be.

After a half hour of chaos, Josh reached for Deanna's hand and tugged her out into the cold night. He faced her toward Denali, wrapped his arms around her waist, and placed his chin on top of her head. "I love you, you know."

"I do. And I love you, too." She leaned against him. "Every dream that's come true for me has been with the High One in the background. I'm glad we're having the ceremony on the Kahiltna."

"Me, too. It will be a day everyone will remember." He breathed in the citrusy scent of her hair. "I'm sorry your dad won't be there to walk you down the aisle."

"Yeah, but I'm hoping he'll get to watch from heaven." She turned in his arms. "I can't wait to spend the rest of my life with you." Her lips reached his, the warmth seeping through to his bones.

He deepened the kiss and held her tight. "Me, too."

"Ahem." A deep voice shattered the quiet moment.

Deanna giggled.

Josh turned and saw Logan, John, David, Zack, and Kyle all with their arms crossed. Now how did they sneak up on them?

John spoke first. "Is he behaving himself, Deanna?"

She winked and pulled Josh close again. "Yes, sir." She kissed him long and hard in front of all of them. "Gotta love my guardians," she whispered and kissed him again.

Kimberley Woodhouse is a wife, mother, author, and musician who lives, writes, and homeschools in Colorado with her husband and two children.

JOIN US ONLINE!

Christian Fiction for Women

Christian Fiction for Women is your online home for the latest in Christian fiction.

Check us out online for:

- Giveaways
- Recipes
- Info about Upcoming Releases
- Book Trailers
- News and More!

Find Christian Fiction for Women at Your Favorite Social Media Site:

 Search "Christian Fiction for Women"

 @fictionforwomen